EMAIL FROM A VAMPIRE

EMAIL FROM A VAMPIRE

NIGEL COOPER

GENERIC POOL PUBLISHING

Published in Great Britain in 2012 by Generic Pool Publishing
www.genericpool.com

A CIP catalogue record of this book
is available from the British Library.

ISBN 978-0-9573307-0-2

Cover design by Jon Iredale.

Set in Sabon LT Roman 10.5/15 pt.
Typeset by the author.

Printed and bound in the UK by
TJ International, Trecerus Industrial Estate, Padstow, Cornwall. PL28 8RW

This book is also available in e-book format, details of which
are available at the author's website below.

www.nigelcooperauthor.com

For Louise

Who has always been behind me and believed in me from the very beginning.

Acknowledgements

I'd like to thank CSI Manager Mark Kelly for giving up his valuable time both in person and via phone and email. Mark, you helped assure that the CSI and forensics scenes maintained accuracy. Also, Deputy Chief Constable John Feavyour and his PA Barbara Warsap for making my communications with Mark possible to start with.

My dearest friend in the world, Louise, for helping me with the proofreading and giving me constructive feedback on a chapter-by-chapter basis as I was writing this book.

My copy-editor Ruth Ekblom, for her professional feedback and constructive comments/suggestions throughout the writing stage. And all her hard work copy-editing and proof-reading.

Karen Howard for her styles and formatting advice.

Jon Iredale for the superb cover design and artwork.

Last, but never the least, I'd like to thank my buddy, Carl. Dude, what can I say, you're the man.

Chapter 1

'Oh, for fuck sake!' exclaimed Tania, as she noticed the time displayed on her bedroom ceiling coming from the LED projection clock.

'Of all the god damn days to oversleep,' she groaned as she exerted huge effort to pull the quilt off her body. She sluggishly dragged her legs around from under the quilt and took a sharp intake of breath as her bare feet came into contact with the cold wooden floor. She sat on the edge of the bed with her head in her hands and tried to nurse her splitting headache.

'Thanks, Merlot,' she quietly groaned as she struggled to her feet. Too hung over to be bothered to bend down and reach for her slippers under the bed, she shuffled in the general direction of the bathroom, eyes still half closed. The short distance of eleven feet from her bed to the bathroom in her hung over condition made her think what it must feel like for an untrained amateur charity marathon runner to make those final hundred metres to the finishing line. Her legs felt like they were made of lead and she was wading through treacle up to her knees. Two bottles of cheap wine the night before can do that to a woman.

'First things last,' she grumbled to herself as she opened the bathroom cabinet and fumbled blindly across the glass shelf in search of the Nurofen, knocking various packets and potions out into the sink in the process.

'Shit, shit, shit,' she said, as she finally laid her fingertips on that ever-welcoming red and silver box. Just as she threw one of the elongated white tablets onto the back of her tongue, she heard the phone ring in the bedroom. Resigned to the fact that, in her hung over condition, there was no way on earth she was going to get to the phone before the answerphone kicked in, she part-filled a plastic beaker with water and took a gulp to wash the tablet down. She exhaled and slumped forward, leaning on the sink with her forehead pressed up against the mirrored cabinet door.

Although her legs were heavy, she somehow found the strength to stand there a minute longer. The cold mirror pressed hard against her forehead felt nice and was doing a great job of soothing her now pounding headache. She slowly pulled her head away from the mirror and gazed back into the bloodshot eyes that were staring back at her. The bloodshot eyes belonged to Tania de Pré: 28 years old; about five foot ten tall; very slim build with long black hair, right now, looking like it had been back-combed with sugar-water. She was quite attractive in a girl-next-door sort of way. But she also had a slightly spooky appearance; she wouldn't look out of place as the head of a witch's coven. In the past, people had often compared her physical appearance and looks to the Canadian singer-songwriter Alanis Morissette, only she was taller and had an outrageous dress sense.

As Tania stood there looking at herself in the mirror the

answerphone kicked in from the handset in her bedroom.

'I pray for your sake that your arse is on its way over here right now, 'cos if you're not at this meeting in fifteen minutes flat, all hells gonna break loose. Savage is on his way in right now, and if you're not here when he arrives he'll go psycho ballistic,' said the anxious male voice on the other end of the phone.

Tania had a sudden reality check, a reality check that took her all of half a second to come to terms with; the race was on. She came back to planet earth and understood that it was vital that she was in that meeting before her boss, Jack Savage, showed up. She had to convince her boss to let her carry on writing her dwindling daily column for the newspaper, without which she would potentially be out of a job. If she wasn't there for this meeting, her column would last about as long as a snowflake in hell. Savage was ruthless when it came to business. He wanted to sell papers, lots of them, and he'd already told Tania that her column was diminishing in popularity and was taking up valuable space, space that could be allocated to something with a bit more impact and tangible saleability.

Tania's typical laid-back morning routine had just missed its turn, it did not pass *Go* and it did not collect £200. Instead she threw some cloths on and hauled her arse straight out the door looking like the night before and jumped into her black BMW Z4 M parked right outside. Tania put her sunglasses on to deal with the blinding bright early June sunlight, then fired up the engine and kicked that 306 horsepower into life. In her keenness to get to her meeting fast, she stamped the accelerator to the floor and screeched away, spinning the rear drive wheels against the tarmac to the dismay of an elderly lady walking her dog. She sped off down the road under hard acceleration.

'Where the hell have you been?' said Seth as Tania exited the elevator on the fifth floor of The Sentinel newspaper offices. 'You look like shit.'

Seth was Tania's co-worker at the newspaper. He was older than Tania by five years and often looked out for her like the older brother she never had.

'Thanks, Seth, but that's not what I want to hear right now. Please, just tell me Savage isn't here yet?'

'He's not, but you'd better get in there and get prepared; he'll be here any second.'

'I appreciated the phone call, I'll thank you later ... if I still have a job,' she said, trying to regain some composure as she dashed towards the meeting room. As she entered she noticed four of her co-workers already seated at the boardroom table, looking efficient, organised, and well groomed.

'Oh dear, this doesn't look good,' said Martin.

Martin Lovejoy had something of a crass sense of humour sometimes, and thought he was God's gift to women. One thing Tania had learned about Martin was that he simply didn't get women and he certainly didn't understand the boundaries. He dressed like a merchant banker and drove a Porsche Boxster S convertible with the deluded impression that it made him look good. He had but mediocre talents as a writer that were more suited to a local rag, than a national well respected newspaper like The Sentinel. He only got to his position through being a brown-noser around his boss,

Jack Savage. However, deep down, Martin did have a heart; he just needed to grow up a bit and think before opening his mouth.

'Look, Martin, I don't need your crap this morning, okay.'

'Morning? Only just; what the hell happened to you, Tania, you look like shit?'

'I've already had that from Seth,' she said, organising her papers in front of her.

'Had anything else from Seth this morning? Is that why you're wearing that just-fucked hairdo? And it really is a wonderful hairdo by the way,' he said, sarcastically.

Tania sighed at his unwanted verbals as she continued to organise her papers.

'I'm not going to get drawn into any of your pathetic banter, Martin, so just drop it, okay.'

'Well at least tell us if it was any good. I mean, did you do it?'

'Oh, just fuck off and grow up!' shouted Tania, as she allowed his crude comments to ruffle her feathers. She was anxious enough this morning and certainly didn't need any of his caustic crap.

'Hey, I'm just kidding around, relax.'

Tania was saved by the boardroom door swinging open. Jack Savage strode in looking as monumental and authoritative as ever. Jack was huge; he was six foot two, tall, big-boned and built like an overweight Russian Olympic shot putter.

'Good morning everyone,' he said in his usual authoritative deep voice.

Tania wondered if he heard her shout the F word just

before he entered the boardroom.

'Everything ok, Tania?' asked Jack, sternly, without even looking up from his briefcase as he snapped the catches open.

'Yes, everything's just peachy' she said, desperately trying not to sound embarrassed as it was obvious that he heard her shout the obscenity at his little minion. The next hour seemed like an eternity as Tania daydreamed her way through the meeting, most of which focused on a dull advertising campaign. Just as she was thanking her lucky stars that none of the discussions so far had involved her column, Jack looked squarely in Tania's direction.

'Tania ...' he paused in an exaggerated style like a cheap TV host who was about to announce the winner of some crap talent show. 'I've been giving serious thought to your column. It's not proving anywhere near as popular as it was this time last year, especially this latest story that you're running. Readers are writing in saying the current story is just plain dull.'

'That's not fair, I get lots of very positive emails from my readers and I have a loyal fan base,' she said defensively.

'Having a loyal small fan base doesn't sell papers, Tania. You've been given plenty of opportunity to turn the column around and make it popular again; we've talked about this before, this isn't news to you.'

'Jack, I've worked really hard on this column. I've been writing this column and working for you for five years now and I've never let you down. Last year my Elvis Presley story was a massive hit. I had emails from die-hard Elvis fans telling me that they were among the single best pieces ever written about the King, and it ran every day for nearly two weeks and sold you a lot of papers.'

'That may be so, but that was then and Elvis has since left the building. Look, Tania, I know you're passionate about the column, but this latest cold war history lesson that you've been running is going nowhere.' He looked down at the papers in front of him, quietly sighed and reflected for a moment. Tania couldn't bear the suspense; after the night she'd just had, she just wanted him to put her out of her misery. If he was going to tell her she was going to lose the column, he should just do it now. But then his head snapped up and he looked purposefully into Tania's eyes.

'I'm going to give you a week. One week to knock on my office door with a tangible idea, preferably one that will leave readers wanting from one day to the next and with a decent shelf life; okay?'

Tania sighed with relief that she still had a job writing her column; for now at least.

'Yes, thank you, Jack.'

'Okay then,' said Jack, as he gathered his papers together and snapped the catches closed on his briefcase.

'Martin, I'm going to need you to stay behind after work for a few hours to go over the details of the D&M advertising campaign.'

'You got it, Jack,' he said in his typical obsequious tone.

Tania shot him a look of sheer contempt as he followed Jack out of the boardroom like his little lapdog. Tania grabbed her papers and handbag, and made a beeline straight for the ladies bathroom.

As Tania pushed open the door, she hoped nobody would be in there as she wanted the privacy to try and salvage something of her hair and slap something on her face so as to look presentable for the rest of the day.

'Thank god,' she sighed to herself, realising she was the sole occupant. She rifled through her handbag looking for a cheap disposable airport travel toothbrush and toothpaste combo, which she knew was still in there from a recent long-haul flight back from America. Just as she placed various items of make-up from her bag onto the sink, Cora walked in.

'Hey you, what happened?' said Cora, in her typical chirpy morning voice.

'I forgot to set the alarm and overslept.'

'No, silly, I mean last night. Your date, how did it go?' she said, in a tone that suggested she wanted to hear all the naughty details. Cora was a pleasant happy-go-lucky well-meaning little thing and she had been a very supportive friend to Tania over the past couple of years, supporting her through her very emotional and messy divorce. Tania's husband had left her for another woman and Cora had been there for her. Recently, Cora had been encouraging Tania to get back out there and go on a few dates and have some fun, but Tania had lost a lot of confidence since she had her accident, which had left her with a very noticeable scar about two inches long going down the right side of her face. In her darkest moments, Tania was convinced that her husband found somebody else and left her because she had lost her looks to the scar.

'It didn't,' she said as she hurriedly brushed her teeth.

'He didn't turn up?' said Cora, with a hint of "the bastard" in her tone.

'Oh, he turned up alright,' as she spat toothpaste into the

sink aggressively.

'The waiter showed us to our table and we had dinner, but the whole time he was on edge and kept fidgeting and looking around. He didn't really pay any attention to anything I was talking about. He just wanted to get dinner out of the way as soon as possible and get me back to my place for a quick shag.'

'The bastard … Are there no decent men left?' said Cora, rhetorically.

'When we left the restaurant he was quite dominating about getting me into his car to give me a lift back home.'

'Oh my, what did you do?'

'Lucky for me, at that moment a cab came down the street and I stepped out into the road right in front of it to get the driver's attention.'

'It can't have been all bad?' said Cora, suddenly feeling a little guilty knowing that she had pushed Tania into the dating scene.

'Yes, actually, it was. From the second we met outside the restaurant he was hardly being subtle about looking at this,' she said, stroking her scar with her right index finger.

'Oh, Tania, darling, I'm so sorry,' she said in a soft sympathetic tone.

'It doesn't matter. To be honest, it all felt very creepy and weird; there was something not quite right about him.'

'Did you get home safely?'

'Well, I actually drove to the restaurant in my own car; but I was parked five minutes away and I felt … well … a little scared and didn't want to walk back to my car. The poor cab driver only drove me half a mile around the corner to my car. Then I drove myself home and crawled into the bottom of a bottle of Merlot to calm my nerves; well, two bottles actually.'

'Look, Tania, you're very beautiful and if the jerk off from last night didn't even want to see past a little scar and get to know you, then it's his loss, not yours. You deserve a decent caring man, and it will happen, Tania, you'll see.'

'Oh, Cora, I know you mean well, but this,' again, gesturing to her scar, 'is not a quality a man finds attractive in a woman. I don't want to be alone for the rest of my life,' she said as she frantically applied foundation to the scarred side of her face, trying to stop the tear that had welled up in her eye from escaping down her cheek.

'You stop right there, Tania de Pré. That scar doesn't make you any less of a woman; besides, it's hardly noticeable once you're made up,' she said, sounding as convincing as she could. Cora moved closer to Tania and put her arm around her shoulder.

'Tania, you'll find your true love one day, you'll see. He will come along right when you're not expecting him.' Cora sounded sincere beyond her typical personality.

'You really think so?' she replied softly, trying to hold back her tears.

'Definitely, you're an amazing woman, Tania de Pré, and a very beautiful one, and don't you ever think otherwise or let anyone tell you different.'

'Thanks, Cora, you're a good friend to me, you always have been.'

'I'm here if you need me, you know that. Look, how about we go out on Saturday ... together ... for a girlie shopping day in the West End?'

'That would be nice.' she said, managing a little smile.

'I'll pop over to your desk to see you later, okay?'

'Okay.'

Cora gave Tania a gentle peck on the cheek and headed back to her desk.

Tania sat at her desk tapping a USB flash memory stick against her teeth as she desperately tried to come up with a new story idea for her column. She launched her email application on her computer and took a mouthful of coffee while she waited for it to launch. Just then, Martin appeared at her desk.

'Hey, look I'm sorry about my crass comments earlier.' Although Martin could be a total dick sometimes – in fact most of the time – he at least had the intellect to realise when he had overstepped the mark.

'Friends?' he said in a soft voice, while pulling a silly puppy dog face and extending his little finger towards her.

Tania let out a brief half-choked laugh and touched his little finger with the tip of her own.

'Sure … you know, you can be a real jerk sometimes,' she said, half-jokingly, with a smile.

'I know,' he said, smiling back, 'but I'm your kind of jerk, right?'

'Go and get me a refill,' she laughed, passing him her all-but-empty mug.

'You got it.' He took the mug and headed off to make Tania a fresh cup of coffee.

PING! Tania's iMac let her know she had new emails. She turned back to her computer to begin the tedious task of dealing with her daily influx of emails.

'Junk, junk, junk, junk, junk,' she exhaled quietly as she clicked the Junk button several times. No matter how well she trained her email application in the art of preventing spam email there was always a new breed of junk and spam email from a new breed of arsehole ready to find its way into her Inbox. Just as Tania was halfway through glancing over a reader's email, Martin returned with her coffee.

'White, no sugar,' he said, as he placed the mug on her desk.

'Thanks, Martin,' she said, as she took the mug and moved it away from her keyboard and onto a coffee coaster.

'Anything interesting?' said Martin.

'Sorry?'

'The email you're reading, anything interesting?'

'Oh, no, just one of my regular readers with a few kind words about yesterday's *dull* column.'

'Well, you never know, somewhere in that Inbox might be a message that'll land you your next big story,' he said, trying to sound encouraging.

'Hmmm, I doubt it. So far nothing but junk, the usual compliments by my regular readers and yet another proposal of marriage from the dear old Mr Making from Manchester, and this time he's sent a picture.'

'Oh, do show!' said Martin, in a camp joking tone as he leaned over Tania's shoulder looking at her computer screen.

Tania clicked on the email and up popped a picture of an overweight bald middle-aged man wearing what looked like a pair of 1970s national health spectacles.

'Nice!' said Martin, taking a swig of his own coffee. They both laughed out loud.

'I'm gonna let you get back to your emails ... catch you later, okay.'

'Thanks for the coffee,' she said, as he turned and headed off across the office floor.

Tania turned back to her computer and trashed Mr Making's email, sighing to herself as she did so. The last unread email subject line read *VERY IMPORTANT – PLEASE READ!!!* She gazed at the subject heading expectantly before clicking on it. Is this it? Could this be the big story she'd been waiting for? ... No. As she opened the email it was nothing more than a short dirty Flash animation cartoon joke involving a skinny cartoon man having sex with a very large cartoon woman.

'Oh, for crying out loud,' she muttered to herself in disgust.

The rest of the day was pretty uneventful, with no ideas for a new story and no interesting emails. Cora appeared at Tania's desk, bag in hand and wearing her denim jacket.

'Hey, it's 5:30; you wanna grab a quick drink with me next door?'

Tania looked at her watch. 'Oh god, where did the day go?'

'Come on, grab your bag and let me buy you a drink.'

'Okay.'

Just as Tania reached for the mouse to put her computer to sleep, her email application pinged to alert her of new mail. She glanced at the subject line, which read *Email From A Vampire*. Tania sighed and clicked the Junk button, then put her computer to sleep. She grabbed her handbag and headed for the elevator with Cora.

Chapter 2

After the relatively short five-mile journey from her house in Islington across the City of London to Canary Wharf, Tania pulled up to the security barrier at The Sentinel newspaper building and smiled at the security man as he lifted the electronic barrier from the comfort of his station booth. She passed through and drove around the side of the building and down the ramp to the underground car park. As usual, she slowed to a virtual stop just before getting to the bottom of the ramp so as to avoid grounding and potentially wrecking the lower part of the front bumper on her BMW Z4 M. She gritted her teeth and cringed during this slow manoeuvre for fear of causing hundreds of pounds worth of damage to her precious car. Once her car was level and past the cringing point, she let out a short sigh of relief.

After exiting her car, Tania scanned the entire car park level, not because she was nervous or expected somebody to jump out and rob her – she knew this was highly unlikely as security was pretty tight at the newspaper's building and there were cameras everywhere, including the underground car park – Tania simply looked around because the lower car park was kind of spooky and reminiscent of one of those lower level car parks you see in American horror and suspense movies. This one had plenty of large concrete pillars and dark corners for monsters, ghouls and crazed knife-wielding killers to conceal themselves behind; at least this was how Tania viewed it. She headed across the car park towards the elevator, locking her car remotely via her key fob as she walked.

The elevator doors opened at the fifth floor and before Tania could get her right foot out, she noticed Cora making a beeline in her direction.

'Hey you, how you feeling this morning?' as usual she sounded all cheerful and happy.

'Not as hung over as yesterday morning. Whether that's a good thing or not, I don't know. Let's see how this day pans out.'

'Look, we're having a bit of a whip around for Jack', Cora smiled, shaking a plastic Tupperware container under Tania's nose. Tania peered down into the container and noticed the loose pile of notes made up mostly of fives and tens, with a couple of twenties in there as well.

'What's this for?'

'It's his fiftieth birthday next week. Of course he's kept it a big secret. You know Jack; he doesn't like to make a big deal out of these things.'

'So how did you know?'

'Martin told me.'

'Martin', she sighed, 'that figures. Why am I not surprised? Martin probably knows how much toilet paper Jack uses to wipe his arse.' Tania checked herself. 'I'm sorry, Cora, I'm still a little anxious and edgy because of my column.'

'Hey, I understand, but everything's going to be ok for you, I've got a feeling something will come up real soon.'

'Well it better come up fast as I've only got six days to come up with something for Jack ... where is he anyway?

'He's not in this morning, he has to help his wife with something, which is why I'm running around now trying to get everyone to cough up a little something,' she said, smiling and shaking the plastic container under her nose again. Tania reached into her handbag and took out her purse and dropped a ten-pound note into the container.

'If he ends up dropping my column next week, I'll want that back,' she said, half seriously.

'Oh Tania, I'm sure he's not going to do that. Even if he decides to drop your column, he'll put you onto something else, but you won't lose your job.'

'I know,' she said, in a soft self-reassuring way, 'but I love my column, it's me, it's what I do and I just can't imagine being able to express myself in another area of the paper.'

'Look, go and grab yourself a coffee and check your emails. You never know, a great story might be sitting right there in your Inbox. I'll pop by your desk later on and see how you're doing.' Cora headed off to collar a few more work colleagues for donations.

Tania carefully put her morning mug of coffee down in its usual place on the coaster just to the right of her mouse mat; within easy reach. As part of her usual morning routine, she hit the Return key on her keyboard to wake her computer from sleep mode, and then clicked on the Mail icon to check her email. While waiting for the application load up, she grabbed her coffee and took a slow sip to avoid burning her lips. The usual ping sound alerted her to the fact that she had new emails. Mid-mouthful she noticed the email from the previous evening with the subject heading *Email From A Vampire* had re-appeared in her Inbox. Strange, as she remembered hitting the Junk button and deleting it the previous evening.

'Great,' she sighed, then purposefully clicked the Junk button and watched the email disappear into the Junk folder. She continued scanning down her new emails in the hope that one of the subject headers might catch her eye and be a potential story.

Tania typically received about one hundred new emails first thing in the morning, of which about fifty per cent were junk. She efficiently selected the ones she knew to be junk and quickly sent them straight to the Junk folder. This was part of Tania's process; she liked to filter down the numbers by getting rid of the junk first, then quickly deal with those emails that she knew would only take a few seconds or a few short sentences to respond to. Eventually she would be left with only possible story ideas. That was the theory, anyway.

Just as she was typing a brief *thank you* email to one of her readers, 'Ping!' a new email arrived at the top of her Inbox.

'Oh, for crying out loud!' she said quietly to herself in frustration as the words *Email From A Vampire* appeared in the subject header at the top of her Inbox. For the third time, Tania junked the email. 'Now stay there,' she said, somehow expecting her stern tone to do the trick. She selected the next email in the queue to deal with, but before she could even read to the end of the first sentence, Ping!

She glanced at the top to see what the new email was; the subject header read *Email From A Vampire*.

'Now you're really starting to piss me off,' she said in a slightly louder voice.

'Everything okay?' said Martin as he strolled passed Tania's desk.

'Yes fine, just having a bit of trouble with a stubborn Junk mail.'

'Maybe I can help, what's the problem?'

Martin was a bit of a wiz with computers and Tania suspected that he liked nothing more than to help a woman in distress, as it gave him a great feeling of supremacy and wellbeing.

'I've junked this damn email three times now, and the junk filtering system refuses to recognise it as junk and it keeps coming back.'

'Let me check your junk filter is set up right.'

He leaned over Tania's shoulder and relieved her of the mouse. She felt a little uncomfortable with Martin in such close proximity to her, especially when his head was only inches away from her face, the right side of her face, the side with the scar on it.

Please don't notice my scar out of the corner of your eye, she thought to herself as she became incredibly self-conscious and tense. Martin put his left hand on Tania's left shoulder to balance himself as he moved the cursor around her computer screen. He didn't quite understand women, and he certainly had no idea what the boundaries and rules were, and what you could and couldn't do. Putting his arm around a woman like this, uninvited, was totally unacceptable. But Tania accepted this and let him have his fun, as long as it didn't take too long, and as long as he sorted this bloody vampire spam out.

'Well, there's your problem,' he said, all pleased with himself.

'What was it?'

'You didn't put it in the Junk folder. You see, you have to highlight the email, then hit that Junk icon right there.' He gestured by scribbling lots of little circles with the mouse cursor over the Junk icon.

'I know, Martin, I do have some computer literacy you know; I did that already.'

'Well, obviously not, as it wasn't in the Junk folder, look.' He opened the Junk folder. 'There were a few junk emails in there, but nothing with the subject *Email From A Vampire*.'

'Look, Martin, I know what I did, and I put it in the Junk folder.'

'Okay, well, let me do it a different way to make sure you don't get it anymore.'

He physically dragged the *Email From A Vampire* junk mail and dropped it into the Junk folder.

'There, from what I can see, your spam and junk filter system are set up correctly, you shouldn't get this email anymore.' He gently took Tania's right hand and placed it back onto her mouse, taking his time over it as if he was somehow getting off on all this physical contact, but in reality, he simply didn't understand the boundaries.

'Thank you, Martin,' she said as she shifted about on her chair uncomfortably to encourage him to take his hand off her shoulder and move out of her close personal proximity.

'Anytime,' he whispered in her ear.

He slowly stood up and slithered away in the direction of his own desk. As she watched him walk away, relief washed over her in an awesome way as she regained her personal space. The Ping sound coming from her computer caused her to swivel around on her chair to get back to dealing with her emails. There it was again! Right at the top of her Inbox, that damn annoying subject header *Email From A Vampire*.

'Oh come on! What the hell is this, a bloody conspiracy?' she said, frustrated. At that exact moment, the phone rang on her desk. She reached to her left and picked it up.

'Tania de Pré,' she answered in her professional voice.

'No, it's not a conspiracy, it's the story that's going to make you famous, Ms de Pré,' said the calm well-spoken male voice on the other end of the phone, as if in answer to what Tania just said out loud to herself just seconds before the phone rang. She looked around the office at her colleagues at their various work desks expecting one of them to be on the phone looking at her with a smile on their face; but nobody was.

'Who is this?' she asked, cautiously.

'Who I am is not important … for now anyway … let's just say I'm the man who's going to make you famous. I suggest you read the email I sent you instead of repeatedly trying to put it in your junk folder.'

'What email are you referring to?' she said, making out she had no idea what he was talking about.

'The *Email From A Vampire*, Ms de Pré, you know which one I'm talking about.'

'Oh that one,' she said, trying to sound blasé and bored with this game. 'You mean the one that I'm in the middle of trashing again right now?' she said, with more than a hint of smugness in her voice. She dragged the email to the Trash icon and watched it vanish from her Inbox.

'Five … Four … Three …' said the voice counting slowly down on the end of the phone, 'Two … are you ready, Ms de Pré?' he said, knowingly.

'For what?' said Tania.

'Watch your Inbox closely,' he paused briefly, 'One!' he said in a shouted whisper. Ping! At that exact moment the email appeared back at the top of Tania's Inbox.

'Oh, very clever, what are you a bloody magician?' she said with a hint of annoyance in her voice.

'Not quite,' he said calmly and quietly. 'Now, might I suggest you be a trifle more respectful and open-minded and read my email. Goodbye for now, Ms de Pré'.

The electronic clicking sound followed by a continuous tone told her that the mystery man had hung up and ended the conversation. She turned back to her computer screen and viewed the subject header intently for a few moments; *Email From A Vampire.*

'Okay, Mr Magician, let's see what you have to say,' she said under her breath as she opened the email.

Dear Ms de Pré

The story that I'm about to unfold to you is going to be very hard for you to take seriously; at first at least. But everything I'm about to reveal to you about myself is absolutely true. I need you to be more open-minded than your career in journalism has thus far required; I need you to read, listen and believe. Finally, I insist that you publish my story. I want you to make it the main feature in your daily column. I want you tell my incredible life story to the world.

For now, at least, my name is of no importance; I will reveal that when we get to the end of my story. What is important is the fact that I am a vampire, and have been for the past thousand years. I was born a mortal human on the 20th June in the year 978 AD. But on the 13th December 1011, when I was 33 years old, I went through a process, known today as vampirification. My mortal age of 33 has been frozen in time for the past thousand years. During this time I have been forced to live in isolation, a solitary and lonely life, as I keep my dark secret from the world. I have had to live in the shadows, only coming out at night to avoid the sun's harmful rays from falling upon my flesh.

During this, my millennium year, I am stepping out of the shadows and I want you to tell my story to the world. I assure you that my story is genuine, and when published via your column, it will prove enormously popular with your readers and it will almost certainly put you back on top with your career; isn't that where you want to be? After publishing my story, you will be headhunted by every major national paper in the country, if not the world.

I'm aware that your column is dwindling in popularity and your boss, Jack Savage, is about to pull it from under your feet. I know you have no other options for your column right now and the clock is ticking, Ms de Pré.

You have nothing to lose, and everything to gain.

Yours sincerely,

The Vampire

'Great, a delusional nut job who thinks he's a vampire,' she sighed. Tania clicked the Reply button with the intent of making this short and quick.

Dear Mr Vampire (whoever you are),

I'd like to thank you for your email and fascinating vampire story, but fictional stories of vampires running around in the dark are not quite what I'm looking for at this stage of my career.
Regards,
Tania

She swiftly hit the Send button and headed across the office floor to make herself a fresh cup of coffee. When she entered the staff room, Seth and Jack were in there. Jack must have just arrived as he still had his briefcase in his hand.

'Good morning, Tania,' said Jack as he turned and walked towards the door with a fresh cup of tea in one hand and his briefcase in the other.

'Good morning, Jack,' she said, forcing a smile.

'Get that for me would you,' he gestured towards the door with his eyebrows. Tania obliged and held the door open for him.

'Good morning, Tania, what can I make you?' said Seth, as he stood poised by the just boiled kettle.

'Coffee, please.' She slumped onto the long leather couch against the back wall.

'Milk no sugar right?' he said confidently.

'Thanks.'

'How are things going with the column, anything new on the horizon?'

'Nothing; just some weirdo who's seen one too many vampire movies.'

'Vampire movies?' said Seth, trying to drum up conversation. 'Tell me more.'

'I got an email from somebody claiming to be a 1000-year-old vampire.'

'That's original,' he laughed. 'Are you gonna run a story about it?'

'Be serious, I need help here,' she said, trying to steer Seth away from the vampire theme, and in the direction of actually suggesting some serious ideas.

'I'm sorry ... kidding aside ... wanna throw some ideas back and forth?' said Seth.

'Yeah, sure. I seem to have something of a mental block right now. Just can't get those creative juices flowing ... do you get that?' she said, looking for him to help with her current predicament.

'Yes, of course, we all do from time to time.'

'How do you break through it?'

'Personally, I have several methods, depending on the severity of the block, or what it is I'm trying to achieve. Sometimes I brainstorm and speed-write anything that comes into my head, it's usually a load of nonsense, but sometimes when I read it back, some little nugget can raise its head and spark something. Other times I'll go down to the lobby and people-watch as they come and go.'

'What do you mean, people-watch?'

'I'll just sit there and watch people. The way they walk, the way they talk, what they're saying, what they're carrying, what they're wearing, if they're smiling, if they're sad, how they carry themselves, their posture and deportment ... lots of things. You'd be amazed how much you can learn about a person, just by watching them, and sometimes this can spark an idea.'

'Has this ever worked for you?' she said in a tone that doubted his methods.

'Yup! Remember the Red Shoes article I wrote a few months back?'

'Yes, of course, very sentimental and heart-felt. I loved that piece.'

'Well, that heartwarming story came from the lobby in this very building.'

'No kidding?' she said, looking a little surprised.

'Straight up. The little four-year-old girl in that piece was running up and down in the lobby reception area when she ran straight into a man and bashed her head against his briefcase,' he said, walking over to the couch and handing Tania her mug of coffee.

'Thanks,' she said, pondering what he had just told her.

'Look, don't sweat it, you're thinking too hard. You need to relax and step back, clear your mind of everything. Then an idea will appear right before you; trust me,' he said, heading for the door.

'Thanks, Seth. I always feel better after talking to you.'

Seth turned to her as he opened the door, 'Don't worry, you'll be ok.'

She took a sip of coffee, momentarily mesmerised by the shadows being cast by the clouds outside as they moved across the carpet floor around her feet.

'Ok, Tania, back to work,' she murmured to herself. *You do still have a column to write, even if the current story is somewhat lacklustre*, she thought, as she got up off the comfy couch and headed back to her desk.

Back at her desk, she noticed the so-called vampire had sent a reply to her email.

Dear Ms de Pré

It would appear that you are not taking me seriously. I can assure you, I speak the truth. It is quite obvious that my words alone are not enough for you, so I'm going to take more drastic action. I'll be leaving you a little gift.

Au Revoir

P.S. I resent the suggestion that I'm just some weirdo who's seen one too many vampire movies.

'What the hell?' she mumbled to herself. Just then, Martin strolled up.

'Hey, how's it going?' he said.

'I'm not sure', she said, sounding somewhere between confused and mildly annoyed. 'Something's not quite right about this guy.'

'What guy?'

'Remember the junk email I was having trouble with earlier?'

'The vampire thing?'

'Yes, well I've since had a phone call from the same guy, and I've now read the email.'

'You mean it wasn't some automated spam and somebody actually sent it?'

'Yes, and he called me on my direct line number right here at my desk.'

'How did he get that?'

'I have no idea, but there's something strange about this, and I don't like it.'

'Strange? How?'

'Well, for starters, when I put the original email in the Junk folder, it somehow, as if by magic, moved itself from Junk right back into my Inbox.'

'No, no, no, that can't happen. He must have just sent it again,' said Martin, confident with his techy knowledge of computers.

'Look, Martin, I know what happened. He didn't send it again, it moved by itself. It's as if it didn't want to be junk, it wanted to be read.'

'Look, slow down and don't get ahead of yourself. It was probably just a corrupted email file, these things happen all the time.'

'Well, I've just got an uneasy feeling about this ... there's other things too.'

'What other things?'

'When he phoned me, he told me to read the email. I basically told him I wasn't interested in his crap and I trashed the email while he was still on the phone. But then he started to count backwards from five down to one.'

'Go on,' he said, encouraging her to tell the rest of the story.

'When he got to one, his email moved itself from the Junk folder right back to the top of my Inbox. At the exact moment he said "one" the Ping sounded on my Mail application, and there was his email.' Martin searched around inside his mental database for an answer.

'There's more ... I was just talking with Seth in the staffroom and I mentioned it to him. I told him that I'd had an email from some weirdo who's seen one too many vampire movies. Then when I got back to my desk a few minutes ago, there's another email waiting for me. Look at the postscript at the bottom.' Martin leaned in to read it.

P.S. I resent the suggestion that I'm just some weirdo who's seen one too many vampire movies.

'What is he, a psychic or something?' said Martin.

'Either that, or he's bugged the entire office. It's like he can hear everything I say.'

'Shit!' he said, sounding somewhat perplexed and unable to offer any technical or other advice.

'So what do you think?' she said.

'I think you should call Ghostbusters,' he said jokingly, but also sounding a little nervous and serious at the same time.

'He said he's going to leave me a little gift.'

'What do you think he meant by that?'

'I have no idea … god, I hope he's not one of those obsessed stalkers who's going to start sending me presents.'

'Well, if he sends you chocolates, you know where my desk is,' he said, smiling.

'Very funny,' she said, looking at him and pulling a sarcastic smile.

'Hey look, I gotta shoot, but let me know how it pans out okay? And I'm around if you need me.' He strutted off back to his desk.

Another frustrating and relatively uneventful afternoon passed with no interesting leads or stories materialising. Tania was still burdened with her mental block, and the fact that this vampire thing kept entering her mind didn't help either. She grabbed her handbag and headed towards the elevator.

'Goodnight, Seth,' she said politely as she passed his desk.

'Goodnight, have a good evening, Tania.'

As the elevator doors opened on the lower ground car park level, Tania paused momentarily before stepping out, scanning the other parked cars. As she walked from the elevator towards her car, she paid particular attention to the large concrete pillars, as usual. Tania found this short walk a little more nerve-wracking at this time in the evening, compared with the morning, especially with the recent vampire activity. She couldn't help but think of those American movies where something horrible happened in underground car parks. She knew it was silly and all in her mind; after all, security here was high and there were easier pickings elsewhere for an average petty thief looking for items left in cars. It was a newspaper office after all, not a bank.

As she got closer to her car Tania took out her keys and pressed the key fob to remotely unlock it. She opened the door and got in and went to put her handbag on the passenger seat just as she always did. Shocked, she took a sharp intake of breath as she noticed a relatively large package wrapped in brown paper on the passenger seat, a package that had not been there when she left her car that morning. Tania stared at the package for a moment, wondering if it could be a bomb or something dangerous, but it was not a shape that suggested it might be an explosive device. This object was rectangular and relatively flat and about twenty by thirty inches in size.

Knowing that she wouldn't have enough room in her small sports car to effectively unwrap this package, Tania got out of the car, walked around and opened the passenger door. She took the package out and placed it on the roof of her car; she carefully peeled away the brown paper packaging to reveal what looked like an old oil painting. She pulled away the few remaining pieces of brown paper and held the picture up to analyse it. It was a portrait of a man and a woman; both looked to be in their thirties. The woman was sitting in a chair, while the man stood just behind and to her right with his left hand on her left shoulder. The man's eyes seemed to stare intently out of the picture at Tania. It was a very romantic looking portrait and incredibly realistic; almost photo-like.

Tania turned the painting over, handling the frame carefully. At the bottom right of the frame, a date had been etched into the wood – 1587. She turned the picture back over and studied the couple in the painting for a few moments before wrapping the brown paper back around it and carefully placing it flat in the boot of her car. She started the engine and headed off home.

Chapter 3

Jack, Martin, Seth and Cora were in the boardroom when Tania entered holding the painting under her arm.

'Okay, I've got something I want to run by you all,' she announced authoritatively without even saying good morning. She placed the painting flat on the large boardroom table and proceeded to remove the brown paper wrapping. As the painting was revealed she took a sharp intake of breath and stared at the painting.

'Are you okay?' said Cora, noticing the shocked and perplexed look on Tania's face.

'Erm … I … no, no … no, I'm not,' she stammered. 'I'm definitely not okay, this can't be,' she sounded confused.

The painting Tania was looking at had changed since she had looked at it in the car park the previous evening. The face of the gentleman in the picture was no longer there. The rest of the painting was perfectly intact; his hair, ears and neck were all there. But his face, well, it was as if his face had never been painted to start with; no sign of any oils, just a perfectly clean and unpainted oval-shaped piece of canvas right where his face used to be.

'What is it?' asked Martin, as he and the others gathered

around to look at the painting.

'Oh my god, I really do hate modern art,' said Jack, paying particular attention to the oval blank face.

'No,' exclaimed Tania, 'you don't understand. The painting was complete; last night there was a face there.'

'What?' said Jack, as he picked the painting up and examined it more closely.

'Last night, when I left the office and got to my car downstairs, somebody had left this on the front passenger seat of my car. When I unwrapped it, his face was right there ... it was a complete painting.'

'What did he look like?' asked Cora.

'I'm not really sure ... he was a bit strange looking. He had quite a pale face with striking hypnotic looking eyes ... kind of like a wolf's eyes. But he was kind of attractive and handsome ... in a seductive and hypnotic kind of way ... I guess,' she said in a soft, slow, surreal tone as she reflected on how strange the man in the painting had looked.

'Earth calling Tania,' said Martin, as he mocked Tania's soft surreal tones.

'Look, I know what I saw ... his face was right here,' she said, as she shot Martin a look to suggest he should tread carefully right about now.

'Okay,' said Jack, taking control of the situation, 'you said somebody left this painting in your car yesterday?'

'Yes.'

'Okay, tell me the whole story, starting from the beginning.'

'I left the office as usual, got to my car and when I got in I was going to put my handbag on the passenger seat but I noticed the painting sitting there, wrapped in brown paper.'

'And you have no idea how it could've got there, or who might be responsible?' said Jack, turning the painting over and examining the date – 1587 – etched on the back.

'Not really, I think it could be the same guy who's been sending me these stupid vampire emails.'

'Vampire emails?' said Jack, more interested now as he turned to Tania and looked her in the eye with his Roger Moore style raised eyebrow.

'Some guy's been emailing Tania, claiming to be a 1000-year-old vampire. At first we thought it was just a junk mail,' said Martin. 'Don't you think we should call the police?'

'No,' said Jack, 'what would you tell them? That someone left an oil painting in Tania's car and the face erased itself during the night?'

'He's right, Martin,' said Cora.

'Tell me more,' said Jack, turning to Tania.

'It's just like Martin said, a man claiming to be a vampire sent me an email. He wants me to tell his life story through my column. Of course I didn't believe him. Well, vampires don't exist do they? I thought the email was a prank, but then strange things started to happen.'

'Go on,' said Jack, keen to hear the rest of the story.

'I don't know; it's kind of hard to explain. I trashed his first email, but it kept finding its way back into my Inbox. I just couldn't delete it, and still can't ... then he called.'

'Called?' said Jack.

'On the phone; my direct line number on my desk.'

'How did he get your direct line number?' said Jack.

'I don't know. I don't have any answers to any of this.'

'Anything else?'

'When he phoned, it was as if he knew I'd been trying to trash his email. He counted down backwards from five and as soon as he got to one, the email appeared back in my Inbox.'

'Spooky! Can I see the email?' said Jack.

'Sure … he said something else too. He knew I didn't believe him and that I wasn't taking him seriously, so in his last email he said he was going to leave me a little gift. I think this oil painting's the gift he was talking about.'

'Okay, so you're saying that when you got to your car last night and unwrapped the painting there was a face there and it was complete?'

'Yes,' she said, with total conviction.

'Right, so the painting wasn't in your car when you drove in to work yesterday morning or you would have noticed it, so … somebody must have put it there during the day while you were up here working. Was your car unlocked?'

'No, I'm quite meticulous about locking my car, I'm security conscious and I love my car, I'd hate for it to get stolen.'

'Okay, I'll check the videos on the security cameras for the car park from yesterday. In the meantime, Martin, I want you to get the painting checked over by an expert.'

'What do you want me to check for?' said Martin.

'Everything you can; find out how old it is for starters. I'm no expert, but it looks pretty old and authentic to me and, if the date etched on the back is genuine, then somebody has just butchered a very old and potentially valuable painting'

'I'm on it,' said Martin as he carefully wrapped the

painting back up in the brown paper.

'Tania, what were the movements of the painting last night?' said Jack.

'After I looked at it in the car park I put it in the boot and drove home. When I got there, I took the painting inside with me and left it in the hallway. Then this morning I ... oh my god,' she said, putting her hand up to her mouth in stark realisation.

'What is it?' said Jack.

'He might have been in my house ... I mean ... to remove the face. He would have had to have come into my house during the night,' she said, sounding anxious.

'You don't know that. Let's gather up all the facts and do a little more research, okay?' he said, in a reassuring voice.

'Okay,' said Tania, still pondering.

'So, this morning the painting was where you left it last night ... in your hallway?'

'Precisely, and wrapped just like I left it. I took it from the house and put it back in the boot of my car and drove to work and brought it straight up here.'

'Have you checked your email this morning?' said Jack, with his Roger Moore eyebrow look.

'No.'

'Well, you should. Go and check right away,' he ordered.

'Ok, I'll just make a quick coffee and then I'll take a look.'

'No, check it now,' said Jack, meaning business. 'I'll make your coffee and bring it over to you. I'll take a look at the emails from yesterday while I'm there, so have them ready.'

'Right,' Tania said, as she turned and headed back over to her desk.

When Tania checked her email, sure enough, there was another email from the mystery man claiming to be a vampire.

Dear Ms de Pré,

I do hope you liked the painting, though I'm sorry that you could only enjoy my face for a brief moment. For your information, the painting in question is, in fact, a portrait of my beloved fourth wife and myself. An artist whom I knew quite well painted it back in 1587.

I'm sorry I had to remove my face; that was an emotionally difficult thing for me to do, but I had to hide my identity in anticipation of what is to come. For now, I only want you to have an image of me in your mind; it will help you when you are publishing the story of my life, which I will shortly be emailing to you as a word document attachment.

I do hope you will start taking me seriously in light of my little gift to you.

Buono ciao, for now,

The Vampire

Just as Tania finished reading the email, Jack showed up at her desk.

'Okay... what do we have?' said Jack, as he placed a mug of coffee on Tania's desk.

'Well, it would appear that the painting was a gift from our friendly vampire. Have a look for yourself,' Tania said.

She gestured towards her computer screen and slid to one side to make room for Jack to lean in and take a look. Jack tapped out a non-descript rhythm on Tania's desk with his fingers as he read through the email.

'Hmm, very cloak and dagger; can I see the ones from yesterday?'

'Sure,' she said, as she opened the other emails. 'Here, have my chair, I'm just going to run this letter over to Cora's desk. It landed on mine by mistake. Back in a sec.' Tania headed off and left Jack to read the emails.

When Tania returned, Jack wasn't there. She sat down to deal with the rest of her new emails, before replying to the mysterious vampire.

Dear Mr Vampire,

It would appear that you have me at something of a disadvantage, the painting appearing in my car, then the face disappearing at some point during the night. All this is very interesting and mysterious, but unfortunately, it proves nothing. Claiming to be a 1000-year-old vampire is simply ludicrous. Vampires are a myth and they simply do not exist. I cannot think why you would try and spin such an outrageous story, but as you can understand, it is not one I can print in my column in any serious capacity.

On another note, did you enter my house during the night?

Regards,

Tania

The very instant Tania clicked the Send button the phone rang on her desk.

'Tania de Pré', she answered, reaching for her coffee.

'Please allow me to retort, Ms de Pré, there's nothing ludicrous about it, and I can assure you that vampires are no myth and they most certainly do exist,' said the very distinctive sounding gentleman on the other end of the phone.

Tania froze mid-mouthful of coffee as she realised it was that of the mysterious vampire.

'I've been a vampire for a thousand years, Ms de Pré,' he said, in a stern tone, 'and I have my reasons for telling my story publicly, which will be revealed in more detail as my story unfolds in your very column. There's nothing outrageous about it, Ms de Pré. One way or another, you will believe me, even if I have to give you physical proof that I can guarantee you won't approve of.'

Tania looked at the Outbox folder on her computer screen and saw that her email had just finished sending, so he couldn't have read it before picking up the phone.

'How did you know what I'd put in the email that I just sent you?'

'Let's just say it goes with the territory of being a vampire; tricks of the trade, Ms de Pré, the same tricks that allowed me to magically remove my face from the oil painting. Now, are you ready to believe me?'

'I can't, I'm a down to earth kind of person. I don't believe in ghosts, ghouls or fairytales, least of all vampires.'

'Very well, Ms de Pré,' he said in a soft, but menacing tone, 'prepare for a second date.'

Tania heard an electronic click on the end of the line; he'd hung up. *Second date, what the hell does that mean*, she thought to herself, as she hung up the phone.

Tania struggled mentally to write the next day's column as she found herself in deep thought about the emails and phone calls from the so-called vampire. While she was pondering, she didn't notice Jack walk up behind her. He put his hand on her shoulder, causing her to half jump out of her skin.

'Jesus, Jack, you scared the bloody life out of me!' She exhaled in relief, putting her hand on her chest.

'Sorry. Come with me, there's something I want you to see.' Jack led Tania to the elevator and down to the ground floor to the security camera control room.

Tania had never been in there before. There was a lone security man in his fifties sitting on a swivel chair in front of a long control desk with about twenty colour monitors mounted along the back wall.

'Okay, show Tania the car park security video from yesterday,' requested Jack. The security man tapped a few keys on his keyboard.

'You're watching monitor six,' said the security man, pointing to the numbered monitor on the wall. Tania watched and saw a man come into view from behind a large concrete pillar. After a brief pause, he walked towards Tania's car. He was dressed entirely in black, wearing a long black coat and what looked like a black Fedora hat with a wider than usual brim. He was carrying the wrapped painting under his arm. When he got to Tania's car, he stood there looking at the passenger side door for a split second, and then his hand extended as he opened it.

'Jack, I'm telling you, the car was locked. I lock it every day,' said Tania adamantly as she watched the video.

'I know you did. I've seen the video from the morning and it clearly showed the hazard lights on your car flash once when you pointed your key fob at it.'

'So how do you explain him just opening the door like that?' she said.

'I don't know,' said Jack, in a soft, serious tone.

They carried on watching. The man in black on the video monitor carefully placed the painting into Tania's car, closed the door, and again briefly, looked at the car before turning and walking away to the left and out of the video monitor's frame.

'That's it, that's all there is,' said Jack. 'At no point do we see his face, nor does he ever look up or directly into any of the security cameras. It's as if he knows where the cameras are and he angles his head accordingly. Just when you think his face is going to be exposed to the camera, it remains in the shadow of the brim of his hat.'

'What about the other cameras? I mean, when he walks out of the frame on monitor six? Surely he pops up on another camera covering the other side?' said Tania, now starting to feel a bit spooked out by having her car space violated.

'That's the funny thing,' said the security man, 'he doesn't. When he walks out of shot on this camera, it's as if he vanishes into thin air.'

'Vanishes, what do you mean? He can't just vanish like that,' said Tania.

'Well, that's precisely what he did,' said the security man. 'I've viewed every other camera angle from in the car park and outside the building, twenty minutes before and after this event, and he's nowhere to be seen ... he's like a ghost. He appeared, and then he disappeared.'

'What's behind that concrete pillar that he walked

behind?' she said, pointing to the pillar on monitor six.

'A fire exit,' said the security man.

'So maybe he came in that way?'

'No, not possible.'

'Have you checked the camera covering that door from the outside?'

'There's no need, there isn't one.'

'Well! What kind of security is that?' huffed Tania.

'No, you don't understand,' said the security man. 'There's no need for a camera there because it's part of the side delivery entrance, and to get there you have to come through the main gate and go through a security check at the barrier, which does have cameras. Of course, he could have landed on the roof via parachute and abseiled down the side of the building,' said the security man with a laugh.

'Ha, that's very funny,' she snorted.

'Okay, thanks for your time,' said Jack to the security man as he opened the door and led Tania back over to the elevator.

As Jack and Tania exited the elevator, Martin was there waiting for them.

'Right, I've got some news on the painting. A friend of mine works next door to an antique dealer who specialises in this sort of thing. He's just arrived. He's in my office with the painting right now,' he said, leading them to his office.

As they entered, the antique dealer was examining the painting closely.

'Jack, Tania, this is Mr Michael Davenport,' said Martin, making the introductions. 'Michael, this is my boss, Jack, and my colleague, Tania.'

'Pleased to meet you,' said Mr Davenport, removing his

round-framed glasses and extending his hand to Jack.

'Pleased to meet you, too,' said Jack, shaking his hand. 'We really appreciate you getting over here so fast and giving up your time to help us out with our little puzzle.'

'Oh, you're quite welcome. I quite enjoy getting away from my premises for a bit of fresh air,' he said, turning to shake Tania's hand and laughing. 'So, you must be the young lady who stumbled upon the painting?'

'That's right,' she said, checking out the odd, but nice little man.

Mr Davenport looked close to retirement age and was quite short; about five foot four. He had an odd round shape that was exaggerated by the hooped pattern on his vibrantly coloured waistcoat. His legs were disproportionally short, compared with his longer upper body. However, he was well turned out and impeccably groomed.

'So what do you make of it?' said Tania, keen to know his findings and first impressions.

'Oh, it's old all right, and I suspect the date of 1587 etched on the back is authentic. Of course, I could take the painting back to my workshop and do some more in-depth scientific tests to be certain.'

'How can you find out the age for sure, with any degree of accuracy, I mean?' said Tania.

'Oh, we have our methods. Age testing a tiny flake of the oil-paint is one relatively accurate method, but based on my experience I'm pretty sure it's authentic.'

'What about the face?'

'Ah yes, your colleague mentioned that. I believe this happened sometime during the night?' he inquired.

'Yes,' she said, tentatively, 'but how could someone remove the paint like that? I mean, leaving a perfect oval of bare canvas? It looks like it was never painted on to start with.'

'Well, in the right hands, there are various methods and modern chemicals that could have been used to achieve this. Do you have any idea why somebody would have broken into your house during the night to do this? I mean, the painting is over 400 years old and potentially quite valuable.'

'No, I have no idea. I'm not sure anybody actually broke into my house … well … I can't be sure,' she said, glancing at Jack for guidance.

'Would you have any objection to me taking this back to my workshop to examine it a little closer?'

'Of course not.' She couldn't say no to this avuncular and sweet man even if she wanted to.

'That's wonderful. I'll have one of my chaps drive over this afternoon to collect it.'

Mr Davenport left the office, leaving Tania, Jack and Martin to ponder.

'Okay, so what we have here is a man who's quite prepared to destroy a valuable antique oil painting. The question is, why?' said Jack raising his right eyebrow. 'Right, this fella's got my attention. Tania, I want you to keep me posted on this vampire chap. I want to hear about everything, every email, every phone call, and especially any more of his weird psychic phenomena, okay.'

'You mean you believe all this vampire stuff?' said Tania, sounding surprised as she always thought Jack was a little cynical and she certainly didn't have him down as somebody who believed in vampires.

'I seriously doubt he's a vampire, but it takes a certain type of person to destroy valuable art, and besides, I've got a hunch about this, and at the end of the day vampires are the flavour of the month. Just look at all the recent cinema movies, TV series and novels. People can't get enough of vampires.'

'I'm a little confused,' said Tania, putting her hand up to her face, unaware of the fact that she was gently stroking the scar down her right cheek with her index finger.

'I'm saying keep me in the loop, there might be a story in this, a big story.'

'You mean a story, or subject matter for my column?' she said, hopefully.

'I'm talking about your column. Look, he isn't a bloody vampire, is he, but I'm sure you can come up with a slant on his story that will get vampire fans hooked and reading your column for a few weeks,' Jack gave Tania a meaningful look, '... right?' he said, authoritatively.

'Yes ... sure ... of course,' she said, trying to contain her excitement, not at the prospect of writing about a phony vampire, but at the prospect of at least keeping her column running.

'Very well, then,' said Jack, 'get on it.' He left and went back to his office.

'Thanks, Martin,' she said, not feeling very comfortable with the idea that she could be indebted to him in some small way.

'Hey, anytime,' he said, looking all smug and proud of himself.

'Ok, well I'm going to "get on it" as Jack said. See you later.' She spun on her heels and headed out of Martin's office before he had chance to make any small talk.

Back at her desk, Tania spent 40 minutes writing up the ending to her current column story; bringing it to a final conclusion, before setting to work on her new mystery vampire story. She then emailed the mystery vampire as she had come up with a comprehensive list of questions to ask him.

Dear Mr Vampire,

Firstly, I do feel a little silly addressing you as Mr Vampire; do you not have a proper name I can use?

Secondly, it appears that since you left the painting in my car, you have got my boss's attention. He is fascinated with the idea and he wants me to find a story in this and run with it in my column at the paper.

So that I can move forward with the story, would you be kind enough to answer the list of questions I've drawn up below:

1. According to vampire myth, they cannot go out during sunlight or daylight in most cases, for fear of busting into flames, or similar. Can you confirm if you go out in the sun or not, and what happens if you do?

2. Can you tell me if you have any extraordinary abilities i.e. super-human strength, night-vision, speed, or other?

3. Do you have fangs? If so, please tell me about them.

4. Do you drink blood and if so, how do you obtain it, how do you go about drinking it and why do you need to do this?

5. Is your skin pale like vampire myths suggest? If so, how did this transformation take place?

6. Anything else you think is relevant.

You mentioned in your previous email that you want me to publish your life story and you have it as a word document. Would you email it to me please?

These questions will satisfy me, for now, but I will be in touch with you again soon.

Regards,

Tania de Pré

Tania then spent the rest of the afternoon making phone calls and doing some speedy research in preparation for her new vampire story.

Later that Friday evening, although she would rather have been relaxing in her own time, she continued with her research at home, which involved several hours on the internet and more phone calls, including one to a north London vampire Goth club called After Dark. She also received an email back from the vampire with the answers to her questions, along with his life story as a word document attachment. He sounded pleased that Tania was now showing some interest and beginning to take him seriously; even if she was prompted by her boss, Jack. Eventually, late in the evening, Tania made a start on the opening column for what she was hoping would turn into one of her most popular column series stories to date. *I hope you're right about this, Jack,* she thought. If ever she needed a break, the time was now! She was so determined to nail this and please Jack, she spent most of the weekend working on it too.

***

'Brilliant, just brilliant, I totally love it!' said Jack with huge enthusiasm as he strode up to Tania's desk on Monday morning.

'Wow!' said Tania, spinning around on her swivel chair, surprised by Jack's reaction. In the past, if Jack felt enthusiastic about a story he would never outwardly show it like this; not with such strong emotion anyway. But Tania figured she would take it while it was there.

'I'm glad you like it,' she said.

'Oh no, I don't just like it, I love it! Though I personally would have been a trifle more diplomatic in places, but I think you have a winner here. I like your angle and I think it will appeal to a wide range of readers. I want this to have a decent run, so make sure you keep the readers hooked in with plenty of energy.'

'Absolutely, I've already started to work out a tangible road map that should keep it going for a few weeks.'

'Great, I want to see them as you write them.'

'As always,' she acknowledged.

Jack left Tania to get on with her work, then just as she turned back to her computer screen Cora showed up.

'Hey, where were you last night? I tried calling a couple of times on your landline and your mobile.'

'Oh yeah, I'm sorry. I turned the volume off on my landline and put my mobile on silent. When I saw how keen Jack was to run with this vampire story, I guess I just wanted to crack on with it and do the best job I could.'

'Yeah, I heard all about it. So, how's it going?'

'Great. I spent Friday evening researching, then over the weekend I wrote up a plan for a series and even completed part one.'

'That's great! I'm really pleased for you,' said Cora, rubbing Tania's shoulder.

'Well, I spent enough time researching and writing it, and I'm pretty pleased, if I do say so myself.'

'Has Jack seen it yet? I saw him leaving your desk as I was coming over.'

'Yeah, he loved it. I mean he really loved it.'

'That's great! I'm genuinely happy for you, Tania.'

'Yeah, I've never seen Jack react so positively to a story before, he was so animated and excited.'

'Well, you know Jack. I'd soak it up while it lasts.'

'That's what I thought. You know, at first I just couldn't see a story in this at all, but Friday night while I was doing some research on the web, it just hit me, and I thought of a really great angle.'

'Can I take a look?' said Cora, clapping her hands together enthusiastically while doing little bunny-hops on the spot like an American teenage cheerleader who'd just been told she'd won Miss Teen USA.

'Calm down, Cora, it's only my opening. Crumbs! First Jack, now you! Has the world gone vampire mad? I'll email it over to you later.' Just then, Tania's desk phone rang.

'Ok, I'll let you get that, catch you later.' Cora headed back across the office floor to her desk.

'Tania de Pré', she answered.

'I trust all my answers were to your satisfaction?' said the unmistakable voice, referring to his recent email.

'Oh, yes, they were perfect, thank you.'

'So does this mean you're going to run my story?'

'Yes … yes I suppose it does,' she said, cautiously.

'That's excellent news.'

'Well, if you want me to be honest, it wasn't my idea. My

boss got wind of it and after he read your emails, he insisted that I run a story.'

'Nonetheless, I won't hold it against you, Ms de Pré. In time I'm sure you'll enjoy publishing my story in your column. Trust me; this story's going to get much more interesting. So when do you expect to go to print?'

'Well, my boss is really enthusiastic about what I've written so far and wants to go to print the day after tomorrow.'

'Excellent. Well, you have my email address, and my mobile contact number is on the signature, so you can get hold of me quite easily if you have any further questions. With regard to the word document I emailed you, I'll leave it up to your professional journalistic skills to condense it down and turn it into more manageable sections for your column.'

'Thank you,' she said, not quite believing that she was having a conversation with a vampire about banalities such as word documents and contact numbers.

'Oh, and I think we should meet, in person. I think it will help you make my story more authentic.'

'Well, I'm not sure that's really necessary for this particular story.' The truth was she was actually too scared to consider meeting him.

'Oh, but it is,' he insisted.

'Perhaps,' she said, in an attempt to lead him off the subject of actually meeting.

'Well, I'll leave you to your work Ms de Pré.' He hung up.

Chapter 4

A teenage boy cycled up to a large, black wrought-iron gate and pressed the button on the intercom system, then looked up towards the security camera while waiting for an answer.

'Good morning, Will,' said a voice via the intercom, in a friendly and familiar manner.

'Good morning, Mr Burnel,' said Will, in his usual polite and courteous way, which didn't quite match his attire.

Will was a skinny 15-year-old with messy shoulder-length light blonde hair, and although he dressed like a grunge rock guitarist from Seattle, his manners and speaking voice were surprisingly impeccable.

'Please, come up to the house,' said Mr Burnel, as the electronic gate started to open.

Will started to cycle along the long winding driveway. He had cycled up this driveway many times before and always enjoyed and appreciated the beautiful surroundings. At this early hour of the morning the grounds of Mr Burnel's estate looked like something out of a fairytale. The tall weeping willows formed a perfect line along either side of the winding drive, shading it from the bright June sunlight, putting it into almost total darkness. At the foot of the trees and beyond them into the distance the ground was a wash of early summer bluebells that were blinding with their vibrant blue colour. With not so much of a hint of breeze, the weeping willows and bluebells lay perfectly still in an eerie and surreal way; the silence broken only by the chirruping song of the many goldfinches that inhabited the grounds.

Although Will was into his heavy metal music and played the electric guitar, he had been well educated in classical music and, although he would not admit it to his peers, he really enjoyed his on-going classical piano lessons, which he'd been having since he was six years old. It was for this reason that he could pause on this regular short journey up to Mr Burnel's house, and mentally hear the first movement of Beethoven's Moonlight Sonata as he gazed along the winding drive at the weeping willows and mass of bluebells covering the ground beneath the trees. The ever-expanding wash of bluebells reminded him of a perfectly placid blue lake. Will always spent a few moments here soaking up this dreamlike scene before continuing up the driveway to the large house.

At the house he carefully lay his BMX bike down on the gravel at the foot of the steps and paused to observe several goldfinches feeding on the various metal feeders hanging from a tree in the open gardens to the side of the house. They looked almost angelic as the bright sunlight hit their feathers. Their gold and black wings, and black, red and white heads, and light tan and white chests made them look like birds from a tropical paradise. Will thought they looked out of place here on the outskirts of north London.

He climbed the four wide stone steps that led up to the large black double wooden doors. At this moment, Will's beautiful scenic fantasy to Beethoven's Moonlight Sonata left him, only to be replaced by a feeling that was somewhat uncertain. He couldn't quite put his finger on why he felt this way, or why he should feel differently. After all, he had run many errands for Mr Burnel over the years.

Although the secure black iron gates from the main road were all very high-tech with a two-way intercom system and security camera, the wooden doors at the house had no such technology. Instead, there was an old-fashioned metal doorknocker, which looked very similar to the female symbol. It had a large circle that was hinged near the top, with a cross coming out of the bottom. Will went to grab the metal cross part to knock the door, but just as he reached up for it, the door opened. Will stood back and moved away from the door, down a single step. This gesture was partly down to Will's surprising manners. Backing away from the door showed respect to the owner of the house; but he also backed away slightly because of the uneasy feeling that he could never quite explain.

'Hello, Will,' said Mr Burnel, in a soft, but distinctive and definite tone.

'Hello, Mr Burnel,' said Will, politely.

'I have the things you wanted, along with The Sentinel newspaper you requested,' he said, climbing back up the final step and offering Mr Burnel a carrier bag via his fully extended arm. By now, Will's uneasy feelings had stepped up a gear, but he was doing a good job of hiding them (or so he thought) as he stood there nervously trying not to look directly into Mr Burnel's eyes. Mr Burnel's eyes looked very fierce and penetrating to Will; like those of his school friend's Siberian husky dog. They were vibrant white with a hint of blue, almost albino-like, with a distinctive black outline and blacker than black pupils, all of which were made even more intense against the bright white area at the edges; an overall very cold and spine chilling look. Although Mr Burnel's frame was quite thin, he somehow came across as a physically powerful man who you would not want to mess with. He was just over six feet tall, with jet-black hair that was impeccably cut and shaped. His cheekbones were well defined giving his face a strong and distinct appearance. Although there was an over-sized porch shading the entire front door from the daylight, his face stood out from the shadow in which he stood, due to its insipidly pale complexion. Will was unable to put an age to Mr Burnel. If he had to guess, he would say mid-thirties; but there was something about him that made it very difficult to say for sure. He could quite easily be fifteen years either side of that; who knew.

'And I have something for you too,' Burnel said as he took the bag off Will and offered him a small flat package about 14 inches across, wrapped in brown paper. Will looked at Mr Burnel uncertainly, not really knowing how to accept his gift.

'It's okay, it won't bite,' he joked, as his bluish red lips turned up into a more welcoming smile. At this, Will smiled back and carefully took the package.

'Thank you,' he said, trying not to sound nervous.

'Well, aren't you going to open it?'

'Oh … yes … sure.' He nervously unwrapped the brown paper. Inside was a framed and signed 10 x 8 inch photo of the late Nirvana front man, Kurt Cobain. Will was about to shout *Un-fucking-believable!!* But then remembered the company he was in and thought better of it.

'Oh my god,' he said, putting his free hand to his mouth unable to contain his excitement. This pleased Mr Burnel greatly. 'He's like … my idol … I'm his …' before he could finish his sentence, Mr Burnel interrupted.

'Number one fan, yes, I know.'

'How? How did you know?'

'Oh, let's just say it was a wild stab in the dark; your attire gave me a clue. I've seen you wearing various Nirvana T-shirts on several occasions, often sporting a portrait of Mr Cobain himself; you even share the same haircut,' he smiled.

'How did you get hold of this? I've never seen this photo of him before.'

'Just something I picked up along the way. Over the years I've picked up many objects and various relics.'

'You're too kind, Mr Burnel,' said Will, thinking he should not really accept the gift, but he knew damn well that there was no way on earth he was going to give it back. Mr Burnel knew exactly what Will was thinking, just as he knew how he was a huge Kurt Cobain fan, and it had nothing to do with T-shirts and scruffy long blonde hairstyles. He could read Will's thoughts as clearly as mortal humans could read the subtitles on a silent movie.

'Well, it's just my way of showing you my appreciation for the many errands you run for me. I really appreciate what you do for me, Will.'

'Thank you, Mr Burnel. If there's anything else you need, you know where to find me.'

'Thank you, Will, you're a good lad.'

'You're welcome, sir.'

'Well then, until the next time.'

Mr Burnel stood back from the door and stepped deeper into the dark shadowy hallway, never taking his eyes off Will. The door closed, seemingly by itself. Will looked down at the framed signed photo, the slightly uneasy feeling now replaced by sheer joy. *This must be worth a fortune!* He smiled to himself and carefully wrapped it back up, put it in his canvas over-the-shoulder bag and cycled back down the winding driveway between the weeping willows towards the main gate; only instead of exiting through it, he turned right off the main driveway down a short track to a cottage just inside the main entrance, on the grounds owned by Tristan Syhier Burnel.

Back at the main house, Tristan took out the newspaper and sat down to read it. He thumbed straight to Tania's column page, but when he found it, the title was not quite what he had been expecting.

SO YOU WANT TO BE A VAMPIRE?
By Tania de Pré

Vampires have never been so popular. During the last five years alone there have been vampire movie cinema releases in abundance, several television series and enough dark vampire romance novels to justify an entirely new genre section in the book stores. It would appear that everybody loves a good vampire story. Adults love the mysterious side of the vampire as they escape the real world and sink into the characters of a good novel. Every teenage girl fantasises about being seduced by a young, dark, romantic vampire, while teenage boys fantasise about doing the dark seducing. The vampire story is popular in every language; the world is in love with the vampire genre.

But do vampires really exist, or are they simply a myth? That is what my column is going to be examining during the course of the next few weeks. As usual, if you have any questions or something tangible that you want to input, you can email me at the usual address at the end of this column.

To start this series I contacted a north London vampire group and recently went along to one of their recent monthly meetings where I spent the late evening and early hours mingling and chatting with some so-called human vampires, most of whom I found to be quite friendly and relatively harmless. However, it was an email that I received from a man claiming to be a genuine 1000-year-old vampire that inspired this new series. So I'll also be examining the mental psychology of those who take the idea to the extreme.

So, what attracts these people to this dark gothic trend and why do many of them so desperately want to be vampires? Based on my research, along with my visit to a recent vampire group meeting, I will give you my findings so far.

Many of the members of the vampire group that I met up with simply want to dress up in gothic clothing, put on make up, and possibly a set of plastic fangs, and have a few drinks and a dance to the gothic rock tunes played out by the hired DJ. This part of the group are harmless in the same way that people following music trends of yesteryear such as Beatle-mania, punk, ska, metal, new romantic, reggae etc. are. But a small minority appear to be mentally delusional and take it a little more seriously; often to ridiculous extremes. Some people are of the opinion that this minority is made up of nothing more than pseudo-vampires or vampire lifestylers. It is this group that I have decided to concentrate on, to see how far this minority attempt to bring about what they call vampirification i.e. the transformation from human to vampire – and why they want to do it? There are many possible answers, most of which are psychological.

I spoke with one such young male, aged just 17. This teenager, who I cannot mention by name, told me that he is a member of several vampire groups both in London and other parts of the UK, and that he has to lie about his age to get into one of the clubs' monthly meetings due to their minimum age restriction of 18. This individual is so obsessed with being a vampire that he seriously believes that he is already halfway through the vampirification process. He has had extreme private dental work done at great expense by having his two canine teeth crowned with metal and porcelain, colour matched and sharpened up to look like vampire fangs.

To get this work done privately he had to use a fake ID, lying about his age. He has also used mild bleaching agents on his face and neck to give himself a paler more vampire-like complexion. He wears wolf-effect contact lenses to make his eyes appear fiercer and vampire-like in appearance, and he even tells me that he has several willing donors who allow him to drink their blood on a regular basis.

This young man has effectively dropped out of society and has become an outcast. He won't go outside during daylight hours or mix with regular people. He is delusional to the point that he seriously believes that there is a real vampire who communicates with him via private messages on an internet forum that he belongs to. When I questioned him about why he feels the need to drink human blood, he has convinced himself that his body needs it, or he will die. This is a seriously extreme and rare case, and I was surprised to come across such a case so early on in my research. Any human vampire who might be reading this should be warned about the dangers of drinking another person's blood. Whether it is in quantity, or just a pinprick off the end of somebody's finger; the dangers are the same. Drinking somebody's blood is nothing more than a stupid and dangerous alternative to eating lots of spinach. With HIV and other modern blood-borne diseases, drinking human blood is a very dangerous game to play and not one that I would recommend participating in.

Perhaps you are a human vampire, or maybe you know one. During the next few weeks I'll be looking deeper into this trend; the fangs, both plastic and dental, the clothes, the lifestyle, the psychology and more. Being a human vampire is definitely more popular with younger people. Perhaps it is because these otherwise adolescent outcasts can feel like they belong to something; a cult. Or perhaps it is a rebellious reaction to being a part of regular society. Vampire groups are more popular than I first thought, with underground vampire cultures in most of the major cities around the UK. There is a very large vampire scene in Paris and New York. More on this fascinating subject tomorrow. In the meantime, feel free to email me, Tania de Pré, with your thoughts.

Tristan calmly put the paper to one side and stared straight ahead, fixing his eyes on a bronze statue of a woman lying in a sensual pose. His calm and cool exterior was at the other end of the spectrum to what he was feeling inside right now. His eyes were so penetrating and fierce it looked like lasers were about to shoot out of them and melt the bronze statue that they were fixed on. To say that he was angry would be the understatement of the century. He thought he was going to get the beginnings of his long and tormented vampire life-story in print; instead, what he got was a total farce.

Tania de Pré had just made a total mockery of him, his life, and everything he stood for; she hadn't taken him seriously at all. Tristan Syhier Burnel was livid, and that was putting it mildly; very mildly. Suddenly he had murderous thoughts, cold brutal blood-curdling thoughts; thoughts that were about to be put into practice to teach Tania de Pré a lesson that she would never forget.

'You will mock me no more, Ms de Pré!' he calmly whispered to himself.

He stood up and looked at the early seventeenth century grandfather clock against the far wall; 8:45 according to the Roman numeral clock face. He then looked towards one of the large windows that were covered with long black velvet drapes from floor-to-ceiling, drapes with a lightproof backing to prevent any daylight from leaking through. For Tristan, dusk couldn't come quickly enough, but his saving grace was that he had the entire day to plan something that Tania de Pré would not forget in a hurry. No more words, no more oil paintings; it was time for action!!

Chapter 5

The following morning at the newspaper office everybody had managed to go about their work up until lunchtime as normal, even though it was Jack's birthday; nobody gave anything away. Jack had said nothing, and neither had any of the staff as they had planned a little birthday surprise for him. While Jack was out for lunch between 1 and 2, Cora and Seth prepared a table not too far from the elevator on which they had placed a birthday cake with a single candle, a bottle of champagne, some glasses, and his present. Cora had told the front desk on the ground floor to call her desk phone to warn them of Jack's return from lunch so everybody could gather around and get ready to surprise him.

At 2pm on the dot, Cora's desk phone rang and the front desk informed her that Jack had just walked through the front revolving glass doors and was on his way to the elevator.

'Ok, everybody get ready, he's on his way up,' shouted Cora across the office floor. Everybody got in place forming a group near the elevator doors. Ping! The elevator arrived. As the doors started to open everybody broke into enthusiastic singing of "Happy Birthday". Jack exited the elevator. Although he was internally happy at this gesture, externally, he didn't give away his emotions.

'Okay, okay, you got me,' he said as he gestured with his hands for the singing to stop.

'Happy birthday, Jack,' said Cora as she stepped forward with his beautifully wrapped present.

'Oh my,' he said, a little embarrassed, 'I wasn't expecting a present.'

'Go ahead, open it,' said Cora, excited.

Jack obliged and unwrapped his present.

'Oh my, what do we have here,' he said excitedly as he took out a copy of The Beatles White Album on 12-inch vinyl. 'Is this what I think it is? Oh my god ... it is!' He had seen the serial number on the album cover.

It was one of the first original 5000 copies to be pressed. He quickly and carefully took the vinyl record out of its sleeve to inspect its condition. Jack was a huge hi-fi enthusiast, and an even bigger fan of vinyl. 'Wow, it's as close to mint as I've ever seen!' He studied the writing on the label in the center of the record very closely. 'It's an original mono pressing from 1968!' He was unable to contain his excitement.

'So who was responsible for tracking this little beauty down?' he asked, scanning his employees.

'Oh, Martin found it, and at a rock-bottom price too', said Cora.

But of course, thought Tania as her lips tightened.

'Well, Martin, you've really come up trumps with this little gem. Is there no end to your investigative talents?' Jack said, happy as a dog with two tails.

Cora proceeded to pour the champagne and invited

Jack to blow out the candle on the cake. Once the brief celebrations were over, everybody headed back to their desks to continue with their work. Jack headed over to his office clutching his prized birthday gift.

Tania pressed on with her human vampire research while continuing to write the next part to her new column. She'd already had several emails that morning regarding yesterday's column with an abundance of interesting comments, suggestions and stories; all very positive feedback, with readers generally loving the opener to this exciting new human vampire series. From these first emails alone, Tania had a wealth of new ideas that would keep this new theme strong and popular for many weeks to come. *Jack was right,* she thought. At that moment she decided it was time for an afternoon coffee so she headed towards the staffroom via Jack's office. She knocked on his door.

'Come!' shouted Jack.

'I just thought I'd pop by and give you an update on some of the feedback I've had from yesterday's column.'

'Yes, it would seem congratulations are in order,' he said, leaving what he was doing and giving Tania his full attention.

'Oh?' she questioned.

'I've had a few emails myself from readers saying how much they liked your introductory story, especially your hard-hitting approach to it.'

'That's great,' she said, remaining totally professional while trying to contain her excitement. Just then there was a knock on Jack's half-open office door and one of the staff from the front desk downstairs appeared holding a square parcel under one arm.

'A courier just delivered this package to the front desk downstairs, sir.'

'Ah, another birthday gift perhaps, be it a bit late in the day' said Jack, grinning to himself and relieving the man of the package. The man looked like he was about to say something else, but Jack cut him short.

'Thank you,' said Jack, ushering him out of his office and closing the door behind him.

'Hmmm, it's quite heavy, wonder what it could be?' he said, putting on a joking sinister voice and facial expression as he placed it on the desk and reached for his pocketknife.

Jack carefully pushed just the first three millimetres of his sharp knife into what he guessed to be the join of the thick cardboard underneath the brown sealing tape. He ran the knife along the entire top edge of the box with his thumb held three millimetres from the tip of the blade to prevent it going through the box too far and potentially cutting into whatever was inside. He repeated the same procedure along either edge to allow him to access the box from the top. Jack gave Tania one final sinister glance, joking around with one raised eyebrow to build a comical tension. Still looking at Tania, he folded up the two top flaps of the box until they were both perfectly upright; he looked down into the box.

'Jesus Christ!!' he shouted in total shock-horror as he let go of the two cardboard flaps and jolted away from the box as if it had just sent a 10,000-volt shock through him. His actions made Tania jump.

'What, what is it!' she shouted.

Jack just looked and pointed at the box, panting and unable to get his words out.

'It's, it's a ...' he continued huffing and puffing with his left hand held against his chest, trying to catch his breath and regain composure.

Tania stepped forward cautiously as she could see that this was definitely not one of Jack's jokes. Although Tania was a cautious woman, she was certain it was not a bomb, as it probably would have detonated during the opening stage. Whatever it was, she felt it was at least safe enough for her to lift the two top flaps up (which had sprung back down) and take a peek. Meanwhile, Jack leaned against the desk and tried to compose himself.

'No, don't look,' he said, able to speak a little better now, but still holding his chest. The curious Tania ignored his advice and carefully opened the two top flaps of the box using just the very tips of her fingers with the gentleness and precision of a surgeon.

'Oh my god!!' she screamed, backing away from the box.

After the brief adrenaline shock rush and a few deep breaths, Tania looked up at Jack.

'Is ... is it real?' she asked in a fast rapid-fire style voice.

'It bloody well looks real to me!' said Jack.

Just then, Martin glanced through Jack's office windows as he walked past and noticed that something was not quite right. He burst in without even knocking.

'Hey, what's going on?' he said, assessing the seriousness of the situation.

'The package,' said Tania, pointing to the box on Jack's desk.

'What about it?' said Martin as he bee-lined towards the package and opened the two flaps before Jack or Tania had a chance to warn him of its contents.

'Holy fucking shit!' shouted Martin, withdrawing his hands from the box with speed that would suggest the box contained live rattlesnakes.

Jack, Tania and Martin had all seen what appeared to be a severed human head, face up in the box. It was held in place and supported with bubble wrap. It was the head of a white male, possibly in his mid-thirties; but it was kind of hard to tell as it had turned quite pale and was a bit contorted.

'Oh no,' said Tania, looking at the courier's address label on the side of the box.

'Jack, it wasn't a birthday gift for you. Look at the name on the courier label,' she said, pointing to the side of the box, 'it's addressed to me!'

Jack didn't hesitate a moment longer. He picked up the phone on his desk and frantically punched 999 onto the keypad.

'Emergency services, which service do you require,' said the female voice on the other end of the phone.

'Police!' said Jack.

It seemed like just a few minutes had passed by the time two police officers arrived in Jack's office. They looked at the severed head and assessed the situation. One of them called it in via his walkie-talkie while the other officer proceeded to move everybody out of the office and cordon the scene off with yellow tape reading

"CRIME SCENE – DO NOT CROSS".

Chapter 6

The entire office floor was empty, except for two CSI's in Jack's office. One video-recorded and photographed the box containing the severed head and the crime scene in general, while the other scrutinised the scene closely for other evidence.

Police officers littered other parts of the building, mainly the lobby area on the ground floor where the package was originally delivered. A detective, Inspector Maldini, was at the front desk questioning the lobby reception staff about the courier who had delivered the box, while another detective, Chief Inspector O'Connor, was questioning Jack, Tania and Martin in a vacant office on the ground floor, away from the crime scene.

'I actually opened the box by mistake. It's my fiftieth birthday today and when the package came up I just assumed it was for me. I didn't bother to read the name on the address label,' Jack explained to Detective Chief Inspector O'Connor.

'Miss? …' said the detective, looking at Tania searching for her name.

'de Pré, Tania de Pré,' she answered.

'Ms de Pré, did you recognise ... the head?'

'No, it just looked horrible, so please, don't ask me to look at it again.'

'Don't worry, Ms de Pré, that won't happen.'

'I'm pleased to hear it' said Tania, sounding anxious and just wanting to get the hell out of the small claustrophobic office they were in. All she wanted to do right now was to go next door to the Italian restaurant and have a large glass of red wine.

'You seem a little on edge, Ms de Pré,' said the detective in a slightly derogatory tone.

'With respect, detective, it's not every day that I get to look inside a box only to be greeted by a severed fucking head!' she said in a louder than usual and quite agitated voice. Jack and Martin both looked at Tania in shock. Although Tania could be a little rebellious and anarchic at times, they were both surprised that she would let rip and swear like that in front of a police detective.

'I apologise ... you're right,' said the detective, realising that he had overstepped the mark slightly with his suggestive tone.

'Look, have you got any idea who could have done this, and why they would send it to you?' said the detective.

'No ... well ... not really.' Just then, Tania's mobile phone rang. The detective looked at Tania questioningly. He gestured with his head to suggest she should answer it. Taking the detective's cue she reached into her jacket pocket and took out her phone. She looked at the screen. *BLOCKED*, read the display. Tania was always a little nervous about answering blocked or withheld numbers, and today was definitely no different.

'Well, aren't you going to answer it?' said the detective. Tania nervously pressed the answer button.

'Tania de Pré,' she said in a slightly nervous, but corporate voice.

'Hello, Tania,' said the voice. Tania immediately recognised it as The Vampire.

'I do hope you enjoyed my little surprise; handsome fellow isn't he? Did you recognise him without his body? Perhaps now you'll start to take me a little more seriously.'

Tania slowly lifted her head and looked at the detective with a look of shock-horror on her face.

'I don't take kindly to being mocked and humiliated, especially so publicly via your newspaper column,' continued the vampire. 'Human vampires, Ms de Pré, are nothing more than social misfits, young people looking for an identity, Goth music fans and reprobates, but they certainly aren't vampires. I, on the other hand, am a genuine vampire and one way or another you will learn this. I expect to see a marked improvement in your column, or more heads will roll. I expect you to start publishing my story using the word document attachment I've emailed you. Do not underestimate me, Ms de Pré ... do we understand each other?'

Tania was silent and stood perfectly still.

'Good, I'll take your silence as a yes.'

He hung up without waiting for Tania to speak. She slowly moved the phone from her ear and lowered her hand; still looking at the detective in a state of shock.

'Everything okay?' asked the detective.

'It's him,' said Tania softly, looking towards Jack, somewhat stunned by the call.

'Who? What are you talking about?' said Jack.

'The vampire.'

'Vampire?' said Chief Inspector O'Connor.

Just then there was a knock on the office door. DCI O'Connor opened it to one of the CSIs.

'Detective, can I talk to you for a moment,' said the CSI.

'Give me a minute, I'll be right out,' said the detective turning back to Tania.

'You were saying something about a vampire, Ms de Pré?' sounding more urgent.

'The man who just phoned me is the man responsible for the head in the box upstairs.'

'Can I see your phone?' said the detective, as he looked at his watch noting the time.

Tania obliged.

'Okay, explain,' said the detective.

'It all started with this email I got last week from a man claiming to be a vampire. Naturally I didn't believe him. I just put it down to spam, or a joke from one of my colleagues, but a few things have since happened.'

'Go on,' said the detective looking at Tania's mobile phone. He noticed the caller blocked the last call. Tania went on to explain to the detective the whole story from the very beginning, including the oil painting that was left in her car. There was a knock at the office door, and then Detective Inspector Maldini entered.

'Sorry to interrupt,' said the detective, 'I've got one of the team tracing the origins of the package via the courier company.'

'Good, I also need you to get onto the service provider

of Ms de Pré's mobile phone and get hold of the number of the last blocked call. Ms de Pré just had a call from a man claiming to be responsible for the severed head.' He handed Tania's mobile phone to DI Maldini.

'Ms de Pré, this is Detective Inspector Maldini. He's going to be working with me on this case and guaranteeing your safety until we know what we're dealing with.'

'Detective,' she said, nodding politely and acknowledging him.

'I'm going to need you to get the phone back to Ms de Pré ASAP in case he calls back and I want you to set up an interception trace on the number; I'm assuming this is okay with you, Ms de Pré?' said DCI O'Connor.

'What does that entail exactly?' said Tania.

'It means we'll be able to listen in and record the phone calls that you receive on your mobile phone and we'll also be able to trace where they're coming from. But we need your permission to set this up.'

'Yes, that's fine,' she said.

'Thank you.'

Detective Maldini left the room and got to work.

'Mr Savage, do you have the address of the antique dealer who has the painting? It's evidence, and I'll need to get it to forensics right away.'

'Sure, here's his card,' said Jack, reaching into his pocket and handing the business card to the detective.

'Ms de Pré, can you show me the emails you mentioned?'

'Sure, they're on my computer upstairs.'

'Okay, just give me a second,' he said, stepping outside the office and closing the door behind him.

'Sorry to keep you waiting,' said the detective to the CSI.

'There appears to be some strange marks on the victim's neck, sir; they looks like some sort of bite marks,' said the CSI.

'Bite marks?' said DCI O'Connor.

'Well, sort of. At the top of the neck below the left ear there are two puncture holes and, between them, four other surface marks.'

'Has the head been put in a body bag yet?' asked the detective.

'Not yet.'

'Okay, let me come up and take a look. You go ahead, I'll be right behind you,' said the detective as he turned and went back into the office.

'I have to go upstairs for a moment. The CSIs have found an unusual mark on the severed head. Ms de Pré, if you come with me you can show me the emails and tell me about that phone call on the way.'

'I'd like to take another look at the head, if that's possible,' said Tania.

'Excuse me?' said the detective, sounding surprised.

'The phone call I just had; he asked if I recognised him without his body ... it might be someone I know.'

'I'm afraid that won't be possible. After the head has been sanitised and photographed it might be possible to show you a photo, but for now we have to find out as much as we can,' said the detective, holding the office door open for her.

'Do you need us for anything else, Detective?' said Jack.

'No, but my CSIs are going to need a few more hours before your staff can return to the office.'

Tania and Detective O'Connor went upstairs to the main office and straight to Tania's desk where she showed him the emails. The detective then had one of his colleagues escort Tania back downstairs away from the crime scene before heading over to Jack's office to view the bite marks on the head.

The two CSIs were finishing up their work and had already placed the severed head into a body bag ready to be taken away. The box had also been placed into a sealed bag all ready to be taken away for closer examination in the hope of retrieving fingerprints off it and other clues.

DCI O'Connor walked over to the CSIs standing next to the evidence.

'Okay, show me these bite marks,' said the detective.

The CSI manager unzipped the body bag.

'Right there,' said the CSI, pointing with the tip of his pencil.

'These four marks resemble a regular bite imprint from another person, but the two larger puncture holes either side are more reminiscent to some kind of fanged animal.'

'Fanged animal?'

'Yes, we'll know more when the pathologist looks at it in more detail at the mortuary.'

'Right! I want a forensic odontologist at the Post Mortem as well,' ordered the detective.

'I'll get on the phone and arrange that right away,' said the CSI manager.

'Good, let me know as soon as you've got any new information.'

'Yes, sir.'

'Okay, you can take these away now,' said the detective to the two CSIs who left with the body bag, box and their equipment.

DCI O'Connor, his deputy, DI Maldini, and the rest of the team worked hard and fast gathering up as much information and evidence as possible during the initial few hours after the two police officers first arrived to assess the situation. There was some conflict, as the police don't usually like any publicity or media around these situations, yet they were in a building full of journalists and press photographers at the newspaper's office. Because of this, DCI O'Connor quickly decided that he was happy that the crime had not happened at the office since the severed head was delivered via courier in a well-packed box. As he was keen to get the head off to the mortuary, he allowed the staff at the paper back into their office to get back to work about three hours later at 5:15pm.

News like this soon spreads and Jack was worried that it would be leaked and picked up by other national newspapers, or worse still, television. He knew that he would not be able to keep this under wraps for long. The final fifteen minutes of the day at the office were quite frantic. Jack spent most of it pacing up and down, trying to figure out how he could deal with things when the news eventually got out. Tania was totally freaked out by the incident and could not concentrate on her writing. Even if she had wanted to, it was kind of hard as she'd got her mobile phone back and Detective Maldini had been given the job of staying with her in case she got another call – for her personal protection or at least until the police knew what they were dealing with. Her saving grace was that it was late in the day and she was due to finish work in about ten minutes anyway.

'Look, is this really necessary?' Tania said to the detective in a polite, but mildly annoyed tone.

'I'm sorry ma'am; I have to stay with you for now. It's for your own protection, just until we're sure you aren't in any danger.'

'How long is that likely to take?'

'I'm not sure, let's just see what the rest of the team comes up with over the next twenty four hours.'

'Okay, but do you have to stand there looking at me like that, you're making me nervous.'

'I'm sorry ma'am,' he said in a soft, but professional voice.

Even though Tania was mildly annoyed at having the detective joined at her hip, he was quite endearing and likable. The detective was a mix between handsome and pretty. He had well defined cheekbones with one of those boyish faces, kind of like a young Johnny Depp. But he also had a handsome demeanor about him and was well turned out, wearing a relatively classy looking suit and expensive shiny black brogues.

'So, Detective Maldini, do you have a first name?' she asked, trying to relieve the tension and awkwardness of the situation.

'Yes I do, ma'am,' he said, politely and a little embarrassed.

'Well, come on then, spit it out', she said.

He looked down at his shoes briefly before looking back up and answering.

'Marion, ma'am,' he said, embarrassed.

Tania laughed out loud.

'I'm sorry, I didn't mean to laugh. Please – forgive me,' she said, still holding her hand over her mouth to cover up her tickled smile.

'It's okay; I get that all the time. My parents are Italian and my mother was a big John Wayne fan, but she felt that John was too common so she chose his real name instead,' he said, smiling.

'Okay, Marion, I'll promise to address you as Detective Maldini, if you promise to quit calling me ma'am and start calling me Tania … deal?' she smiled holding out her hand inviting for him to shake on it.

'Deal,' he said, shaking her hand and smiling.

She couldn't help thinking to herself how soft and smooth his hand felt, under the firm grip of his handshake.

'You look pretty young for a detective … Detective?'

'Well, I'm 34 years old, ma'am … sorry … Tania,' he said, trying to get comfortable with the idea of addressing her by her first name.

'Well, you look a lot younger.'

'Thank you,' he said, sheepishly.

'So, do you really think I'm in any danger?' she asked, thinking she possibly could be, or they would not have assigned the detective to stay with her temporarily.

'I can't say for sure as we don't have enough information yet. It's just a precaution. I'm sure there's nothing to be overly concerned about,' he said, trying to reassure her.

'How long is all this going to take?'

'I'm sure we'll know a lot more within a few days.'

'A few days, and you're going to stay by my side during

that time?'

'Not exactly,' he said, smiling, 'we can place you in a safe house; there's one not too far from here.'

'A safe house?'

'Yes, somewhere you can stay for a few days until we know what we're dealing with. I'm assuming as a journalist you could work from home, or in this case, a safe house?'

'I'd rather not do that, Detective.'

'It will only be temporary, and it's for your own protection.'

'Look, I just don't think I'm in any serious danger.'

'How can you be so sure?'

'He needs me for his story. Besides, something just tells me I'm in no imminent danger from him ... call it gut instinct, Detective.'

'Well, we can't force you to go into a safe house; we can only suggest and give you advice. If you choose not to, that would be your prerogative, but I'd strongly advise against staying at your own house, at least until we have more information.'

'Thank you, Detective, but I'll be fine.'

'Okay. Well, then at least let me escort you back home. My car's already parked opposite yours in the office car park. When you leave, I'll escort you to your car and follow you back to your house in mine and, if it's okay with you, I'll come into your house to establish security.'

Tania was finding Detective Maldini more and more likable by the minute and although she noticed he was not wearing a wedding ring and found him quite attractive, she figured this *nice* man would not be able to handle her fiery and often unruly ways. She couldn't even handle herself sometimes. *Wait a minute, back up. Reality check*, she thought. Detective Maldini is only here to do his job, to protect me.

'Would you like a cup of coffee, Detective? I'm parched after all the questions from your boss,' she said, getting up to go and make one herself.

'That would be nice,' he said in a tone that suggested he was well overdue a caffeine fix.

She looked over her shoulder as she walked across the office floor towards the staffroom. Detective Maldini was right behind her.

'I'm sure nothing's going to happen to me on the way to the staffroom, Detective.'

'I know. I thought I'd come along just the same.'

'I figured you would,' she said smiling.

One of Tania's work colleagues gave her a knowing smile from her desk after clocking the handsome detective right behind her. Tania smiled back at her and shook her head with a silly smile on her face to suggest he was not her type. Surprisingly, most of the office staff had managed to put the head-in-the-box thing if not totally out of mind, certainly to the back of it, to allow them to go about business as usual, for the final minutes of the day.

In the staff room, Tania flicked the switch on the kettle.

'How do you take it?' she asked.

'Oh, just plain old black will be great, thank you.'

'Do you think you'll find him?'

'The man responsible for the severed head … yes!' he said.

'You sound very confident, Detective.'

'Well, anybody doing anything as drastic as this is bound

to have slipped up somewhere. He'll have left a clue or some evidence along the way. If he's made a mistake, and I'm sure he has, we'll find it ... every contact leaves a trace.'

'I'm sorry?' said Tania, questioning the detective's last five words.

'Oh, a famous forensic scientist once said, "Every contact leaves a trace." ... Look, if this guy's slipped up, we'll spot his mistake and find him.'

'Have you ever had a case like this before?' she asked.

'Well, this is the first time I've ever been on a case involving a severed head, if that's what you mean,' he said, not really sure if that was what she meant.

'But don't worry, we're pretty experienced at this kind of thing and we have a good team of people working on it. We'll find him,' again, sounding confident.

'Always get your man, Detective?' she said, handing him his coffee.

'Pretty much, yes,' he said, taking the cup of coffee from Tania.

'Thank you,' he said, taking a gentle sip being careful not to scald his lips on the fresh black coffee. Just then his mobile rang in his jacket pocket. He put his coffee down.

'Detective Maldini,' he answered. Tania watched the detective patiently as he listened to the voice at the other end of the phone for what seemed like an age. The phone call had given Tania a short reality check, and she was starting to get a little anxious again. The detective looked at Tania as he listened to the other speaker.

'Okay, thanks,' he said, looking a little disappointed as he put his phone back in his jacket pocket.

'Anything wrong?' she asked.

'All the leads we were chasing have run into a brick wall.'

'What do you mean?'

'They tracked the parcel back through the courier company. Apparently, they collected it from a coffee shop over on the Embankment from a homeless guy who paid the driver cash.'

'A homeless guy?'

'Yes, apparently some homeless guy had been paid £50, plus money for the courier, by someone to go into the coffee shop when it opened, order coffee and wait there until the courier company came to collect it from him.'

'Well, could he tell your people what he looked like … the man who paid him I mean?'

'Unfortunately not; it was an hour before dawn when he was given the parcel, money and instructions. It was still dark. All he could remember was that he was smartly dressed, all in black and wearing a black hat. He said the brim of his hat shaded his face from the street lighting. But he did say something about the man's eyes.'

'What about them?'

'He said his eyes scared him, something about looking evil … like the Devil's eyes. He said he was scared to say no to the man; he thought he was the devil and that he would kill him if he disobeyed him.'

'The devil?'

'Yes, he said the devil looked straight into his soul.'

'What about the emails and the phone call I had on my mobile?'

'We got the number from the phone company for the

blocked call. But it came from a pay-as-you-go number. The person who bought the mobile from the shop gave a fake name and address and he has either ditched the phone or it isn't switched on as we can't get a GPS fix on it.'

'And the emails?'

'Same story. Our forensics IT experts traced the origins of the email address and it turned out that the email address was set up using a free online service at a regular high street internet café over in Wembley. They pinpointed the date and time the email address was set up and when they were sent, but this particular internet cafe doesn't have any security cameras so there's no video evidence we can look at.'

Tania sighed and took a large mouthful of her coffee.

'So what now?' she said.

'Well, it looks like I'll be escorting you home … are you sure I can't convince you to stay at our safe house?'

'No, really, I'll be fine' she said, sounding a little unsure.

The detective could see that she was uneasy. 'Tania, everything's going to be all right, we're going to catch him … okay?'

She looked at the detective and nodded tentatively in acknowledgement before heading back to her desk to wrap up her work for the day. She put her computer into sleep mode and grabbed her handbag.

'You ready?' said Detective Maldini.

'Yes.'

As they walked across the car park to their respective cars Tania noticed the detective scanning the car park floor.

'Kinda spooky isn't it?' she said, noticing the focused look on his face.

'Doesn't it worry you doing this walk from the elevator to your car every night?'

'Not really, it looks worse than it is. I know there are security cameras down here with a team of big strong security men at the other end of them. Besides, this building is pretty inaccessible to anyone other than staff and authorised visitors; you can't just walk in here.'

'I'm glad to hear it,' he said, pausing by his car. 'Well, this is me,' manually putting the key in the door lock.

'Interesting choice of car for a police detective,' she said, studying his classic Volkswagen Karmann Ghia. 'How old is it?'

'It's from 1974, one of the very last ones off the production line before they stopped making them,' he said proudly.

'Well, I'm just over there,' she said, turning and unlocking her BMW Z4 M Sports via her remote key fob causing the interior lights to illuminate inside the car.

'I prefer something a little more modern,' she smiled, walking to her car.

'I'll follow you, don't race off and lose me now,' he shouted.

As Tania put her hand on the door handle, she glanced inside her car and noticed something on the passenger seat. She turned back to the detective who was about to close his car door.

'Detective!' she shouted. He got out of his car and ran over to her to see what the problem was.

'What is it,' he said.

'Whatever that is on the passenger seat, it wasn't there when I left the car here this morning.'

The detective cautiously walked around to the passenger side, looking around the car park as he did so. He studied the door handle and paused for reflection.

'Ok, I'm gonna get a CSI response team down here,' he said, taking out his phone. He hit the speed dial number for his boss DCI Sean O'Conner.

'Sean, it looks like our man's been here today,' he said, into the phone, 'We've just got to Ms de Pré's car in the basement and it looks like some kind of old sword has been left on her passenger seat ... the doors were locked ... I'm going to need a CSI team to get down here right away ... okay.' Maldini hung up. 'A CSI team is on the way.'

Two CSIs arrived pretty fast and spent an hour video-recording the scene, taking photographs and checking the car for prints and other clues, but they found nothing. The sword was photographed and checked for prints and blood before it was bagged up ready to be taken away for further investigation back at the CSI examination room.

'Ok, we're done here,' said the CSI manager, 'I'm gonna go to the security office and check the video for the car park security cameras to see if anything shows up.'

'Can I go home now?' asked Tania, bored and starving hungry, as she hadn't eaten all day.

'Certainly ma'am, only not in this car I'm afraid,' said the CSI.

'What?' said Tania, frustrated.

'I'm sorry ma'am, we're going to have to take the car away to a secure location so the forensics team can go over it with a fine tooth comb.'

'Is that really necessary?' she said, hopefully, but then realised just how stupid that must have sounded.

'I'm afraid so, it's absolutely necessary, there might be vital evidence on or in your vehicle … you do want us to catch him don't you?'

'Yes, of course.'

'Don't worry, I'll give you a lift back home in my car, and then I'll arrange for a loan car for you to drive until forensics have finished with yours,' said Detective Maldini, who then turned to the CSI. 'Let me know what the security camera video shows.'

'You got it,' said the CSI.

'When can I get my car back?' said Tania to the CSI.

'Not long, about three or four days.'

'Please, just take good care of it,' she said, worried for her much-loved car.

'Don't worry, it's in good hands,' said the CSI, reassuring her.

Detective Maldini and Tania left in his classic car; leaving the two CSIs to continue finishing up their work.

Once they reached her house, Tania unlocked her front door and invited Detective Maldini inside so he could satisfy himself that she was in no imminent danger.

'So how does this work?' she said, dropping her bag and walking through to the kitchen.

'I'll have a quick look around to make sure everything's okay, then I'll head off to arrange a loan car for you.'

'Are you in any rush, Detective? I'm about to cook, if you're hungry that is?' she said, out of politeness as she knew the detective had not eaten all afternoon since he had been with her at her office.

'Oh, no thank you, I still have work to do and I have to get back to the station for the de-brief,' he said politely. Detective Maldini did find Tania very attractive, but did not want to take her up on her offer; instead he kept his self-control and remained totally professional.

'You know, you can't live on junk food alone, Detective,' she said, suspecting he was a bachelor with not much time to cook due to his long working hours.

He smiled back. 'Do you mind if I quickly check the house?' he said, trying to get off the subject of food and the dinner invite.

'Be my guest, but I must warn you...'

'Warn me?' he said.

'My bedroom isn't your typical neat and tidy feminine bedroom,' she joked.

'Huh,' he laughed, and went off to check the house.

Tania threw some ingredients for a stir-fry into a wok and reached for a glass and a bottle of Cabernet Sauvignon; after today, she needed it.

'Everything seems to be okay,' said the detective returning to the kitchen. 'What time do you leave for work in the morning?'

'About half-eight.'

'Okay, if I don't get a hire car for you this evening, a police officer is going to be arriving here any minute. He's going to be parked up outside watching your house during the night. He'll give you a lift to work in the morning if need be. In the meantime, here's my card and contact details,' he said, handing Tania his business card.

'You can get me on that mobile number, any time, day or night.'

'Thank you, Detective,' she said sincerely.

'Seriously, if you're at all worried or suspect anything's not right, call me,' he said, authoritatively.

'I will.'

'Okay then, I'll let myself out … make sure you lock up behind me,' he said, closing the front door behind him.

He then paused momentarily on her doorstep, turned and raised his hand to ring the doorbell, but he didn't, instead he quietly sighed. *Don't be silly, stay professional, Marion*, he thought to himself as he walked down the steps and back to his car.

Chapter 7

In the crime scene examination room the next morning, the forensics staff had found traces of blood on the blade of the sword found in Tania's car, but no fingerprints on the handle, or other parts of the weapon. The CSI manager had also called in the services of an expert in ancient weaponry to establish its age, type, and value and anything else that could give valuable clues to help lead the police to its owner. The expert had several reference books and various papers with him to help with his evaluation of the sword.

'Well, because of its incredible condition, upon first inspection you'd be forgiven for thinking that it's a relic from the battle of Culloden that took place back on 16th April in the year 1746. But this one's actually much earlier than that and of a unique design too. What you have here is a two-handed Claymore, otherwise known as a Broadsword, and I'd say that this fine example's from as early as the mid-fifteenth century,' said Mr Bradshaw excitedly.

'Have you any idea what it's worth?' said the CSI.

'Well, that's the question. The thing is, there are only three Claymores in existence from the fifteenth century, and none of them come remotely close to the condition of this one. Somebody's meticulously maintained and cherished this beauty throughout the centuries. It doesn't look a fraction of its age; it really is quite remarkable. I'd like to do some further age testing on it if I may, to find out for sure. But if this is what I think it is, this unique example is probably worth over half a million.'

'You've got to be kidding me?' said the CSI.

'Oh, I take my work very seriously, Mr Drayton, especially when it comes to ancient swords such as this one, so no, I'm not kidding.'

'And in your professional opinion, this sword could be capable of beheading somebody ... today I mean, not historically speaking?'

'Well, in the right hands and used in the right way, executed at the right angle by somebody who had the strength and power ... I'd say yes, it probably could.'

Just then the CSIs mobile rang.

'Mark Drayton,' he answered.

'Mark, we've had the DNA results back from both the severed head and the blood samples taken off the sword; they both match ... but there's something else,' said the voice on the other end of the phone.

'Okay, give me a minute, I'll call you right back,' Drayton said, turning back to Mr Bradshaw.

'I'm afraid you won't be able to take the sword away for further age-testing, as it's evidence.'

'That's a shame. Will there be any opportunity for me to spend some time examining the sword in more detail at some point in the future?' said Mr Bradshaw, hopefully.

'Perhaps. I'll see what I can do once the case is closed.'

'Thank you, Mr Drayton; I'd very much appreciate that. It really is a rare and fascinating piece.'

'Let me escort you out, and thanks again for lending us your expertise,' said the CSI, as he held the examination room door open for Mr Bradshaw.

'Oh, you're quite welcome, the pleasure was all mine.'

The instant the CSI had escorted Mr Bradshaw off the police premises, he returned the phone call from his colleague regarding the DNA results to get all the details.

* * *

At The Sentinel newspaper office, Jack had decided to pull the vampire story that Tania was running in her column since the severed head arrived. Although the vampire story had only gone out twice, Jack didn't want part three to hit the streets for fear of more severed heads turning up at his offices. The whole ordeal had thrown the newspaper into a state of disarray and Jack was right in the middle of it, trying to maintain composure throughout the workforce as well as keeping a lid on things.

Tania was at her desk staring at a blank word document on her computer screen while tapping her fingers on the desk as she searched for inspiration for a new story to replace the vampire one that Jack had just pulled the plug on. Detective Maldini walked up to her desk.

'Good morning, Tania.'

She spun around on her chair. 'Oh, good morning, Detective.'

'I'm sorry I didn't drop the courtesy car off to you

personally this morning. Things have been pretty crazy back at the station, what with one thing and another. Is the loan car okay for you?'

'It'll suffice, for now.'

'Good, there're a few things I need to speak to you about,' said Detective Maldini.

'Well I'm about to break for lunch if you want to join me at Giovanni's next door … it's an Italian restaurant, Detective.'

'I kinda figured it was; the clue was in the name,' he said, smiling at her.

'You'll like it, the coffee's great.'

Inside Giovanni's, Tania ordered a quattro stagioni pizza and a cappuccino. Detective Maldini just ordered a latte.

'You don't strike me as the pizza type,' he said, waiting for the waitress to get out of earshot.

'Typically, I'm not. But every now and then a good Italian pizza really hits the spot … besides … I figured when it arrives, if you change your mind about eating, you can have a slice of mine … I hate eating alone.'

'Huh,' he laughed, 'perhaps.'

'So, what do you need to talk to me about, Detective?'

'Well, there're a few things. First, I'd like you to come to the station to have a VRI.'

'A what?' she questioned.

'Sorry, a video recorded interview.'

'I don't understand. Why would I need to be interviewed on video? Am I a suspect, Detective?'

'No, of course not,' he said, reassuring her. 'You're a significant witness and we need to get as much information from you as possible. A VRI is routine, and it could help us with the case.'

'I can't see how, Detective. I'm as much in the dark as you are.'

The waitress arrived back at their table with Tania's cappuccino and the detective's latte.

'Well, perhaps you aren't as in the dark as you might think,' he said, taking on a more serious tone.

'What do you mean?' she asked, reaching across the table for the sugar.

'I'd like you to take a look at a photograph of a man,' said the detective, reaching into his inner jacket pocket. He showed Tania a police mug shot.

'Oh my god!' exclaimed Tania putting her hand up to her mouth as she clearly recognised the man in the photo.

'Do you know him,' said the detective?

'Yes ... well ... kind of, I had a date with him recently.'

'Are you sure this is the same man?'

'Yes, I'm totally sure.'

'How long had you been dating him?'

'It was our first date.'

'How long had you known him?'

'Just a few weeks; it's kind of embarrassing,' she said, not wanting to go into detail.

'Please, this is important,' Maldini urged gently.

'We met on a dating website and bounced a few messages back and forth, then we arranged a dinner date. That was the first time I'd ever met him in person.'

'I'm assuming you know his name?'

'Yes, his name's Allan. Look, why do you have a picture

of him and more to the point, why are you showing it to me; is he a criminal or something?'

'I'll get to that in a minute. But first, it's very important that you tell me where you met him and how long you've known him.'

'Like I said, I met him on an internet dating site about two weeks ago.'

'Did you give him your address?'

'No, I am actually quite streetwise and clued up, Detective,' she said, dismissing his suggestion that she might be a little wet behind the ears.

'Of course, did he give you his surname?'

'No, he didn't say. We didn't really get that far. Look, what does he have to do with all this? He's somebody I had a date with recently. I have a right to know, Detective!'

'Well, his name's Allan Bar ... he was a known sex offender.'

'What!' she said, sounding totally freaked out and utterly alarmed.

'Tania, listen to me. Allan Bar was an incredibly violent sexual predator ... he'd been stalking you for some weeks. To be honest, I'm surprised he gave you his real name.'

'How do you know all this? And what do you mean, he *was* a sexual predator? Isn't he anymore?'

'Not exactly no ... he's dead.'

'What!'

'Okay, bear with me for a minute. We took a DNA swab from inside the mouth of the severed head and put it into the DNA database ... the severed head is that of Allan Bar ...'

Tania interrupted him. 'Oh my god, the head in the box

is the guy I dated recently?'

'Yes.'

'But when opened the box and looked at it ... well, it didn't look familiar, not that I gave it that much attention, of course.'

'Well, it wouldn't, people have a habit of looking a bit different in that situation.'

'You mean when their head is removed from their body?' she said, a little too loudly, getting the attention of the couple sitting behind them. The horrid realisation washed over her and soaked deep into her inner core. Tania sat there feeling like she was in the middle of a dark cold nightmare. Just then the waitress walked past.

'Excuse me,' shouted Tania, not wanting to miss getting her attention.

'Yes, ma'am,' answered the waitress.

'Can I have a double brandy, please?'

'Certainly, just give me a moment and I'll bring it right over.'

Tania turned back to the detective.

'I didn't realise there was a database with everybody's DNA on it?'

'Not everybody, only about ten percent of the population, and most of the people on it are convicted criminals. When a person is arrested, we routinely take a DNA buccal swab from inside their mouth ... it's a way for the police to build up a DNA database; this makes catching criminals easier in the future.'

'I'm sorry, I'm just finding all this a little hard to get my head around ... please, continue, Detective,' she said, desperately trying to keep up.

'The DNA swab we took from the severed head matched up with Allan Bar on the database. That's how we know who the head belongs to.'

'I still don't understand how you know he's been stalking me?'

'I haven't got to that part yet. We went to his apartment this morning and found photos ... photos of you, Tania.'

Just as Tania sat there in silence trying to get her head around it, the waitress sent a pile of plates she'd just collected from the next table crashing to the floor with a loud smash right behind Tania. This caused Tania to half jump out of her skin. She let out a short sharp scream that was loud enough to get her some attention from other nearby diners.

'You okay?' asked Maldini.

'Yes, I'm fine,' she said, still holding her chest and taking a few deep breaths. 'Where the hell's that bloody brandy?' she muttered to herself. 'Sorry, Detective, carry on.'

'From the evidence we found in his apartment, it looks like he'd been taking pictures of you secretly for a couple of weeks preceding your recent date at the restaurant. He'd printed the photos off via his computer and they all had digital date stamps on them. You were lined up to be his next victim ... or at least you would have been if your mystery vampire friend hadn't beheaded him first.'

Tania just listened, without responding. She was trying to take it all in – and was still waiting for her damn brandy.

'Last year he committed a brutal sex attack that left a 19-year-old Brazilian girl in hospital fighting for her life. We knew he'd done it and we had stacks of evidence, but it got thrown out on a technicality ... the bastard walked out of the courtroom whistling *The Girl From Ipanema*.'

'Was she okay?' asked Tania, genuinely concerned.

'Yes, she pulled through just fine; physically at least ... I can't imagine she's going to forget the ordeal anytime soon though. He's a nasty piece of work, Tania ... or at least he was.'

Tania sat there contemplating all this, while Detective Maldini looked around the restaurant admiring the Italian style décor. Tania was so deep in thought that she didn't notice the waitress place her double brandy on the table in front of her.

'Are you okay?' said Detective Maldini.

'Huh ... apparently, yes ... thanks to my vampire,' she mumbled quietly.

'I'm sorry?' said the detective.

'Oh ... nothing,' she said, picking up her double brandy.

'Do you think you should be doing that at this time of day?' he said, as she was about to put the glass of brandy to her lips.

'Abso-bloody-lutely!' she said, knocking the drink back in one go.

'Feelin' better?' asked Maldini, surprised at her action.

'Oh yeah!'

'Look, do you think this is a coincidence, or do you think this mystery vampire guy knew what Allan Bar was up to and decided to save your life?'

'I don't know ... how would he have known that I was about to become the next victim of a serial sex predator?'

'Well, that's what I'm trying to establish ... there's something else.'

'You mean there's more?' she said, as if this wasn't enough.

'I'm afraid so.'

'Please, enlighten me, Detective' she said, with bated breath.

'There were some bite marks on the victim's neck.'

'Bite marks!' she said, in disbelief.

'Yes, bite marks. We took DNA swab samples from around the bite marks. If somebody bites somebody else, they would normally leave a saliva residue around the area they'd bitten.'

'So what's the problem? You should know who bit him, right? ... Oh, don't tell me ... he wasn't on the DNA database?'

'It's not that simple. It wasn't a person that bit him – well, not exactly.'

'What are you saying; that he was bitten by an animal?'

'Sort of ... perhaps ... not really,' said the detective, trying to figure out how best to explain the scientifics to her.

'Please, Detective, try and be a little less cryptic.'

'Whatever bit him left saliva and another strange substance around the wound. When we got the DNA results back from the lab there was something strange about them.'

'Strange ... strange how?' she said, confused.

'The DNA appears to have other elements to it, apart from the human one.'

'How's that possible? What other elements were there?' she said, sounding a little anxious now.

'Well, the DNA appears to be made up of three parts. Part human, part wolf and the third part is something else entirely. It's not an animal, at least not an animal that we know of. The lab people were totally perplexed by it. They said they'd never seen anything like it. It's as if the DNA from the third part doesn't exist, or it's dead.'

'Dead, I don't understand,' she said, now totally confused.

'Well, if it's any consolation, neither do we.'

'Well what are we talking about here, some sort of wolf-man, Detective?' she said, desperate for an answer to this riddle.

'No, the wolf strand was only a very small part of the DNA, but it was there.'

'You said there was another strange substance around the bite marks, apart from saliva?'

'Yes, some sort of venom.'

'Like snake venom?'

'Kind of, but this wasn't snake venom; it was something else entirely. It contained a very powerful kind of nerve relaxant, like that found in the venom that snakes use to stun their prey and stop them moving; but it also contained a strange looking DNA that the guys at the lab had never seen before. They don't know what to make of it.'

Tania just sat there pondering everything the detective had told her. She desperately wanted to piece it all together so it made sense.

'We also took DNA samples from the dried blood on the blade of the sword that you found in your car; it's a perfect match for Allan Bar's severed head. Plus we found traces of metal on the bone that matched the metal on the blade. So it looks like it was definitely the sword used to decapitate him.'

'And that sword was in my car ... oh, Jesus!' she said, thinking of the horror behind this new enlightening cold fact.

'The sword is an ancient Scottish Claymore ... it's over 500 years old and, according to the expert we brought in, it's worth over half a million pounds.'

'Oh please, this just keeps getting better by the minute. So you're saying that whatever bit Allan Bar, before deciding to play chop suey with his head using a priceless antique sword, was part human, part wolf and part something else, perhaps a vampire?' she said, in total disbelief.

'Something like that … yes,' said Maldini; embarrassed that he could not give a more logical answer to this weird puzzle.

'Why the hell would he hack somebody's head off with a half a million pound sword, and then leave it in my fucking car!' she said, loud enough to cause the customers in the neighbouring booth to look over in disgust.

'I'm sorry,' she said to the couple eating across from them, realising that they'd heard her F word.

'Oh my god, he's trying to prove to me that he's a real vampire,' she said, as the penny finally dropped.

'They also confirmed that the oil painting left in your car is authentic. It was painted in 1587.'

'So, what are we dealing with, Detective? A psychopathic antiques dealer who's half man and half alien, or is he a real fucking vampire?' she said, sounding a little frustrated and disheveled.

Just then, her pizza arrived.

'One quattro stagioni pizza,' said the waitress politely, as she placed it on the table in front of Tania. 'Can I get you anything else?'

'Actually, I've kind of lost my appetite. Can you put this in a takeaway box for me, please,' said Tania.

'Oh, certainly ma'am … is everything all right?' asked the waitress.

'Yes, everything's fine, really. I'll eat it back at the office.

'Very well, ma'am,' said the waitress as she took the pizza away.

'What about the face in the painting ... I mean ... when, where, how and why did he remove it?'

'Well, it looks like it was removed during the night while it was at your house.'

'You mean he was inside my house while I was upstairs sleeping!' she said, freaked out.

'Possibly, it might not have been him that did it; he could have had someone else do it for him. The face was probably removed with chemicals, but why it was removed still remains a mystery. If it was a more recent painting, or photograph, I'd say it was removed to hide his identity, but this painting is over 400 years old so it's safe to assume the man in the painting has been dead for quite a long time now,' said Maldini.

'Dead, yes ... but, perhaps not buried or dead in the way that you and I know,' she said, as she searched the previous week's events in her mind. A cold chill shot down Tania's spine as it dawned on her that all was not as it first appeared. There was something about this mysterious man, something dark, something quite unworldly, something she couldn't explain.

'What do you mean?' said Maldini.

'Well just look at the evidence or lack of it as the case may be. We have a guy running around in the dark who disappears into thin air off security car park video recordings like David-bloody-Blaine. He appears to be unlocking and locking my car door as if by magic, he might be creeping in and out of my house at night through locked doors and windows and it would appear that he has some sort of sixth sense as he seems to know what I'm thinking and doing at any given moment!'

'Are you saying you now believe he's a real vampire, and that he's speaking the truth about being around for the past thousand years?' said the detective, in a half serious tone, trying to get a handle on where Tania was going with this.

Tania just looked at him intensely with serious eyes that suggested yes, she did, but she wasn't going to allow the words to pass over her lips out loud. Just then the waitress reappeared with Tania's pizza in a takeaway box.

'Here you go ma'am,' said the waitress placing the box on the table.

'Thank you,' said Tania.

'Look, I really think you should come to the station for the VRI. A specially trained officer will help you through it … it could be a great help to us, Tania.'

'You really don't have anything to go on, do you, Detective?' she said, sounding more serious now.

'No, I'm afraid not, which is why it's important that you do this interview. Even though you don't think it'll help, we might get something out of it that could give us a valuable lead.'

'When?'

'How about right now,' he said, perfectly seriously.

'Now!'

'If it's not too much trouble. I can drive you in my car.'

'How long will it take?'

'Not too long – two hours, maybe three. We need to get as much detail and background information leading up to the severed head delivery as we can.'

'Well, okay. I'm at a loose end since Jack pulled the plug on my vampire story.'

'What do you mean?' asked the detective.

'I'd written the first few columns about vampires, well, human vampires actually. The feedback from readers was great. But this morning Jack told me I couldn't run it anymore. I have to start over and find a new story for my column … he's worried more severed heads are going to turn up in his office.'

'Oh, I can understand that. Okay, you ready?'

'Yes, I'll have to quickly clear it with Jack first. Let me get the bill.'

'Please, let me,' he said, insistently as he reached for his wallet.

'You don't have to do that.'

'Don't worry, it's my pleasure … I'll put it on my expenses if it makes you feel better,' he said, smiling.

She grabbed her boxed up pizza and they left.

The VRI at the police station ended up taking over three hours. Tania was glad she took the pizza along because about half way through she was almost passing out with hunger. Trying to remember the details of the events leading up to the severed head being delivered had her brain demanding fuel. It was all a rather drawn-out and boring experience and now she'd had enough. Her breath smelt of stale coffee and pizza. Her clothes smelt like the inside of the police station and she just wanted to go home and take a shower. She could almost hear the officer who interviewed her sighing at her answers, although he didn't sigh aloud;

she could see it in his eyes. She suspected her answers didn't really give the police anything else to go on and they were desperate for a lead. The police don't like unsolved murders and they certainly didn't want this case unsolved, especially when they only had a severed head and no idea of the whereabouts of the body.

After the VRI at the police station, Detective Maldini drove Tania back to her office, not that she could really get down to any serious work, as there was only an hour of working day left to go. They pulled up in the car park back at the newspaper's offices.

'Look, I really appreciate you taking the time to do the interview. Police stations are hardly the most pleasant places to spend an afternoon,' he said, gratefully.

'It's okay, I don't think I was much help though.'

'Actually, you were. I've had a few ideas already.'

'Really?' she said, surprised.

'Yes, I just want to run it by my Senior Investigation Officer first, and then I'll need to speak to your boss about you running this vampire's story in your column.'

'What? I don't understand,' she said, sounding somewhat perplexed, but also happy at the possibility of being able to at least resume her column again.

'Don't worry; I need to work a few things out. I'll explain it all in the morning after I've spoken to the SIO at the de-brief tonight.'

'Ok, I'm sure you know what you're doing, Detective.'

'How's your loan car?'

'It's a Mondeo,' she said, in a sarcastic derogatory tone.

'Ha!' Maldini laughed out loud. 'Sorry about that. But

hey, you should have your own car back tomorrow.'

'Really?' she said, excitedly.

'Yeah … they're going to drop it back here at some point tomorrow and take your loaner back.'

'Thank god for that!' I don't know if I could have stood driving this mundane thing around for a minute longer.'

'Ok then, well I guess I'd better get back. I'll walk you over to the elevator,' he said.

'You don't have to do that; I'll be fine, Detective. To be honest I'm only going up to grab my things, and then I'm going home to soak in a hot bath with a glass of wine.'

'It's no bother, I'd like to,' he said, in a soft tone. They then looked into each other's eyes for a fleeting moment, which felt slightly uncomfortable to Tania, so she broke the contact by gracefully reaching for the door handle and letting herself out of the detective's car.

'I'm sorry, I didn't mean to embarrass you,' he said to her across the roof of his car.

'I'm not embarrassed, Detective,' she said, feeling slightly better now that she wasn't in quite such close proximity to him. The fact was, she had quite enjoyed the slightly romantic moment between them – but for now at least, she didn't want to go there. Her feelings for Detective Maldini were mixed. She fancied him for sure, but on the other hand, he was just too nice for her and she felt that he deserved a nicer, less volatile woman who would treat him right.

'I just meant I wanted to make sure you got back upstairs safely.'

'It's okay, Detective,' she said, putting her hand on his shoulder and smiling. But her facial expression gave him no green light, and being a detective, he read and understood this loud and clear.

'Okay, walk me to the elevator,' she said, leading the way.

Ping! The elevator arrived at the basement. Tania stepped inside and turned to face Detective Maldini who waited outside the elevator.

'I'll come and see you in the morning after I've seen your boss to explain my plan,' he said. 'You have a good evening.'

'Thank you, Detective, you too,' she said, pressing the button for the fifth floor.

The elevator doors closed, cutting the line of sight between them.

Chapter 8

Jack's office door burst open and Martin flew in with a look of total panic and urgency written all over his face.

'Jack, there's a television news crew and a reporter downstairs setting up camera equipment in the lobby!' he said, out of breath from running to Jack's office.

'What?' exclaimed Jack, as furious as hell.

'They've got wind of the severed head; somebody's bloody leaked it,' said Martin.

'Fuck!! … Right, make sure nobody from this office speaks to them, and I mean nobody, no interviews, nothing!' said Jack, adamantly.

'Okay, I'll inform everyone,' said Martin.

'Good, do it now. I'm going downstairs to get rid of them. The last thing I need is this severed head business all over the bloody Six O'Clock News,' he said, practically jogging out of his office to the elevator.

As Jack exited the elevator in the lobby, he was relieved to find that the cameraman and reporter hadn't been allowed past security in the reception waiting area. The female reporter was trying her hardest to sweet talk one of the two security men into letting her and the cameraman through, but he wasn't having any of it. Jack noticed the commotion going on between the female reporter and security man and instantly recognised her; not only from television, they had spoken in person in the past. Jack made a speedy beeline towards the security office holding his hand up to the side of his face to avoid being recognised by her.

'Jack!' shouted the female reporter. 'Jack Savage!' she shouted again.

Jack turned to face her and smiled the fakest smile imaginable. Luckily for Jack, her cameraman was having a technical issue with a corrupt memory card so he wasn't ready to start filming just yet.

'Natalie, nice to see you again,' said Jack, in a tone suggesting he was surprised to see her and a cameraman in the lobby of his newspaper's building.

'Oh come on Jack, don't give me that who, me, he, she routine; you know why I'm here,' she said, determined to get her story.

Natalie Sturgess had built up a reputation for being a ruthless TV reporter. She knew every dirty trick in the book when it came to television reporting and getting a story, and more often than not, she was happy to put them into practice when needs must.

'Look, Natalie, there's no story here, there's really nothing to tell,' said Jack, trying to sound as convincing as he possibly could.

'Come on Jack. A severed head turns up at your offices, and you're trying to tell me there's no story. Oh, please!' she said, sarcastically.

'Where exactly did you get this information?' said Jack,

scratching his chin and raising his right eyebrow.

'You know me, Jack, I have my sources.'

'Yes, lots of them, from what I've heard … so, was it the police or somebody from my paper?'

'Oh come on, Jack, you know I can't tell you that.'

Jack figured that she would never reveal her private sources of information, so he didn't bother insisting. Instead, he turned to the head security guard and took him to one side out of earshot of Natalie Sturgess, leaving the other security man to keep the cameraman and Sturgess at bay.

He instructed the guard that if anybody showed up who looked even remotely like a television news crew, reporter, journalist or photographer, that under no circumstances whatsoever were they to be allowed into the building, let alone into the lobby reception area. He then instructed the security man to go back to his colleague and escort Natalie Sturgess and her cameraman off the premises before heading back over to speak to Natalie.

'Sorry, Natalie, I've got nothing more to say on this matter, and I really must get back to work. I've got a newspaper to run, remember,' said Jack, as he casually headed back to the elevator.

'Come on, Jack, just one quick interview?' she shouted after him.

'Sorry, Natalie,' shouted Jack, as he pressed the fifth floor button to close the elevator door behind him.

Natalie abruptly turned and looked at her cameraman, who was still fiddling around on the floor with his camera. She shot him a seething look, which was about to be followed up by a severe vocal outburst, but the cameraman was spared her insults and abuse by the two security men, who promptly escorted them both out of the building.

When Jack got back upstairs he sat in his chair and peered out through his office windows across the desks on the main office floor, as he tried to figure out if it could have been any of his own staff who had leaked the information. He had to try and think of a positive angle on this, an angle that would be good for his newspaper. He certainly didn't need any bad publicity or to be a laughing stock for the competition. Just then, the phone on Jack's desk rang. He could see on the phone's display screen that it was the receptionist from the lobby.

'Savage,' he answered.

'I have Detective Maldini at the front desk to see you, sir. He doesn't have an appointment, but he says it's important.'

'That's fine, send him up.'

'Can I get you a tea or coffee, Detective?' said Jack.

'No, I am fine, thanks.'

'So what can I do for you this morning?' said Jack, gathering some papers up on his desk.

'I'd like you to allow Tania to continue running the vampire story in her column,' said the detective, in a tone that suggested he wasn't really asking for permission.

'I'm sorry, Detective, but I pulled the plug on that story for a very good reason, a reason that your CSI team recently took away from this very office in a body bag.'

'I understand that, sir, but I'm asking you to consider reinstating the story.'

'Are you crazy, Detective? Why would I want to do that?'

'Because it could help us catch him … and if I can be

candid with you, we don't have anything else to go on. ... no leads, nothing. Tania's column is our only link to the man who left that head in your office.'

'Detective, it's not down to me to catch this man for you, that's your job.'

'I understand that, but, believe it or not, many crimes are solved with the help of the public ... besides, it could be very good publicity for your paper, and it could boost sales too,' said the detective, trying to dangle a carrot in front of Savage's nose.

If the detective didn't have Jack's full attention before, he certainly had it now. Jack put down his papers, leaned back in his chair, and was all ears.

'Okay, Detective, what do you have in mind?'

'I think we should play along with this guy. Let Tania run his story in her column. He'll see his story unfolding in the paper the way he wants, and he'll let his guard down. We'll monitor his phone calls and emails to Tania, and when he slips up ... we'll be there.'

'And what if he doesn't slip up?' said Jack.

'They always slip up,' said the detective, confidently, 'besides, you have to put a positive spin on this severed head business, before your competition put a negative one on it. Jack, if you don't publish this story, he'll go to another paper ... and they'll publish it for him. So you might as well publish it your way with your own slant and boost sales of your paper at the same time.'

Jack sat and stroked his right eyebrow while pondering the idea for a moment, weighing up the pros and cons. After thinking about it he realised that there were a lot more advantages than disadvantages to running the story.

'Okay, Detective, I'll tell Tania to run the story, but I hope you know what you're doing because I don't want any more damn heads turning up in my office.'

'You seem to be forgetting something,' said the detective.

'Oh? What's that?'

'He only sent Tania the severed head because she didn't publish his story and because she decided to go off on a tangent and publish something else entirely.'

'Fair point, detective.'

After the detective left, Jack got busy. He told Martin to call the TV reporter Natalie Sturgess to invite her back with her cameraman to do a personal interview with him. He put Tania back on the story with specific instructions to run the vampire's real life story in keeping with how he wanted it. He then spent the next couple of hours writing notes in preparation for his interview.

The rest of the day went well for both Jack and Tania, despite the pressure they were under. Tania had emailed the vampire to inform him that the paper was now going to run his life story exactly how he originally wanted it. She then spent the rest of the afternoon writing up the column introduction.

Although Jack was pleased with the way his television interview went with Sturgess, he was not looking forward to seeing himself on television. Meanwhile, the police had set up an electronic interception on Tania's office desk phone as well as her mobile and were monitoring them both closely. They'd also brought in a high-tech forensics electronics internet expert to trace the origins and exact log-on times of any future emails that come in from the vampire.

Come six o'clock, the vampire story was all over the television news. Natalie Sturgess stood in the lobby at The Sentinel newspaper offices with a hand-held microphone reporting to camera. In the background was the plush reception area and on the wall the newspaper's name and logo made out of rather fancy glass with tasteful blue lighting shining through it from below.

'There have been some unusual developments here at The Sentinel newspaper offices in London over the past few days. It all started when the paper's daily columnist, Tania de Pré, received an email from a man claiming to be a 1000-year-old vampire. The man wanted the paper to publish his life story via Tania's column. But when the paper ran a different angle on the story, it angered the man so much he went out and brutally murdered the known sex offender, Allan Bar. The killer then sent Bar's severed head in a brown cardboard box to The Sentinel's offices here in Canary Wharf via courier and then, later the same day, he managed to get through the office's sophisticated security system undetected to leave the murder weapon responsible in Ms de Pré's car in the underground car park. In another curious twist to the tale, the weapon used to behead Allan Bar was a unique fifteenth century Scottish Claymore sword that's since been valued at over half a million pounds,' said Natalie, reporting the news on national television.

***

Over in north London, a barman and a DJ were busy setting

up for their regular monthly meeting of their vampire club night, at the After Dark club. They saw the news story on one of the large wall-mounted LCD HD televisions and stopped what they were doing to watch it. After Dark was one of the better-known vampire clubs in London. Its members strictly followed its code of practice for human vampires and took it all very seriously. This was especially true of the people who ran it, so naturally the news reporter on television had the barman and the DJ's full attention. They both stood there in total silence, transfixed by the story, absorbing every word that came out of Natalie Sturgess's mouth.

'So far, the police have been unable to trace the source of the emails and telephone calls from the man who's simply calling himself, The Vampire, and they've been unable to find the missing body to go with the severed head. This is Natalie Sturgess, reporting for ASTV, at The Sentinel Newspaper offices, Canary Wharf, London.'

As the news article finished the barman and DJ both looked at each other.

'Should be a bloody good night tonight after that news piece,' said the barman.

'You got that right,' said the DJ, excited.

After the Six O'Clock News aired, the vampire story became hot property. A local radio station set up a phone-in discussion show and their switchboard was jammed with listeners phoning in with their opinions not only about this story, but vampires in general. A young female member of the After Dark club in north London had phoned in with her opinions about the vampire story on the news. She had a unique, but annoying voice and had a lot to say on the subject. Her long phone call concluded with her putting the mystery 1000-year-old vampire down to nothing more than a phony attention seeker. She even managed to plug the After Dark club on air at the same time. Another caller, a mother of two young children, was defending the mystery vampire and approving of him killing and beheading the violent sex offender, Allan Bar. Opinions from callers who phoned in to the radio show were varied, but one thing was for sure, it had become obvious that the nation were fascinated with the idea of real vampires living secretly and undetected amongst humans.

By 11pm the After Dark club was heaving with its regular human vampire members. The turnout was greater than usual, with every single member turning up in full vampire dress. Even non-members had turned up and paid at the door to get in. There was no doubt that the news story four hours earlier was responsible for all the extra custom that the After Dark club was receiving.

This particular vampire club was well known in the area and had a regular niche following, but it did have a rather cliquey feel to it, and regular dedicated die-hard members frowned upon the general public just walking in off the street; especially tourists who just wanted to take photographs of them. Some members would make it blatantly obvious that they didn't want the general public in there by intimidating them and trying to scare them away. In the past a few select individual members had got quite nasty with tourists, with threats of feeding off their blood if they didn't leave. Needless to say, nobody was ever on the receiving end of one of these threats as they never stuck around long enough to find out if the threat was genuine or not.

The After Dark club was in a basement. Members had to go down six concrete steps from the street level to get to the main door of the club, a solid black wooden door with no windows. There was an intercom system with a small camera to the side, so the person answering from inside could see who was there. Members were generally recognised on the security monitor inside and buzzed in via the electronic door lock.

For non-members, somebody would generally come to the door to check them out via the security monitor. Once inside the door, there was a small reception area where they would check people in and take a £5 entrance fee. From here, there was a long corridor covered with various pieces of vampire memorabilia. A movie poster from the film, *Interview With The Vampire*, a framed and signed photograph of Christopher Lee and a genuine black wooden coffin lid were just some of the vampire artifacts on display.

At the other end of the corridor was another solid black wooden door that led into the main club area. Once inside, it was surprisingly plush, considering the clientele that frequented the place. Along the shortest wall nearest the door was a dimly lit bar illuminated by a combination of red and white LED lights strategically placed along the bar itself, as well as in the mirrors behind the bar. There were large white LED lights underneath the clear Perspex floor where the bar staff stood, the under lighting giving them a ghostly appearance.

The main area where the human vampires socialised was

a slightly staggered elongated room with various alcoves situated around the walls. The alcoves were dimly lit with more red and white LED lights, and were fitted with black and wine-red leather sofas and black smoked-glass coffee tables. There were large black velvet floor-to-ceiling drapes covering the bare brick walls. Not only did these drapes look the part, but they also helped the acoustics of the club enormously by taking the harsh bright edge off the often-loud Goth music that the DJ favoured.

Sitting in what was probably the dimmest and most secluded alcove was a man and two young women. He was a young looking 38-year-old, and although he wasn't sporting what regular members would call full vampire attire, there was definitely something about him that smacked of vampire. He wore a smart black shirt with the top three buttons open revealing part of his chest, with a pair of trendy black trousers and black ankle boots. He was tall, about six foot three, and strong looking although not in a bodybuilder muscle-bound way; but you could tell that he wouldn't have much of a problem bench-pressing 250lb without breaking a sweat. He had black shoulder-length hair with a hint of purple about it. His complexion was paler than average, which emphasised his jet-black eyes.

The two women talking to him were both about 25 years old. They were dressed in full vampire attire for the evening, complete with full make-up, coloured contact lenses and fake push-on individual fangs that were held in place with dental putty. They were both incredibly attractive, in that Goth/vampire sort of way.

They were obviously very good friends; in fact at first

glance they could almost be sisters. One had long black hair with thin deep red highlights to the front and sides, while the other was a dark brunette. They were both well-known members at the club and took the whole vampire thing quite seriously. They each had a few tasteful artsy tattoos and several piercings in their ears. The black haired one also had a small diamond stud in her nose and a tongue piercing.

'So, how come I've never seen you here before mister?' said Miss Tongue Piercing, taking a large gulp from her double vodka and coke.

'Well, let's just say that this isn't really my typical kind of establishment,' said the mysterious man, in a well spoken, but very deep rough voice, with a very faint Russian accent.

'So what is your kind of establishment?' she said, in her high pitched annoying voice.

'Oh, something a little more ... let's say ... organic,' said the mysterious man.

'Well excuse me, aren't we organic enough for you?' she laughed sarcastically, taking another gulp of her drink.

'Well, the evening's still young ... I'm sure I'll get something out of it before the night's through,' he said, looking straight at her with a twinkle in his dark sinister eyes.

'Ooohh, I like the sound of that,' she said, emphasising the "th" sound to show her tongue stud in a seductive way. 'So what's your name anyway?'

'My name is Raven,' he said, the faint Russian accent a trifle more detectable.

'Well, that's original, I've never heard that one before,' she said, giggling away like a silly little schoolgirl.

'You were the girl I heard on the radio earlier, am I

right?' said Raven.

'Yeah, that's right,' she said, all giggly and proud of herself. 'You have good ears'.

'So what makes you so sure that the man they speak of on the news is not a real vampire?' said Raven.

'Oh come on, that guy's a total faker,' she said convincingly, as if she had some sort of psychic powers that told her this.

'And what do you think?' Raven said, turning to her brunette friend.

'Well, it's an interesting story. I guess we'll just have to wait and see,' said Miss Brunette, sounding more grown up and grounded than her scatty friend.

'Yes, I guess we will,' said Raven.

'Well, I know for a fact he's not genuine,' continued the ever-annoying Miss Tongue Piercing.

'Oh, how so?' said Raven.

'Because I've met a real vampire and I can tell the difference,' she said, continuing to knock back her vodka and coke like it was going out of fashion.

'So, what do you make of me? Am I a real vampire?' said Raven, toying with her.

'Ha! No way,' she laughed.

'How can you tell?' he said, mocking her.

'Trust me, honey, you're a pretty good imitation, and I must say you look the part, especially with those black contact lenses and the pale foundation make-up, but you're not the real deal,' she said, adamantly.

'What makes you think I'm wearing contact lenses and foundation?'

'Oh come on, no human has eyes like that.'

'You're quite right, no *human* has eyes like mine,' said Raven, now totally bored with this dull conversation.

'How come you're not drinking?' said Miss Brunette in a serious tone.

'I'll drink later,' said Raven, in an equally serious tone, giving her a piercing look.

'Anyway, the police are gonna catch the guy soon enough and he'll go to jail ... then you'll see that he's not a vampire and you'll see that I'm right,' Miss Tongue Piercing said, knocking back the last of her vodka and coke.

'Well, I can assure you, the vampire whom they speak of on the news is most certainly real ... and so am I,' said Raven, serious as hell. Miss Brunette was starting to worry about their mysterious male guest.

'Excuse me,' said Miss Tongue Piercing, belching, 'I have to go visit the little girls' room.'

She got up and nearly knocked her friend's drink over with her knee in the process. Raven watched her amble pathetically across the floor in her half-cut state. The second she disappeared around the corner and was out of sight, Raven turned back to her friend.

'Please, excuse me ... I think it's time to feed,' he said, in a sinister tone.

Raven calmly got up from the large leather sofa and pursued Miss Tongue Piercing to the ladies room, leaving the brunette sitting there scared stiff and not really knowing what to do.

Raven walked down the dimly lit corridor to the ladies bathroom. He opened the door and entered. Inside was a stark contrast to the rest of the dimly lit club. It was brightly lit with pristine white tiles on the floor and walls, more akin to the clinical décor of a dentist's surgery. It had large brightly lit mirrors on the wall above the sinks. Miss Tongue Piercing was alone and fixing her make-up in the mirror. She got to the end of re-applying her lipstick, then turned around to leave and bumped straight into Raven, who was standing right behind her. She took a very sharp intake of breath in shock as she thought she was alone. Then a cold chill ran down her spine as she had a stark realisation. She turned back to the mirror and could not see a reflection of Raven in it.

'Oh my god, you're real … I mean … you're a real vampire!' she murmured nervously as she backed away and started to tremble in fear.

Raven calmly walked over to her. As he did so, she moved away from the mirror and backed even further away from him. Raven continued to approach her while she continued to retreat from him until she was backed right up against the white tiled wall and had nowhere else to go.

Raven paused just a few inches away from her. Her heart was beating like a drum and the alcohol she had consumed throughout the evening did not take the edge off the fear that was now consuming her. He moved his face in closer to hers and looked deep into her eyes. A cold chill shot down her spine like a bolt of ice-cold lightning as she felt his cold breath against her face. But as she felt his cold hand caress her right cheek, something happened … it was like she was being hypnotised. A strange, but pleasant feeling washed over her entire body as she fell into a state of calm relaxation. It felt kind of good, somehow sexy, she thought.

'How would you like me to help you discover your infinite supply of orgasms … all at once?' he said, 'I feel like I should at least allow you to experience one last ultimate pleasure … before you die.' His tone was slow, quiet and seductive, yet spine-chillingly cold all at the same time. She stood silent and unable to move as Raven lowered his right hand down to her waist, unbuttoned her black jeans and slipped his hand down the front of her knickers.

She sucked in a short gasp of air as her head kicked back in a reflex reaction to what Raven was doing to her genitalia. She gazed in a mesmerised state at the ceiling as his cold fingers manipulated her clitoris. Her heart started to race faster and beat harder, making her pant and take in deep gulps of air. She let out cries of pure ecstasy as tears mixed with black and purple eye make-up ran down her face. She was in a state of shock, fear, and pleasure all at the same time; a totally fucked up cocktail of emotions were cascading frantically around inside her. Her heart was beating so fast and hard it felt like it was about to explode out of her chest as she came close to orgasm.

Her body writhed and spasmed violently as multiple orgasms started to fire off rapidly down below. These were no regular orgasms; they were like nothing she had ever felt before, ultra-strong and super-electrifying. Her hypnotised state was slowly clearing. She slowly tilted her head forward to look at Raven's face; orgasms still rapid firing, her body still jerking and twitching. She looked into his eyes and noticed they were transitioning from black to purple, then back to black again. He opened his mouth wide and she noticed two large canine fangs that hadn't been there before, and then she noticed a clear white substance dripping from them. Terror washed over her as her body jerked and spasmed uncontrollably. Her adrenaline was now in overdrive mode, her heart slamming against the inside wall of her chest. She took a deep intake of breath and tried to scream, but before she could, Raven grabbed her windpipe in a tight grip with his left hand, causing the scream to get caught in her throat. He lifted her a few inches off the floor, pinned her to the wall, snapped her head backwards and launched his head forward at lightning speed to sink his fangs deep into the side of her neck, puncturing her jugular artery, forcing blood to spray out and up over the white wall tiles behind her. The venom released from his fangs paralysed her body, causing it to stop thrashing around. She was all but dead and pinned upright against the wall a few inches off the ground held only by the pressure of Raven's palm pressed hard up against her pubic bone with his fingers still jammed hard into her genitalia. Her toes were lightly twitching involuntarily as they dangled a few inches above the floor with a pool of blood starting to form beneath them.

As Raven continued to feed off her, Miss Brunette came in to check that she was okay. She saw her friend pinned up against the blood-splattered wall and screamed in horror. Raven turned and shot her a look to suggest that she would be next. She panicked and quickly ran out of the bathroom, the door slamming shut behind her.

Raven pulled his right hand out of the girl's knickers, which, up until then, had been keeping her propped upright against the wall. Miss Tongue Piercing dropped to the floor – dead. He looked down at his hand and noticed menstrual blood all over his fingers.

'How ironic,' he said, smelling his fingers, then putting them in his mouth and licking them clean. At that moment, two men came bursting into the ladies room, one of them holding a 6-inch bowie knife in a leather sheaf.

'Okay, you son of a bitch, you're dead!' shouted the one holding the bowie knife, as he removed it from its sheaf and advanced fast upon Raven. The man swung his arm sideways and tried to stab Raven in the side of his stomach. But Raven was faster, much faster. Raven grabbed the man's fist. He didn't remove the knife from the man's fist; instead he used it as an extension of the knife's handle and swung the fist, knife and all, up and under his assailant's chin … the blade penetrated through the man's lower jaw from underneath, through his tongue and up into the roof of his mouth, pinning his jaw closed.

The man stood there and let out an agonizingly painful gurgling gulp, still gripping the handle of the very knife that pinned his mouth shut. Deep red, thick goopy blood filled his mouth, half choking him as it oozed out from between the gaps in his closed teeth, forcing its way between his lips and down his chin.

Raven left him standing there dealing with it, and turned his attention to the other man who was standing in front of the door blocking Raven's exit. Raven covered the ten feet of space between them in less than a second and grabbed him by the throat, lifted him a foot off the ground and then threw him ten feet across the room, sending him smashing into the wall and crashing to the floor, breaking several wall tiles as he did so.

Raven flung open the door and made for the exit. As he paced meaningfully through the bar area and down the corridor, blood still dripping off his chin from his savage attack on the girl, everyone gave him a very wide berth. When he got to the door to the street, there was an overweight middle-aged woman dressed like a Goth standing in his way. Raven grabbed a fistful of her blouse and pulled her face to within a few inches of his own. She let out a sharp shriek as he did so. He looked deep into her eyes, which instantly put her into a deep trance, causing her head to flop backwards. He held her in this upright position in his strong grip and turned to examine the several club members who had gathered in a terrified group at the other end of the corridor.

'So you want to know what it's like to be a real vampire? Well, this is what it's like, it's bloody, it's brutal, and its name is Raven Xavier, and it has absolutely no remorse … none whatsoever,' said Raven, in an ugly, angry, aggressive voice, his Russian accent much more prominent. While keeping his eyes focused on the club members, he grabbed the woman he was holding in mid-air by her throat with his free hand, forcing his fingertips behind her windpipe and applied a powerful ever-increasing vice-like grip until blood started to ooze out from the top and bottom of his fist.

Then suddenly, while maintaining his strong grip, Raven snapped his arm back like an archer on speed, bringing with it part of the woman's windpipe, leaving a gaping bloody gorge where her throat used to be. He released his grip on her blouse, and she dropped to the floor, dead, with blood still pumping out of the cavernous hole in her throat. He stepped over her body, dropped the handful of flesh on to her chest as he did so, opened the door and departed. He left the onlookers inside the club in a state of absolute terror, unable to comprehend what had just happened.

Chapter 9

It was a beautiful sunny morning and the grounds of Tristan Syhier Burnel's estate were quiet with nothing stirring. The only signs of life were from the odd squirrel hopping around the open grounds, various finches in song, and a pair of magpies making their presence known quite vocally.

The cottage at the foot of Tristan's grounds near the main entrance gate was also perfectly still. Inside, Will's mother was in the kitchen listening to the radio while having a late breakfast after doing a few Saturday morning chores. Will's father wasn't around anymore; he had been murdered when Will was just two years old. However, Will did not know this; he thought his father's death was an accident. Will's father's death was a blessing in disguise as he had been a violent alcoholic and had nearly killed Will's mother on more than one occasion, and almost killed Will too.

The days of Will's mother being battered black and blue by her violent husband were well and truly over. They had spent the past twelve years living a safe, peaceful, and happy life as Mr Burnel's tenants in the cottage on the grounds of his estate. Will had been given the opportunity of a good education through Mr Burnel's generosity and his mother had done an excellent job of bringing him up. She was incredibly grateful for the way her life had turned around, and was more than content with the little slice of heaven and security that she and her son had.

Although the cottage was about 200 metres away from Mr Burnel's main house, Will and his mother pretty much had the run of the entire grounds and its beautiful scenic gardens and small wooded areas to themselves. Despite the fact that the grounds were very beautiful, Mr Burnel was rarely seen outside enjoying his beautiful surroundings, especially during the hours of daylight.

Will ambled into the kitchen wearing some baggy shorts and a Led Zeppelin T-shirt, still half asleep with his eyes half closed. It was 10:30am, but as it was the weekend, he had no school.

'Hi Mum,' he said, in a half asleep teenage groan.

'Hey, good morning, sleepy head,' said his mum, in a very up-beat and cheery tone. She was always pleased to see her son for the first time in the morning, even if he did have the conversational skills of a lobotomised zombie for the first twenty minutes immediately after getting out of bed.

'Want some breakfast?' she said; as she ruffled his bedhead hair-do with her hand, causing it to take on an even funnier appearance.

'Just a slice of toast, please.'

'Tea?'

'I think I'd better have coffee; I need to try and wake up. I've got to run a few errands for Mr Burnel this morning.'

'Well, it's half ten, so you'd better get a move on.'

'I know. He said it wasn't urgent, so I'm okay for time.'

Just then, the news on the radio came on.

'*Late last night there were two brutal murders, and a third person was left in a critical condition at a north London nightclub called After Dark. The After Dark club is a well-known haunt for vampire fanatics and Goths...*'

Will's mother stopped in her tracks with her fingertips still paused on the toaster's down lever as she listened to the radio announcer.

'*... Several members of the club witnessed a man, who they were convinced was a genuine vampire, kill a woman right in front of them. Another young woman witnessed her best friend being murdered by the same man in the ladies bathroom. The young woman entered the bathroom to find the man apparently drinking blood from her friend's neck.*

She ran to get help, but the two men that came to her aid were no match for the attacker, who the members at the club are now claiming to be a real vampire. The mysterious man left one of the two men in a critical condition after stabbing him in the jaw with a knife. He is now in hospital fighting for his life. The other man survived and explained how he was lifted off the ground and thrown ten feet across the room into a wall.

As the killer was leaving the club he proudly announced to onlookers that he was brutal, had no remorse and that his name was Raven Xavier, and that he was a real vampire ...'

'Are you okay, mum?' said Will, noticing that the news

announcer on the radio had her undivided attention.

'Just a minute,' she said, wanting to listen to the rest of the news story.

'... *Whether there are any connections between the murders last night and the recent case involving the severed head of the known serial rapist, Allan Bar, remains unknown. For now, the police aren't giving anything away. But one thing's for certain ... last night's brutal murders and the recent Allan Bar beheading, both appear to involve some sort of so-called vampire. Whether it's the same person responsible in both cases still remains to be seen.*'

'Will, can you keep an eye on your toast, I just have to run up to Mr Burnel's house. I need to speak to him for a moment,' his mother said, with her mood changing rapidly from chirpy to deadly serious.

'Sure, but you know he doesn't like to be disturbed during the day, unless it's an emergency ... is everything okay?'

'Everything's fine, honey. I'll be back shortly.'

She left hastily, leaving Will to butter his own toast and finish making the coffee.

***

The police now had a second team dealing with the murders that happened at the After Dark club. In typical police fashion, they had cleared everybody out of the club, cordoned it off and secured the building. CSIs were there most of the night and well into the next morning trying to gather up as much evidence as possible.

The bodies of the two dead women had been put into body bags and taken away to the mortuary for a post mortem examination. As with the Allan Bar case, the police SIO had requested an odontologist to be at the PM along with the pathologist as there were clear bite marks on the younger woman's neck. Just like with the Allan Bar case, the results of the DNA swab taken from around the bite marks proved to be very unusual; part human and part something else. The something else part was similar to that of the DNA found on Allan Bar's bite marks, but not exactly the same. So the police were now looking for two separate killers; killers whose strange DNA results look like they were of a similar kind.

The CSI team found absolutely nothing in the club as far as trace evidence was concerned – just rivers of blood all over the ladies bathroom and near the front entrance. All they had was a description of what the man looked like, and his name – Raven Xavier – if, of course, that was his real name. The police asked two of the key witnesses to give a description of Raven Xavier to the police sketch artist so she could draw up an accurate artist's impression of him to go out to the media and television stations.

The first police team was getting desperate regarding the case of Allan Bar's beheading. Evidence was still virtually non-existent, so, out of pure desperation, they decided to publish an artist's impression of the man they thought was responsible. Although going public is normally a last resort for the police, unless they feel that the suspect could be a danger to the general public, they were struggling with their investigation and needed all the help they could get. In addition, they believed that the man responsible for the Allan Bar murder could well be a danger to the general public.

They called in Tania de Pré to describe the face from the missing oil painting, as she was the only person to have seen it before it mysteriously disappeared during the night when the painting was at her house. They didn't believe for one second that the man in the oil painting was responsible for Allan Bar's beheading; after all, the painting was over 400 years old. But they had concluded that the man responsible might actually look like the man in the painting. It was a wild stab in the dark, perhaps, but as these were desperate times for the police and they had nothing else to go on, it was worth a try.

Tania didn't have to exert too much effort to help the police sketch artist come up with a likeness. After all, only the actual face had been removed from the painting, the hair, ears, neck and body were all still intact. She described the missing face from the painting as very pale with chiseled cheekbones and striking hypnotic looking eyes; like a wolf's eyes. She also told the artist that he was quite attractive; the police sketch artist could make of the attractive part what she wanted. The police sent both this, and the Raven Xavier artist's impressions to the regular national newspapers and television stations. Now all they could do was sit ... and wait.

Chapter 10

Tania's new column on the vampire proved to be a massive hit. She had done an amazing job of putting together the first part of the vampire story in her column, doing exactly what the vampire wanted. Tania still did not know the vampire's name and was referring to him throughout the column simply as *The Vampire*. She had taken sections from the lengthy Word document that he had sent her via email, abridged them, and got his life story off to a great start.

EMAIL FROM A VAMPIRE
By Tania de Pré

Off the back of the 'So You Want To Be A Vampire' story I ran recently, I have decided to take an abrupt change in direction regarding vampire stories. Having done more background research on some emails that I received from a man claiming to be a genuine 1000-year-old vampire, I have agreed to publish his story via this very column. He refuses to reveal his name, for now, so I will refer to him simply as The Vampire. I have been in communication with him via telephone and email. He has emailed me a rather lengthy word document detailing his entire life story from his birth date as a human, the change to a vampire, and his life as a vampire thereafter, right up to the present day. Over the next two weeks I will be publishing the key parts of his incredible life story in abridged form; most of which are written by the vampire himself. This is as real as it gets!

The mystery vampire has assured me that by the time this story concludes, readers will be left with no doubt that real vampires do actually exist and have been living among us for a very long time. At this stage, even I don't know what he means by this and how his story is going to truly end. In the meantime, follow and enjoy his story.

The remainder of this column and the on-going story are smaller sections that I have cut and pasted from some of the more relevant parts of his story, written in his own words.

I was born a mortal human on the 20th June in the year 978 AD. My birthplace was a small village in western France, close to the border of Switzerland. As was typical of that period, I remained in the village throughout my entire childhood and teenage years working as a peasant on the land of a local nobleman. When I was 14 years old, my father died of consumption, while my mother died eighteen months later from pneumonia. I then had to fend for myself, and I eventually settled down with my bride when I was seventeen. My bride was unable to bear children, but we had a strong, unbreakable love for each other, which never faded as the years went by.

It was when I was 33 years old that I became a vampire. It happened on the 13th December in the year 1011. My becoming a vampire was not planned, it was accidental. I was simply in the wrong place at the wrong time. I was out hunting in a nearby forest on a winter's evening. Although I didn't know it then, that was the last time I would ever see daylight. The sun had gone down and it was getting very late. I had still not been successful in my hunt but there was a full moon and the light was pretty good, so I decided to continue hunting for another hour. It was during this hour that I was savagely attacked by a pack of five starving wolves.

Then, out of nowhere came my rescuer. To this day, I do not know who, or what my rescuer was. All I could remember was that he moved incredibly fast and appeared to have super-human strength. He killed three of the wolves very easily, while the other two ran away deep into the forest.

My memory of the events that happened that night are hazy, but not because it happened a thousand years ago. They are hazy because at the time I was half-unconscious on the cold snowy ground and bleeding heavily after the savage attack by the wolves. I had lost a lot of blood. I can vaguely recollect an outline of what looked like a man wearing a long black hooded cloak. As the cloaked man stood there looking down at me, I saw his eyes peering out from inside the large dark hood. They were red, so red they looked like two small balls of fire burning brightly in the moonlight. The strange hooded man knelt over me, crouched down and whispered something in my ear. Although I was freezing cold from the forest floor, feeling faint and on the verge of passing out, I will never forget the words that my rescuer whispered to me.

'You will live to see tomorrow, but you will never see the light of day again.'

I barely knew what was going on as I was on the verge of passing out due to the sheer amount of blood that I had lost. The strange man bit his own wrist, and held his arm out so that his blood dripped into the open wounds on my neck, the wounds made by the wolves. He then moved his wrist higher so that his blood ran into my slightly open mouth and down my throat.

It is obvious now that the mysterious rescuer was some sort of vampire who had saved my life. However, the price to pay for being immortal meant that I would never be able to step out into the light of day ever again. Some of the wolves' DNA had already found its way into my system via the numerous bites and wounds on my arms and neck, before the vampirification process had completed. This is why, today, my eyes look like that of a wolf's, because essentially, they are. So, I became a rare breed of vampire; a kind of hybrid. I had all the strengths and powers of a vampire, but with the hunting instincts and acute hearing and eyesight of a wolf. I had become the ultimate nocturnal hunter and killing machine, I was right at the very top of the food chain. Why the mysterious hooded vampire saved my life that winter's night has remained a mystery to me for the past thousand years.

The story continues to unfold in the vampire's own words in tomorrow's edition.

***

There was no doubt that the first part to the vampire's story had the nation gripped and riveted. They wanted more – much more. The paper had received thousands of emails within hours of the story hitting the streets. Readers couldn't get enough of the mystery vampire's story.

Later that day, the police received a phone call from a

woman who knew the whereabouts of Allan Bar's missing body. She had spotted his body hanging upside down and stripped of his clothing, high up on the side of an old disused warehouse building along a canal path where she walked her two dogs. He was suspended from the metal guttering that ran along the edge of the roof by a single rope that was tied to one of his ankles.

The police suspected his body had been left hanging naked to humiliate him and to kill his dignity, just as he had humiliated his numerous female rape victims.

How it had taken somebody this long to spot the body was a mystery to the police, considering how publicly it was displayed. The lady who phoned in to report it to the police had only noticed it because she heard loud *cawing* sounds from above. When she looked up, she saw a crow pecking away at the suspended corpse. The police could not figure out how the headless body had been attached to the metal gutter sixty feet off the ground, as there were no signs of forced entry into the warehouse and no fresh footprints inside – and it would have been easy for the police to spot them as the floors were very dusty since nobody had been inside for years.

The police had also concluded that it would have been virtually impossible for somebody to approach the warehouse rooftop from any of the neighbouring buildings without the use of specialist equipment, of which there was no evidence. There was simply no trace evidence whatsoever; nothing. The police were totally perplexed over how the body got all the way up there. Although there was no new evidence, the body had turned up so that was at least some small token of relief for the police.

Chapter 11

Back at the newspaper offices Tania continued to work on her column, abridging additional parts of the story that the vampire had emailed to her. She had heard about the After Dark club murders from Detective Maldini and her work colleagues and wondered if it was her vampire that was responsible. She had sent him an email asking the question, but so far had no reply. She was starting to wonder if he was going to contact her again any time soon, as she was complying with his wish to publish his story. Deep down, she suspected it wasn't her vampire; she couldn't quite explain it, but killing innocent people just didn't seem like his style somehow. Besides, she had read his entire life story that he had emailed her, and feeding off people was something that he tried to avoid at all costs; instead he generally fed off the blood of animals, and on occasion got human blood from other sources that did not require hurting anybody.

Tania was keen to get away on time today, as a new DVD movie had arrived mail order in the post that morning and she was looking forward to getting home and relaxing in front of the TV with a glass of wine. So she wrapped up the work on her column for the day, quickly sent a few last minute emails and then headed off home.

When she got home she made herself something to eat, caught up on the phone with her mother for an hour, and then had a long therapeutic soak in a lovely candle-lit hot bath. She removed her new DVD from its shrink-wrapping, grabbed a wine glass and her half-eaten box of Maltesers from the fridge, and then turned to get her bottle of red wine off the kitchen worktop. It was only when she picked the bottle up that she realised that there was only about a glass left in it. She opened the kitchen cupboard where she kept her reserve stocks of wine, but it was empty.

'Oh great!' she sighed, as she stood there in her bathrobe, all cozy and looking forward to chilling out on the couch in front of the TV. *What the hell, one glass will just have to do,* she thought.

After her movie finished, she just wasn't tired at all, even though it was now 10:45pm and she'd had a hard day. So she decided to do some more work on her column on her home computer. She glanced at the clock and decided that if she rushed out the door now, she could probably get to the off-licence down the street before it closed.

So, without further ado, she threw on a pair of loose-fitting grey toweling jogging bottoms and a T-shirt, grabbed her jacket and walked briskly to the off-licence on the corner.

As she approached the counter she realised that she had left her purse at home and had no money to pay for the bottle of Merlot that she was clutching. This didn't prove problematic, as the owners of the shop knew Tania well because she was a regular; it just went on a tab until next time.

As she walked back up the street Tania thought about how she appreciated the owner of the off-licence for not forcing her to walk home to get her purse and come out a second time. Then she began to reminisce over the movie she had just watched. Suddenly, she heard a voice call out to her from inside a doorway she had just passed.

'Good evening, Ms de Pré,' said the distinctive familiar voice.

Tania freaked and jumped out of her skin as she spun around, clutching at her chest and dropping her bottle of wine, sending it smashing to the ground.

And then she saw him as he slowly stepped out of the shadowy doorway where he had been standing. A tall slender man, dressed all in black, wearing a black Fedora hat with its wide brim throwing a shadow across his eyes, revealing only the lower two thirds of his pale white face. His eyes, white and wolf-like peered out fiercely from the shadow of the brim of his hat. Tania could do nothing but stand there, frozen to the spot.

Chapter 12

Tania stood there, suddenly feeling a cold chill, even though the late evening June temperature was quite mild. She felt like she was paralysed on the spot, unable to move. All she could do was stand there and wait to see what he was going to say – or do.

'You look like you've seen a ghost, Ms de Pré ... please, don't be afraid. I can assure you that I have absolutely no intention of hurting you in any way; not now, or ever,' said the vampire, in soft reassuring tones.

Tania had instantly recognised his voice as the man who had phoned her, the same man claiming to be a 1000-year-old vampire. Now that she was looking at him in person, and heard him speak to her face to face, she couldn't quite explain why, but she actually believed him, even trusted him. The initial shock slowly started to subdue.

'Let me apologise for startling you. I would have much preferred to arrange a more formal meeting, but something tells me that you wouldn't have agreed.'

'Have you been following me?' she asked, nervously.

'Oh, no, no, no, Ms de Pré. I simply wanted you to meet me in person.'

'And you're not here to kill me?' she said, seeking his reassurance.

'Please, Ms de Pré, the world is a far more interesting and beautiful place with you in it. My intentions are honorable,' he said.

She let out a little nervous laugh.

'The murders … at the After Dark club the other night … I wasn't responsible for them.'

'I know,' she said, confidently.

'Oh, how's that?' said the vampire, surprised.

'It just didn't seem like your style somehow.'

'Please explain.'

'Well, although you're a vampire … I mean … a real vampire, you seem to be a nice one, based on all your writings about your life story. If what you've written is true, then you have morals and decency and would not have brutally murdered innocent people like that.'

He tilted his head to the side slightly and looked deep into Tania's eyes. 'You're very perceptive and you're not judgmental, Ms de Pré … I like that.'

'Well, I'm still sitting on the fence regarding the Allan Bar beheading.'

'Ah yes, Mr Bar. The man responsible for brutally attacking and raping several women, almost killing three of them,' he said sternly.

'I'm still not sure that gave you the right to kill him.'

'You were lined up to be his next victim, Ms de Pré, who knows, he might have killed you?'

'Yes, you're quite right, I never thanked you for that,' she said, tentatively.

'You're quite welcome.' Just then, the vampire noticed blood dripping down her ankle and over her white training shoe.

'You appear to have cut yourself,' he said, looking at the deep red blood trickling down over her ankle.

'Oh, it must be from the broken bottle,' she said, looking down at it. The vampire got down on one knee to take a closer look. She quickly backed away.

'Please Ms de Pré; we can't have you bleeding all over the pavement like this. Relax. I just want to see how bad it is.' He proceeded to roll her jogging bottoms up her ankle to reveal the cut, which was only about a centimetre long, but bleeding slowly nonetheless. The vampire picked up a small piece of broken glass and slowly cut the palm of his own hand with it, causing it to haemorrhage blood. Tania looked shocked at his action, but before she could protest, he had grabbed her ankle and pushed the palm of his bleeding hand against her cut ankle.

'What are you doing? ... This won't make us blood related will it? ... Like blood sister and brother?'

'No, and you won't become a vampire either. I'm simply healing your wound,' he laughed, removing his hand from her ankle and standing up.

'There, all better now,' he said, smiling.

She knelt down and examined her cut, just in time to witness it healing right in front of her very eyes. It was like watching a 14-day time-lapse shot of a cut healing up. *How's this even possible*, she thought as she watched her cut heal up completely without so much of a hint of scar tissue, and all in the space of about ten seconds?

'How did you do that?' she said, in total disbelief at what

she had just seen.

'Oh, just one of the perks of being … a vampire.'

'So, do you know who was responsible for the After Dark club murders?' she asked, getting to her feet.

'Yes, I do,' he said, in a very serious tone.

'Well who was it? I mean, was it the man who they mentioned on the news?'

'Yes, his name is Raven Xavier.'

'Yes, I know that, but who is he?'

'He's like me, a vampire. But he's different.'

'Different how?'

'When I became a vampire, I retained an element of humanity. As my life story document that I sent you clearly states, I am something of a unique hybrid, made up of three parts. The two smallest parts are made up of wolf and human, with the third, the lion's share, being vampire. Raven Xavier on the other hand, is 100% vampire, and a very evil one at that.'

'I'm confused. How come vampires are springing up all over the place all of a sudden? First you, and now this Raven Xavier monster; and while we're talking about names, I don't know yours.'

'And that's the way I'd like to keep it … for now, anyway.'

'Oh, why's that?'

'All will be revealed in good time, Ms de Pré, have a little patience.'

'So why is this other vampire brutally murdering innocent people?'

'I don't know, not yet. But I suspect it has something to do with me.'

'What makes you think that?'

'Because I've broken the vampire's ancient code, the rule of silence.'

'Rule of silence?'

'Yes, since the very beginning, vampires have done a great job of convincing the world that they didn't exist. It was vampires who invented vampire stories and urban myths, simply to throw humans off our scent. This is how my kind have been able to survive and go unnoticed, living among you for thousands of years. And now, because I've come out of the dark to tell the world my story through your column, our secret is almost out.'

'Almost out?'

'Well, right now, most readers will assume that my story in your column is nothing more than the writings of somebody with an elaborate and vivid imagination. Don't get me wrong, I'm sure your readers are thoroughly enjoying every word I've written, but I'm also sure they don't actually believe it. Most people simply want to believe in vampires, ghosts and other myths because they want to believe that there's more to life than the harsh reality they are stuck with. But deep down, they know that none of it is true. But by the time my story ends, there will be conclusive proof that vampires do exist, and when that happens, our secret will be out in the open for the first time in over 3000 years.'

'So why is Raven killing people in public, and so brutally, if he wants to keep the vampire secret under wraps I mean?'

'He's angry, angry with me for going public.'

'I still don't get it. By killing those people at the After Dark club the way he did, so publicly, he's let the cat out of the bag without any help from you … right?'

'No, not really; people still won't believe it. They will put Raven down to nothing more than a psychopathic delusional murderer. They'll want to see something else, something more concrete. And in time, when my story concludes, they will.'

'What do you mean?'

'Patience, Ms de Pré, patience; you'll be the first to find out, I promise.'

'Is Raven going to kill any more people?'

'Probably, yes.'

'Can you stop him?'

'I don't know. It's been a few hundred years since I last came up against Raven Xavier.'

'What! You mean you know him … you've met him before … when?'

'It was back in 1706; I remember it well. Johann Sebastian Bach had just finished composing his famous Toccata and Fugue in D minor. A local aristocrat had invited me to a dinner dance. Back then I got out a lot more than I do these days, especially in the evenings after dusk.' The Vampire fixed Tania with his hypnotic eyes and started to recount his tale.

* Friday 26th November 1706 *

The large ballroom was very quaint and tasteful in typical baroque style with lots of fine detail around the gold-themed room. There were eight large chandeliers, holding a hundred candles each, hanging from the high ceiling, illuminating not only the room, but also the very detailed painted ceiling containing lots of romantic looking angels and cherubs.

I was dancing the minuet with one of the other guests that I had met that evening, when I suddenly became very aware of an uneasy presence, a presence like I hadn't felt for a long time. As I moved gracefully around the floor with my beautiful dance partner to the sound of the small string ensemble, the uneasy feeling continued to wash over me, getting stronger and deeper by the second. Although the feeling was uncomfortable and edgy, it was somehow strangely familiar at the same time. Then I saw the cause of my uneasy feelings. Over against the far wall stood a man, deep in conversation with one of the other female guests. He was very tall, about six foot three, and very strong looking. His complexion was very pale and his eyes were as black as a midnight ocean on a moonless night. His hair was black and perfectly straight. There was something very different about him. He had a very seductive and hypnotic way about him with the opposite sex; a way that I instantly recognised.

The young woman he was in conversation with was about 17 years old and stunningly attractive with very long blonde hair in impeccable ringlets. They both appeared to be having a good time, drinking and laughing together. But his intentions were of a sinister nature. It was obvious that she'd had way too much to drink. She was more than a little tipsy and could hardly stand up. She was falling for his hypnotic powers and was all over him.

I don't know how I knew, but I could sense his evil intentions towards her. It was as if I had a built in sixth sense; I was tuned into his frequency. Anyway, the next thing I knew, he was leading her out of the main dance hall to somewhere more private. So I politely excused myself from my dance partner and followed them out into the entrance hall.

I saw him guiding her, laughing and joking, up the stairs and along the wide corridor to one of the bedrooms. He had his arm wrapped tightly around her waist to support her as she stumbled along in her drunken state. He pushed the bedroom door open and encouraged her inside by moving his hand down onto the lower part of her bottom, gently nursing her through the door, before closing it behind them.

My acute hearing meant that I could hear everything that was going on inside the room from my position outside in the corridor. They were laughing away. She was giggling like an immature little girl as he hypnotised and seduced her further. Raven liked to take his time with his seduction ritual. It was clear that he thought it was great fun to torment and tease his victims sexually, before eventually killing them. I have since learnt that, for Raven, sex and killing go almost hand in hand – both excite him equally. The only thing that excited him more was doing them both at the same time.

That evening, he must have taken at least forty minutes over this particularly squalid encounter, really taking his time to slowly remove her ballroom gown, corset, petticoat and many other silky layers one by one; with her panting and begging for him as he did so. I slowly opened the door and put my head through to see the young woman standing there totally naked, except for her stockings and garters, at the foot of the bed. He stood right up close to her, still fully dressed, toying with her like a cat with a mouse, only in a sexual way that was getting her worked up and incredibly frustrated, sexually. It was obvious that he liked it as he slowly caressed various parts of her body, soaking up every moment, knowing that he was going to be the last man to touch her naked body alive.

He put the palm of his hand flat against her chest and pushed her hard, and sent her flying backwards onto the bed. He leapt off the floor and landed with his knees either side of her chest and his hands either side of her head; he then gazed down into her eyes. At that moment, something happened; she saw something in his eyes and started to struggle. She tried to scream, but he clapped his right hand over her mouth before she could really get it out. She had a look of absolute terror in her eyes. He grabbed her hair with his free hand and snapped her head over to the side, revealing the perfect blemish-free skin on her neck, while licking his lips and exposing his fangs.

At that moment I flung the door fully open and used every ounce of my powers and speed to get across the bedroom to him. I was moving so fast that when I collided with him I knocked him clean off her and into the far wall eight feet beyond the bed. He was very strong; he put his feet into my chest and launched me high and far across the room, causing me to smash into a large oil painting on the opposite wall. He then stood up and let out an evil roar. His eyes had changed from black to vibrant purple and his fangs were fully extended, dripping with venom. I jumped to my feet to confront him as I fully expected there to be a fight between us, but to my amazement there was not. Instead, he looked me up and down for a few moments, then dove through a closed window and vanished into the night, leaving the shocked but unharmed woman alone with me. I threw the terrified girl her clothes and told her curtly to get dressed and go home.

'You see, Tania,' said the Vampire, finishing his story, 'unlike men, whom Raven can slaughter without hesitation, women are different. He can't just kill and feed off a beautiful woman in the same way he can a man. Instead he has to go through his whole sexual ritual thing with them first; it excites him.'

'And you haven't seen him since?' she said.

'No, that was the first time I'd ever met him. I've heard stories about him over the years through other vampires, but I haven't seen him personally since 1706; until the other night.'

Although Tania was alone in a dark shop doorway with the vampire, she was starting to feel a little more comfortable in his presence – strangely.

'Can I ask you a question?' she said.

'Certainly.'

'Am I under any kind of influence by you right now … I mean, have you put me into some sort of hypnotised state or anything like that? Like Raven did with that girl in the story you just told me?'

'No,' he laughed, 'I haven't hypnotised you.'

Tania couldn't quite explain why, but she didn't doubt his words for a second; but if she wasn't under any kind of hypnosis, where were the strange emotional feelings starting to stir deep inside her coming from? To Tania, the vampire was starting to seem more appealing and attractive, than frightening. He had a dark, seductive way about him, to which Tania found herself magnetically drawn.

She had to snap out of this right now; after all, *he's a vampire, a vampire capable of killing,* she thought. But no matter how much she tried, the vampire was becoming more and more magnetic to her by the minute. She could feel herself being drawn to him. Was it his human part that she was finding herself becoming strangely attracted to? Or the vampire part? *Or perhaps a combination of the two,* she wondered.

'Are you ok, Ms de Pré?' he enquired.

'Oh, yes … I'm fine,' she said, shaking herself out of her current thought processes, while still looking deeply into his eyes.

'Well then, please allow me to walk you back to your house.'

Although he said this in a soft gentle tone, she felt like it wasn't really a question, but she didn't mind. When they arrived at Tania's house, the vampire waited at the foot of her steps and watched her climb them to her front door. There was no way on earth that she was going to invite the vampire inside. But the scary thing was that for a moment, the thought did actually cross her mind.

'Look, you don't have to call me Ms de Pré all the time, you can call me Tania. In fact I'd prefer that,' she said, as she put her key in her front door and unlocked it.

Tania turned around expecting him to acknowledge this, but it was too late; he was nowhere to be seen – he'd vanished. She glanced up and down the street, but he was nowhere to be seen, so she went inside and made herself a drink; she had to settle for a cup of tea, as there was no way she was going to go out to the off-licence again. She settled on the sofa to ponder over the conversation she'd just had with the vampire. She put her feet on the coffee table next to that day's newspaper, which was open at her column page. She figured that he must be happy with the way his story was going; otherwise he would have said something. She looked at the headline of her column and thought, *yes, that's a damn good heading for a story.*

EMAIL FROM A VAMPIRE – Part 2
By Tania de Pré

Continued in the vampire's own words.

The mysterious hooded vampire vanished into the night; leaving his blood to take effect on the human body that he had left behind on the forest floor. As the effects of the hooded vampire's blood started to work their magic, I began to regain full consciousness.

As I slowly came around, I was aware of the cold snow falling on my face. The ground beneath me was cold and damp and I could feel wet leaves underneath my head, wrists and hands. When I slowly opened my eyes, I could see the frosty branches on the large trees moving in the wind high above me. Although it was dark, I could see very clearly, not because of the light from the full moon, but for another reason.

It was as though I had developed some kind of super-human

night vision while I lay there on the forest floor recovering. Everything was very bright and incredibly clear. When I turned my head against the sodden cold snow-covered ground I could see clearly for about 300 metres to the edge of the forest, even through the darkness and dense mist that had come in while I lay unconscious.

I noticed that the white snow around me was splattered with blood. Although it was quite dark, the deep red blood appeared quite vibrant, lit up in the moonlight against the bluish white snow. What had happened to me and why did I suddenly have incredible night vision when only the previous day my eyesight was far from what is today known as 20/20, even in good daylight. This was the immediate question that sprang to mind as I lay there feeling surreal, yet somehow incredibly invigorated. I drew my hands across the ground up towards my chest, raking the damp leaves under my fingers as I did so. I pushed on my hands and got to my feet, which felt strangely effortless considering that I'd recently been savagely attacked by a pack of wolves.

I wasn't sure exactly how long I had been lying on the forest floor, but I felt no compulsion to stretch as I stood there. I had woken up feeling like I had slept for a year while my body had totally re-built and regenerated itself, but there was something else; my body felt powerful. I felt like I had inherited the hind legs off an energetic young stallion. I felt incredible, I felt alive; I felt like I could run for a hundred miles.

Then I became uneasy, there was an eerie feeling around me; what was it? The strange and dark feeling was coming from within my own body. I felt like my human emotions were being replaced by something else, something dark and sinister, and I didn't like it. As this transformation took place, there was nothing

I could do. It was too strong to fight off. It wasn't in my head; it was in my soul. What was happening to me? That was it, my soul didn't feel right anymore, I was becoming somebody else, or something else.

As I stood there in the forest, an ice-cold feeling washed over me. Whatever was going on inside me had now completed its course. I could remember who I was, but I was also very aware of how I now felt. It was surreal, eerie, and with a feeling of the unknown, yet at the same time, it felt incredible.

From my frozen stance there in the forest, I slowly turned my head, first to the left, then to the right, as I scanned the area. I was looking for something. I was suddenly aware that I was hungry, that I had to feed, but this was a different kind of hunger. I wasn't hungry for bread or wine; I had to feed on a human – human blood to be more precise. This thought would have repulsed me and made me feel sick the day before, but that day it felt like I needed to drink human blood like a drug, and I needed it desperately. I had an overwhelming need to feed for two reasons; one, to survive, and two, because I felt like I was going to enjoy it.

I was aware of the extra senses that I had acquired while I was unconscious on the forest floor. I had an acute awareness of everything that was going on around me, everything within several acres. I heard the distant sounds of horses pulling a wagon at the edge of the forest area about 300 metres away. I moved across the forest floor to the dirt track road that ran alongside it in what seemed like just a few short seconds. I kept myself hidden from view behind some trees alongside the track. Then I saw the wagon led by two large horses about 100 metres up the track. There was a man sitting at the front guiding the horses. He was wearing a long dark coat with a hood to shelter him from the snow as he whipped the horses, demanding more speed.

As the wagon drew nearer, I could sense two more people inside the rear section, which was covered in detailed painted cloth: they were female. The horse drawn wagon was now close enough for me to smell the occupants in the back. I don't know how, but I somehow knew that the driver had consumption. My instincts told me that I could feed from a human with this disease and it would not affect me that much. I would simply feel slightly weak for a couple of days, but with this in mind, I knew I was going to have to feed on one, or both of the female occupants inside.

Continued tomorrow.

As Tania sat there on the sofa drinking her tea, reflecting on her meeting with the vampire, she became more aware of the strong emotional feelings that continued to stir inside her – and it felt good.

Chapter 13

The following morning the police artist's impressions of the two vampires had been published in most of the national newspapers and they were all over the television news. By lunchtime most of the country had seen the artist's impressions and were familiar with the Allan Bar decapitation and the After Dark club murders. The story was front-page news with most of the papers that published it. The Sentinel newspaper had also put the story, along with the artist's impressions, on the front page, but they had also put in a plug to Tania's column, which simply read:

Sentinel columnist, Tania de Pré, currently has unprecedented access to this shocking news story. See "Email From A Vampire" in her weekday column, to read the life story of a man claiming to be a 1000-year-old vampire – and who, coincidently, is also a suspect in the Allan Bar murder case. Read Tania's column exclusively on page 7.

Will had seen the news along with the artist's impressions on his iPhone during his school lunch break and had cycled home in a desperate hurry to see his mother so that he could speak to her. He had recognised one of the sketches as having a remarkably similar resemblance to his landlord, Tristan Syhier Burnel. When he got home, his mother was in the kitchen sitting at the table with a cup of coffee. There was a copy of The Sentinel newspaper in front of her open on Tania de Pré's column page.

EMAIL FROM A VAMPIRE – Part 3
By Tania de Pré

Continued from yesterday, in the vampire's own words.

As the horse drawn wagon passed, I moved at un-human lightning speed and leapt onto the side of it, ripping its cloth covering open. The two female occupants were about 30 years old and obviously quite wealthy. One was wearing a black cloak and scarf covering her neck and although it was winter, the other one was wearing a low cut blouse and a relatively lightweight overcoat. Her neck was pale, almost pure white in the bright moonlight. She was by far the easiest and most appealing target, as her neck was already exposed.

They were both stunned to silence by my fast and uninvited arrival as I appeared out of nowhere on the side of their wagon. I focused my attentions on the woman with the exposed neck and looked straight into her eyes. As she looked back into mine, she screamed and had a look of pure terror all over her face. My powerful legs propelled me forward and straight at her with incredible force and speed. All in one swift movement, I lunged forward and grabbed her shoulder with my right hand and her hair with my left. I snapped her head to the left and sank my teeth deep into the side of her neck, piercing her jugular artery with uncanny accuracy. My newly acquired knowledge told me that large volumes of blood travelled through the jugular veins, allowing me to feed faster.

The ruckus caught the attention of the driver. He yanked back hard on the reins, bringing the horses to a somewhat clumsy halt on the snowy wet muddy track. By now, the other female passenger looked as white as a ghost, she had gone into a state of shock as I proceeded to feed off and slowly kill her fellow passenger.

The driver turned around and parted the cloth covering the rear to see what the commotion was. When he saw me, and all the blood splattered around the interior of the wagon, he grabbed the crossbow that he kept next to his seat, loaded it and aimed it at my chest. Like a flash, I jumped forward and grabbed the crossbow, pushing it upwards, causing the bolt to be fired through the cloth roof of the wagon and high into the night sky. Still holding onto his crossbow I hit him square in the face with it, sending him flying backwards off the wagon, causing him to land painfully on his back on the cold snowy ground several feet away. I then leapt off the wagon, and flew down and slammed into him, like a peregrine falcon launching an attack on a pigeon in mid-flight. I felt, and heard, his ribs and back break upon the impact of my knees smashing into his chest. His consumption became instantly obvious. My knees, together with the weight of my body slamming into him, caused a colossal amount of blood to project violently from his throat and mouth, hitting me in the face. I looked down at him and watched the last few traces of life drain from his face as he lay there in the snow spluttering blood and struggling for breath.

The other female passenger had come out of her state of shock and had jumped off the wagon and was screaming hysterically as she ran back down the snowy track in the direction from which they had just come. She stumbled and kept falling as she desperately tried to flee in the snow and escape death. At this point, she was of no interest to me, so I let her struggle on through the snow. Although the snow was only ankle deep, it must have felt like treacle up to her knees as she fled in fear.

The moonlit snowy track had become very quiet and still, with only light snow falling silently onto the wagon and the ground around me. I leapt back onto the wagon and looked at the woman I had been feeding off. She was still alive – just. Even though I only had my jaw locked onto her neck for a few brief moments, I had taken quite a lot of blood from her. Because I had severed her jugular artery, it had been jetting blood out all over the cloth interior and seat of the wagon while I was dealing with the driver. She had lost a great volume of blood, and if she looked pale before, she was positively white now. She could barely hold her head up as she stared at me. Her look of terror had been replaced with a resigned look of imminent death.

In her final words she managed to say, "What are you?" in a very faint whisper mixed with the sound of gurgling blood in her throat. I could not answer, as I didn't really know myself, so I said nothing. I watched her eyes slowly close, as she died right in front of me. The tiny part of human emotion that I had left inside me surfaced. I now had mixed emotions about what I had just done. I had killed and fed from a woman out of pure vampire instinct; the instinctive need to feed. I had woken up on the forest floor that night a vampire, a vampire with an urge that needed to be instantly satisfied. But after the experience of killing and feeding was over, I knew that I would find it very difficult to kill a human again, and go through life killing; there had to be another way.

I turned to get out off the wagon, and then paused briefly to look down at the dead driver. The snowflakes were melting on his still-warm body, washing the blood away down his cheeks and neck. I leapt from the wagon and my feet didn't touch the ground until I landed at the edge of the forest twenty feet away. I fled with great speed into the dark depths of the forest with mental torture and emotions clashing and fighting inside me as I struggled to come to terms with what I had become.

Continued in tomorrow's edition.

***

Will knew that his mother had seen the police artist's impressions on the front page of The Sentinel newspaper and read the news of the murders. And it looked like she had read Tania de Pré's daily column too.

'Mum?' said Will, looking for answers, concerned and fearing the worse.

'Sit down, honey,' she said, softly, 'there's something I've got to tell you.'

'It's Mr Burnel, isn't it … it's Tristan, in the paper and on the TV?' said Will, shocked and scared.

His mother paused for a moment and glanced at the newspaper on the table. Then she slowly looked up at him.

'Yes … he's involved,' she said, softly. She always knew that she was going to have to tell her son the entire story about Tristan and how they came to be living in a small cottage on his estate, but she never expected that day to be today, and she certainly didn't expect it to be like this.

'I don't understand ... what's going on? The papers are saying he killed a rapist; is it true? And what's all this stuff about vampires?' he said, agitated, confused and overwhelmed by the enormity of the situation.

'Will, it's a long story, and it's not one that we should get into during your lunch break. I'll tell you everything this evening when you get back from school.'

'Mum, I'm not going back to school this afternoon. Not until I know what's going on – tell me now.'

He was adamant and wasn't going to change his mind. He wanted to know why their landlord, the man whom he and his mother worked for on a part-time basis – and above all, their friend, or at least his mother's friend – had made the front-page news. She could see in his eyes that he was not going to move on this, so she didn't even attempt to play the strict parent by sending him back to school as she knew it wouldn't work on this occasion.

'Okay, sit down,' she said, trying to figure out how she could encapsulate a very long story, into a nice easy digestible bite-size chunk that Will would be able to swallow and understand. Will moved around the table and pulled out a chair.

'Will, I need you to promise me that you won't repeat a single word of this to anybody, ever, not even your future wife if you ever get married,' she said, more seriously than she had ever meant anything before.

'Okay, Mum, I understand,' said Will, recognising the

fact that his mum was being deadly serious.

'I mean it, Will, what I'm about to tell you doesn't leave this room – ever!'

'Okay, Mum, you have my word.'

Will had been brought up well. He never lied and if he made a promise or gave his word on something, it was as solid as oak. His mum knew this and trusted him implicitly to never speak a word of what she was about to tell him to anybody.

'Tristan ... Mr Burnel and I first met when you were just two years old. He knew I was going through a rough time with your father.'

'Did Mr Burnel know my dad?'

'Only briefly, she said, moving on swiftly as she didn't want to be questioned in detail about this, 'but the important thing is, Mr Burnel helped me and he even saved your life one night.'

'Saved my life! How?'

'You were only two years old when your father died so you don't really have any memories of him, and in a way I'm glad.'

'What do you mean, Mum?' he said, concerned.

'He was an alcoholic, quite a violent one actually.'

'Did he hurt you?'

'Yes ... yes he did, sometimes quite badly. He put me in hospital a few times. Sometimes he would just come in drunk and other times he would steadily get drunk at home. Either way, he always needed somebody to shout at and vent his anger on; and that somebody was usually me, and the shouting usually led to beatings too.'

'Oh, Mum, I'm so sorry,' said Will, sincerely, getting up to give her a hug.

'It's okay, it wasn't your fault and I'm all right. The thing is – I could take his abuse and beatings. But when he started to focus his anger towards you I knew I had to get us both away from him.'

'I was too young to remember. What did he do?'

Before answering, she got up and went to the kitchen cupboard and grabbed the small bottle of brandy, which she kept there for medicinal purposes such as this. She poured herself a double before continuing.

'Well, at first he would just shout and scream at you if you cried. He slapped you quite hard across the face on a couple of occasions, for silly things like you knocking over an ornament or running around the living room. One time you knocked his glass of gin and tonic over on the coffee table. He slapped you so hard on the side of your head that it knocked you out. You were unconscious for nearly five minutes.'

'Oh my god! That's horrible,' he said.

'I haven't got to the horrible bit yet,' she said, taking a large gulp of brandy.

Will gave her his undivided attention and he waited with bated breath.

'One night he got really bad. He was looking for somebody to vent out on and you had a tummy ache and were crying in pain, so he tried to get to you. I stood between him and you to stop him hurting you and I refused to get out of his way. Well, he proceeded to beat me black and blue, but I still wouldn't move. He grabbed me by the hair and threw me straight into a glass dresser against the wall.

Then he slapped you around the side of the head, knocking you to the ground. I was on the floor and could hardly see as I had blood pouring into my eyes from a deep cut on the top of my head. As I wiped the blood out of my eyes I saw him pick you up by one ankle and carry you outside. Back then we lived on the fourth floor in a council flat. I didn't know what he was going to do so I jumped to my feet and ran outside after him. When I got there, I couldn't believe my eyes. He was dangling you over the edge of the balcony by your ankle with one hand. He told me that if I didn't go to the off-licence and buy him two more bottles of gin, he would drop you onto the concrete car park below. I was panic-stricken and didn't know what to do. He then told me that he didn't want a screaming brat anymore and said he was going to drop you anyway. He outstretched his arm and said, "Say goodbye to the screaming brat." It was then that I met Mr Burnel for the very first time. Just as your father was about to let go of you, he appeared out of nowhere. Anyway, Mr Burnel managed to grab you by the leg just as your father dropped you. He saved your life, Will … and he saved mine too. He took us in and gave us a decent shot at life, taking us away from the drug-ridden council estate. He let us live in the gatehouse cottage on his estate; he paid for your education and your entire private tuition along with private piano lessons. He even paid me to do housecleaning for him part time.'

'Why, why would he do all that for us?'

'Will, Mr Burnel's a decent man. He's got compassion and he's very generous and it's because of him that we have the good life that we do; it's because of him that you and I are still alive today. But...'

'But what, Mum?'

'He's not like other people.'

'What do you mean?'

'Will, I know you're a clever and intelligent boy, so I need you to be open minded, more open minded than you've ever been before.'

'What is it?' he said, preparing for the next words to come from his mother's mouth.

'Mr Burnel's a vampire,' she said, as serious as can be.

Will did not laugh, or crack any jokes. He could see that his mother was deadly serious and even though he didn't believe in vampires, he didn't quite know how to react in light of this new information.

'The front-page story in the paper is only a part of it. You should read the column on page 7,' she said.

'Column?'

'Yes, the paper's been running Mr Burnel's life story via a column for the past few days. It's expected to run for a few more weeks until his story concludes.'

'Mum, there are no such things as vampires; they're a myth.'

'Will, I know you're probably finding all this very hard to take in. But I want you to bear with me. The other day when I had to leave you at breakfast to go and see Mr Burnel up at the house, we spoke about this and he wants me to bring you up to see him later tonight.'

'You mean after it gets dark?'

'Yes, but not for the reason you're probably thinking. Mr Burnel can see people in his house during the day; he's just resting right now.'

'But only behind closed curtains out of the sun, right?'

'That's right,' she said.

'So he can't actually go outside during the day. Is this why I've never seen him out on his estate during daylight hours?' he asked.

'That's right, Will. Look, later this evening after dinner I'll take you up to see him. He wants to explain his condition to you himself.'

'The paper thing has got me confused. If they want to arrest Mr Burnel in connection with the murder of the rapist, how can they be running a story about his life in a column in the very same paper that contains news of the rapist's murder? I mean, why don't they just come and arrest him?'

'Because they don't know his name. The column refers to him as the vampire and they have no idea where he lives.'

'But surely the police could track him down ... I mean, in a digital age with all the electronic information and stuff?'

'Will, Mr Burnel has been around for a thousand years. He's had a lot of experience in life; he's lived the equivalent of fourteen lives. He's incredibly smart and he's always one step ahead.'

A nervous laugh escaped from between Will's lips. 'Wait, you're telling me that he's been a vampire for a thousand years?'

'Yes, he was born a human in the year 978 and became a vampire in 1011.' Even as she said it out loud, she could hardly believe it herself, but she had witnessed things that proved his status to her without a doubt.

'So, does he drink blood ... I mean from people?'

'Well, that's a question that you can ask him yourself later this evening.'

'Our landlord's a vampire … cool!'

That was about all Will could come up with at that particular moment. He needed to get his head around everything that his mum had just told him.

'Look, I think I'm going to go back to school for the afternoon after all. I need all this to sink in without thinking about it too much.'

'Are you okay?' she asked.

'Surprisingly, yeah, under the circumstances,' he said, as he got up to leave the kitchen table.

'Are you sure?'

'Yeah Mum, don't worry, see you after school.' He turned and walked towards the kitchen door.

'Don't forget …'

'I know Mum,' he said, interrupting her, 'I won't speak to anyone about it.'

Chapter 14

Later that evening at about 9:30pm, Will and his mother walked across the grounds of the estate to go and visit Mr Burnel. Will was quite anxious about this and felt very nervous during the short walk. Will's mother rapped the metal door knocker five times; four in succession, then a brief pause, then one final one. She stepped backwards a few feet and waited.

Will looked at her. She could see that he was looking at her out of her peripheral vision, and she also knew that he suspected she had some sort of secret knock so that Mr Burnel knew it was her. Neither of them said anything. The door opened with a slight creaking sound to reveal Mr Burnel standing there. He was impeccably turned out as usual, wearing highly polished black custom-made brogues with a slightly pointed toe design, immaculately pressed black trousers, a white starched shirt with the top four buttons open revealing quite a lot of his chest, and a deep purple waistcoat with a very subtle black flowered outline pattern. His hair was perfectly groomed and his skin looked silky smooth, as if he had shaved just five minutes earlier.

'Ah, good evening, Angela,' he said, addressing Will's

mother in a familiar way.

'Good evening,' she replied.

'Will,' said Mr Burnel, politely, 'please, come in.'

He opened the door fully allowing plenty of room for Will and his mother to enter. Although Will had lived on the estate grounds for thirteen years, he had only ever seen inside the hallway from the door, but had never actually set foot inside. As they entered the large hallway, Will looked around like an excited kid being taken on a tour inside an ice-cream factory. He was too overwhelmed by the magnificence of the house to remember his previous nervousness. The hallway floor was an expanse of very light, almost white-coloured marble with tiny black speckles. There was a double-staircase with sixteen steps going up either side leading to the first floor. The staircases had modern and tasteful black carpeting, subtly patterned, with thick white piping down either side. The walls were finished in white on the ground floor and magnolia on the ceiling and first floor. Even though his mother had described inside the house, Will thought it was surprisingly modern and streamlined and not at all what he had expected.

Between the double-staircase on the ground floor was a large open double-door that led into a huge room with a black grand piano off to one side, and double patio doors that led out to some steps and the beautiful gardens. Hanging from the ceiling in the hallway was an enormous chandelier with hundreds upon hundreds of tiny crystals. It looked like a beautiful snow storm frozen in time.

Will was snapped out of his state of overwhelming awe by Mr Burnel's voice. 'Please, come this way,' he said, leading the way through a door to the right.

Will followed his mother and Mr Burnel into a large living area.

'Make yourselves comfortable,' Mr Burnel said, gesturing towards the two large elongated black leather sofas. Will and his mother sat on one of the three-seater sofas facing the large panoramic bay window. Again, Will found himself in total admiration for what he thought was really cool interior décor. The long floor-to-ceiling black lightproof drapes were open, revealing the night-time sky full of vibrant white stars and a crescent moon; it was an exceedingly clear night.

'Angela, would you care for a drink?' It was taking Will a little time to adjust to somebody calling his mother by her first name. Although Mr Burnel and Will's mother had spent considerable time in each other's company over the years – after all, she did work in his house part-time and they did live on his estate – he had rarely seen Mr Burnel and his mother together and he had never heard Mr Burnel address her by her first name.

'I'm quite alright, thank you,' she said, politely.

'And how about you, Will? Can I get you anything?'

'Oh, I'm fine, Mr Burnel, thank you,' said Will, fidgeting nervously and not quite knowing what to do with his hands.

Mr Burnel walked over to the other three-seater sofa and sat right in the middle of it, making himself comfortable. And then, he came right out with it and dove right into the crux of the subject in hand.

'So Will, I understand from your mother that you're up to speed on the rather ghastly events in the newspaper and that you're having a little trouble with all this vampire business?'

'Erm … well … it's …' Tristan read his mind and interrupted him.

'It's okay, Will. If I were in your shoes I'd be having some serious doubts too. And once upon a time, I was your age, and human too,' he said laughing and trying to make light of it. 'What your mother has told you is all true. I'm a genuine vampire, what you would call the real deal. I was born a human, just like you, on the 20th June in the year 978 and lived quite happily right up until the year 1011 when I was 33 years old. That was the year I became a vampire, and I've been one ever since.'

Will looked at him, politely, but he was finding all this vampire stuff very hard to believe. He was polite enough to at least be open-minded and not outwardly show his true thoughts on the subject. However, Tristan read Will's mind and knew exactly what he was thinking, but he respected Will for being diplomatic and respectable in the way he engaged in the conversation.

'So, do you have any questions you'd like to ask me?' said Tristan, looking into Will's eyes intently while reading his thoughts.

Will thought about the usual ones: *Do you drink blood? Do you kill people? Can you shape-shift into a bat and fly? Are you allergic to garlic and crucifixes? Will a stake through the heart kill you? Will the sun's rays make you burn up and explode into a ball of flames?* But there was no way on earth that he was going to ask any such questions. Will was just about to open his mouth to say something polite and futile, but Tristan got in there first.

'Okay, let's take a look at those questions shall we,' said Mr Burnel. 'Yes, I do drink blood. Yes, I have killed people in the past. No, I can't turn into a bat or fly. I'm not allergic to garlic or crucifixes. Yes, a stake through my heart will kill me, but it has to be a certain type from my home region and from a specific time in history, and the sun's rays won't make me burn up and explode into a ball of flames, but yes, they will kill me.'

Will sat there speechless and totally blown away by Mr Burnel's ability to read his mind, or was it coincidence that Mr Burnel had answered the typical questions in the same way that Will had thought of them. Tristan read this thought also and got up from the sofa and walked over towards Will taking a small silver pocket knife out of his waistcoat pocket as he did so. Tristan knelt down in front of Will.

'Give me your hand,' he said, extending his free left hand.

Will looked at his mother nervously for guidance.

'It's okay, do as he says,' she said in a soft reassuring tone.

Will slowly gave Tristan his right hand. Tristan turned Will's hand palm up and using the compact silver knife in his right hand he quickly made a short slash across the middle of his palm. Will winced and pulled his hand away in mild pain. He opened his hand and looked at the blood seeping from the cut that was about an inch long. Tristan moved the knife to his left hand and made a short slash across the palm of his own right hand. Will looked on in disbelief at what was going on, but he trusted his mother implicitly, so he went along with it.

'Okay, give me your hand.'

Will slowly held his right hand back out to Tristan, blood dripping from its palm. Tristan took hold of it with his own bleeding right hand in the style of a handshake. He gripped Will's hand firmly for about eight seconds, and then let go.

'Now, take a look,' said Tristan.

Will looked down at the palm of his hand to witness the cut healing in front of his very eyes. First the blood stopped, then the cut closed up, then there was some pink scar tissue, then a thin white hairline, then nothing. As if by magic the cut had healed and vanished completely. Will was no longer shocked. He was more blown away and massively impressed by Mr Burnel's really cool mind reading and wound healing skills.

'Fuck me! ... I'm sorry,' he said, realising he just swore out loud, 'I mean, wow, you really are a vampire!!' He was hardly able to contain his excitement.

'Yes, that I am,' said Tristan, getting up and moving back to his position in the middle of his sofa.

'I always knew there was something different about you,' said Will. 'I mean, you're different. I don't just mean the way you look, I mean ... there's just something about the way you are ... I can't really explain it.'

'Well now you can, is it okay with you?' said Tristan.

'Is it okay? It's more than okay, this is so cool!' said Will, all excited.

'Your mother tells me that you're good at keeping secrets, Will, is this true?'

'Yes, sir,' he said, adamantly.

'Good, because this is one secret that you'll never be able to tell anyone. You do understand the importance of this?' he said, in a very serious tone.

'Yes, Mr Burnel. You have my word. I promise I'll never tell a soul,' said Will, looking down at the palm of his hand to double check.

'Okay then, so I think we're done here,' he said, getting up from the sofa.

Will and his mum got up also as Tristan led them out into the main hallway. As Tristan walked across the marble floor towards the front door, he stopped and turned to Will.

'Oh yes, I nearly forgot. I have killed people throughout history, but not for a very long time and most of them were bad; murderers and serial rapists like the late Mr Allan Bar for example. A part of my humanity remains, Will. So I'm what you could call, a good vampire. I need blood to survive, but I don't kill people for their blood. When I first became a vampire it was difficult. But as the years went by, things got a lot easier.'

'These days I have several sources for my blood supplies including butchers for animal blood, several willing human donors and a few nurses, who are friends of mine who I pay to supply me with blood from the hospital blood banks where they work. So you see, it's not quite how they portray vampires in the movies,' he said, smiling.

'Okay,' said Will, thankful that Mr Burnel had cleared that one up.

'And if you want to know anything else at any time, feel free to come and knock on my door. I'll always be happy to talk to you, Will ... I can probably help you with your history homework too,' he laughed, which caused Will to smile.

'Thank you,' said Will.

Tristan opened the door for them.

'Thank you,' said Angela, gratefully, as she passed through the door after Will.

As they walked across the estate back to their cottage, there was an unusually calm feeling of normality. Of course, Angela had known the truth about Tristan since Will was just two years old, so she'd had plenty of time to accustom herself to it. Will, on the other hand, had only just found out about Tristan being a vampire. But as he walked with his mother down the winding path between the trees admiring the bright stars in the clear night sky, he too felt comfortable with it, like this was the most natural thing in the world.

Chapter 15

The following morning the continuing story of The Vampire appeared as usual in The Sentinel daily newspaper. The nation was absolutely riveted and sales of The Sentinel had soared and reached an all-time high.

EMAIL FROM A VAMPIRE – Part 4
By Tania de Pré

Continued from yesterday in the vampire's own words.

Explaining to my wife Amelie that I was now a cold dead creature was far from easy. In fact, it almost ended our relationship. It took several months for me to regain her trust, but eventually we managed to work it out.

After the torrent of abuse and hatred that my wife and I had endured from the other villagers during the winter of 1011, we were left with no choice but to leave. The locals had noticed that there was something different about me. My pale complexion and fierce looking eyes did not bode well with them, and the children in the village were frightened of me, or rather my new facial looks.

But, the worst part of it was their jealousy. With my new vampire status came many advantages and strengths, one of which was my ability to easily hunt down and kill deer and other wildlife in the forest. Many of the villagers were often unsuccessful with their hunts, especially during the winter months, and the fact that I now found it so incredibly easy angered them all the more.

After we moved, Amelie and I lived a happy life together in a peaceful, but somewhat remote location off the beaten track and far away from people. We worked around the vampire part of me, which was the majority part, compared with the tiny wolf and remaining human part. Amelie was never in any danger from me, thanks to the tiny human part that remained. Although I had vampire instincts and needed to feed, they were always under control where Amelie was concerned. She helped me come to terms with what I had become, and even gave me ideas as to how I could control it and live life without having to kill people for their blood.

Over the years I hunted animals and drank their blood. I would then bring the dead animals back to our home so that Amelie could cook and eat the meat. I always drank their blood immediately after I had killed them. Animal blood was just okay as a source of sustenance for survival, but for reasons unknown to me, it doesn't taste as good as human blood, especially when cold. So Amelie and I never ate together. I would kill the animal in the forest, feed from it right there on the spot, then bring the dead carcass home and Amelie would cook and eat while I sat with her.

She understood that animal blood didn't really satisfy me, so every now and then she would offer herself to me by holding out her extended arm so I could feed from her wrist. I always refused, except for one time just before she died. I have Amelie to thank for teaching me how to control my feeding habits. I told her all about my various skills and powers as a vampire, and she then taught me the best way to control and use them; we learned together, and eventually we found a harmony as an un-dead and living couple.

As part of my vampirification process, my canine teeth fell out and new pointed fangs grew in their place. My fangs are also retractable and slightly transparent, as well as replaceable. Just like some venomous snakes lose and replace fangs often, so do I. My fangs are hollow, this allows me to inject venom directly into my prey or human victims and I can control the amount of venom that I release. The amount I inject comes down to whether or not I want to kill, or simply immobilise the prey or victim just long enough for me to feed.

With animals, I would typically inject a large enough dose to kill them, as I knew I would be taking it home as food for Amelie. If my craving for human blood got the better of me, I would not kill a human to feed. Instead I would hypnotise them and put them into a state of trance; this was another of my inherited vampire powers. I would then bite them, typically on the neck or wrist simply because these parts of the body were already exposed. While they were in a state of hypnosis, my razor-sharp fangs would pierce their skin and I would release just a tiny amount of my venom into them, just enough to relax their muscles and mildly anesthetise them, so they did not struggle. I would then drink their blood, usually about half to a pint, before finally leaving them to come around.

At the beginning, I would stay nearby and watch them from a hiding place just until they woke up. Normally, my venom and hypnosis would wear off and they would start to come around after about fifteen to twenty minutes. They would get up, somewhat confused and disoriented, and then go on their way, with no recollection of what had happened to them. I later found out about a few people who had complained about two mysterious puncture holes in their skin, either on their neck, or wrist. So from then on, after I had fed off a human, I would nick the end of my thumb on one of my own fangs, then press a few drops of my own blood into the two puncture wounds and hold it there for several seconds. I learned by accident that my blood had huge healing properties, so by doing this I could heal the two puncture holes leaving no wound or scar tissue whatsoever.

As the years went by, Amelie noticed that I didn't appear to be aging. I looked just the same as I did the day I became a vampire thirty years previously. Amelie had a very long life and although she had various illnesses and two deadly diseases over the years, she survived. Whenever they happened I would cut my wrist and she would drink my blood in order to survive and make a full recovery.

She knew of my blood's healing powers and she would recover overnight as the healing effects took place and regenerated her body. Eventually, she died of old age when she was 104 years old. Dying of such an old age was unheard of back then. She knew she was going to die that night, and so did I. She didn't ask for my blood, and I didn't offer, as I somehow knew that she felt that her natural life had come to an end and it was time for her to depart this earth.

That was the night that I drank blood from Amelie for the very first time. She told me that she wanted a small part of her to be inside me, to go on living inside of me, so she could always be a part of me. She explained that she could die peacefully knowing this, and she also said it would help me after she was gone, knowing that a small part of her was inside me. I took my beloved Amelie's hand and delicately sank my fangs into her wrist. She didn't wince; she simply smiled at me with contentment. She told me that a lovely warm feeling washed over her entire body while I gently drank. I had never seen her look as happy and peaceful as she did that night. I laid her arm to rest back by her side as she looked meaningfully into my eyes and said, "Always remember me, my darling, I love you." She peacefully fell asleep and passed away.

Continued tomorrow.

*** *

As the nation slowly started warming to the vampire and his incredibly emotional story, the police continued with their on-going investigations, which had proved very frustrating since they ran into dead end after dead end. But Detective Maldini had been putting in countless hours looking deeper into the mystery vampire case and the Allan Bar murder. He had been doing a lot of detecting in his own time, as well as in police time; he was determined to get his man and solve the case.

At the police headquarters, Detective Maldini was giving an early morning briefing. The After Dark club murders had been covered in much detail by the senior investigating officer DCI Sean O'Connor. Now, Detective Maldini had stepped forward and was discussing the Allan Bar murder case involving the vampire.

'So far the so-called vampire has been very smart. Whenever he phones Ms de Pré either on her mobile, or at the newspaper, he calls from a mobile that we know to be a pay-as-you-go type, and when he bought it, he gave a false name and address so we can't trace him that way. He only ever turns the phone on immediately before making a call and he turns it off when the call's over, so there's no electronic signal for us to trace either. He isn't on the DNA database. We don't have his fingerprints and he never leaves any. He's very smart when it comes to leaving trace evidence – he simply doesn't do it. I also get the impression that if there is a clue left behind, it's left there because he wants us to find it. I believe he knew that we would discover the unusual characteristics of his DNA. He's very good at sneaking around unrecognised and dodging us; he's always one step ahead.

'But, I believe we're getting closer and we will catch him. Our forensic IT technician has been busy and is making serious inroads. Based on the emails he's sent to Ms de Pré at The Sentinel, we've been able to establish that he's not sending them from a personal computer at his house. Instead, he's using high street internet cafés and a free public domain email address system. We've been able to establish exactly which internet cafés he's used so far and we know the exact time and date that he sent them.

'He's smart and can't be underestimated. So far, he's only used decrepit old internet cafés in the seedier parts of the city and ones that are typically open until late at night. The ones he's used so far have closing hours of 11, 11:30 and midnight, with one open 24-hours. His patterns so far show that he typically turns up at internet cafes to send emails between 10:30pm and midnight. In addition, the places he's used so far don't have any security cameras on their premises. He's also very aware of public CCTV cameras on the streets. We've looked at footage from several cameras located on the streets outside the internet cafes he's used so far, based on the times the emails were sent we've come up with a loose description of somebody who we think could be our man. He usually dresses all in black, with a long overcoat and a black Fedora wide-brimmed hat to hide his face. We haven't been able to get a proper look at his face yet, so we can't establish whether or not he's making any attempt to seriously disguise himself.

'So we've been collaborating with other police stations and, based on the locations he's been visiting so far, have looked into all the internet cafés in and around these areas and have eliminated any that have security cameras on their premises and any others that are in prime public locations. For the remaining ones, we've put undercover officers in them to stake them out between the hours of 10:30pm and midnight. These internet cafés are in the main and secondary zones on the map on the wall.

'Our forensic IT technician has set up computer equipment right here at the station. We now have this guy's password, so the second he logs into his email account, we'll know about it. We'll also know exactly where he is at the time. Hopefully it will be at one of the internet cafés that we have staked out. Now, we only have a vague description of him from the CCTV footage from The Sentinel's car park security cameras and we can't be sure that Ms de Pré's description from the painting can be used with any accuracy due to the painting's age. But based on what we do have, if one of the undercover officers suspects he's turned up, they all have a secret code to use on the computer they'll be stationed at in their designated internet café. Once they use this code, we'll be aware of it instantly and we can send further undercover officers and reinforcements.

'Now, he won't be arrested and we won't be blowing our cover. We need to do a lifestyle assessment before we do anything else. So, we'll be following him for two or three days to find out as much about him as we possibly can. We'll be trying to find out who he is, what he does, what he eats, the places he visits, where he lives and so on and so forth. Then, when we've gathered up enough evidence we'll move in, but not before.

'Remember, the man going by the name of Raven Xavier who's responsible for the After Dark club murders struck again in the early hours of this morning, killing an innocent woman in Soho. We can't have this evil character running around leaving dead bodies in his wake all over the city; we need to catch him, and we need to catch him fast. Also, I have a gut feeling that that the man responsible for the Allan Bar beheading might be able to shed some light on Raven Xavier, after all, they're both claiming to be vampires.

'I want to know about everything that happens in this case, as it happens at every step of the way and on every level. Does anybody have any questions?' said Maldini, wrapping up his brief.

Raven had killed a 22-year-old oriental woman in the seedier part of London's Soho at about 1:30am, just six hours prior to Detective Maldini's morning briefing. His victim was a street prostitute who was simply in the wrong place at the wrong time. Raven had propositioned her for his own amusement with the sole intent of toying and playing with her before bringing her life to a brutal and bloody end. He'd taken her to a cheap nearby B&B, where the owner was happy to rent rooms by the hour, furnished with a double bed and a fresh set of sheets.

The rather deviant looking skinny middle-aged white dude who was working the reception that night phoned the police after discovering what was left of the prostitute's body. He was next door to impossible with regards to helping the police. When one officer asked him if he could describe the man, all he could say was, *"Hey, I get fifty creeps in here every night. One creep looks just like another, what can I say? This motherfucker, well, he looked extra creepy, ya know what I'm sayin'? Ha ha ha."*

However, he did tell the police that he took payment from him for three hours with extra payment for fresh sheets. He told the police that after the three hours were up, he noticed the man leaving alone and when he shouted after to enquire where the hooker was, he simply answered, *"She needs cleaning up, just like the rest of the room."*

He told the police that after the creep had been in the room for about two hours, he had heard a lot of noise and commotion going on upstairs, but general banging, crashing and yelling and even screaming was not unusual for this kind of establishment – he'd heard worse – so he'd ignored it. But the sight that greeted him inside the room afterwards was nothing less than a total bloody massacre. Raven had nailed the prostitute spread-eagled to the wall by her wrists and ankles in the style of Leonardo da Vinci's *Vitruvian Man*, using a hammer and several four-inch nails.

The woman was as white as a ghost, as Raven had pretty much drained her of all seven pints of her blood. What he didn't drink had run out from the deep fang penetrations from various arteries around her body. She hung there on the wall, blood dripping down her head, neck, arms, torso, legs, looking like some sort of horrific ritualistic sacrifice. The bed itself looked like a blood bath, the white sheets now entirely blood-red. The room was so horrific one of the first police officers to arrive on the scene couldn't stomach it and vomited involuntarily, to the dismay of his colleagues.

Later that night, in the early hours, Raven continued his bloody killing spree by murdering an innocent man who was simply waiting on a street corner for a taxi to pass by. Raven was absolutely furious and livid beyond belief that Tristan had let the cat out of the bag by letting the world know that vampires exist; for real. Up until now, Raven had spent the past seventy years or so feeding discretely by not killing the people he fed off and he certainly didn't bring any attention to himself. Vampires had, until now, remained a myth and their secret had been closely guarded. They had adapted and had been allowed to go unnoticed in the civilised human-occupied world. If Tristan was going to tell the world his cute little story so publicly in the press, Raven was going to send out his own message to the world: bloody and brutally.

How many actual living vampires there are in the world, nobody in the vampire community really knew for sure. Tristan suspected that there were between twenty and thirty in Great Britain, but this figure was a wild stab in the dark, based on those vampires who had actually come forward and made themselves known to other vampires, or from these vampires picking up the psyche of other vampires from time to time. This figure was also based on other pieces of information and evidence that had come to light during the past thousand years.

Of the few vampires who were known, some liked to be in touch with their kind, while others preferred to remain recluses, unknown to other vampires, choosing to have contact only with humans. Tristan fell into the latter camp and he had not seen or spoken to any other vampires since he first encountered Raven back in 1706 when he picked up on his psyche in the ballroom during the Baroque dance. Tristan had always been aware that other vampires existed in the UK, as well as the rest of the world, as on rare occasions he had seen evidence of vampire traits and sensed their energy.

Throughout the centuries, Raven had always been reckless with his feeding habits, leaving bodies and carnage in his wake without a care in the world; but even he was intelligent enough to know that times change. The police have prevailed and, in more recent years, technology has made it much easier for the police to catch criminals, particularly reckless cold-blooded murderers. Raven hadn't been quite so reckless for about seventy years or so, but now he had thrown away the rulebook. He had super human strength, he could move at ten times the speed of humans, he could leap as high as thirty feet from a standing position and was able to jump from building to building and, above all, police bullets could not kill him. To all intents and purposes, he was at the top of the food chain by some considerable margin; mere mortals couldn't catch him or stop him, and he knew it.

He was running all over the city on a blood-curdling killing spree without any thought to the consequences, as he knew there wouldn't be any. He needed to feed and because Tristan had so publicly announced to the world that vampires existed, he had no reason to be discreet anymore. He enjoyed what he was doing, so he was going back to his old ways, just like back in the good old days.

The following night at 11:15pm he struck again. This time, Raven had picked on a young couple who were walking home from a restaurant just off Brompton Road in Knightsbridge; only he didn't kill the young woman. Just to be contrary, he killed only the man. The killing was fast and brutal. He leapt out from a dark doorway and launched himself at the man, savagely ripping into the jugular artery on the side of his neck with his razor sharp fangs. Raven's jaw locked onto the young man's neck, like a pitbull in a dogfight, while he fed off him, drinking his blood. The man's wife stood there screaming hysterically. Her high-pitched screams bellowed into the night and were so loud they must have been heard all over Knightsbridge. Within about thirty seconds, blood had jetted out of the man's neck and was all over the alcove walls, floor and shop window where Raven had dragged him after his attack. It was all over very quickly. Once Raven had finished he held the man upright by his throat for a few seconds before dropping him on the pavement clutching his neck. Then, like that, he vanished into the night and was gone. He spared the woman's life, but left her there, frozen to the spot, to watch her husband die on the pavement right in front of her eyes.

The undercover police officers had been in place since 10:30pm at several internet cafés dotted around various north-west and central London areas, in the hope that the vampire would show up at one of them at some point or another, to send an email to Tania de Pré at The Sentinel newspaper.

Then it happened. At 1:30am, one of the undercover officers staking out an internet café in north Finchley noticed a man come in to use one of the computers. He fitted the description of the so-called vampire that they were after. He was dressed in black with a long overcoat and black Fedora hat. His complexion was quite pale and there was something unusual about him. He approached the counter and paid cash in advance for use of one of the computers for a period of thirty minutes. The Indian man behind the counter did not recognise him from the police artist's impressions that had been published in the national newspapers; if he had done so, Tristan would have known about it via his mind-reading capabilities.

The undercover police officer was just around the corner in the L-shaped café. Tristan briefly glanced at him, and then made his way to the computer that the clerk had allocated to him. Tristan didn't bother reading the officer's thoughts, as the undercover cop looked the part. He was an English Caucasian man, about 32 years old. He could almost be described as a white Rastafarian; he had long blonde messy-looking dreadlocks held in place with a red, gold and green striped sweatband, two piercings in his left ear and another on his right eyebrow. He wore a T-shirt sporting the rock band, Black Rebel Motorcycle Club, which revealed a few strategically placed tattoos on his upper arms, one of which was a black rose. He sat there drinking a can of Red Bull, while seemingly browsing the internet.

Tristan loaded up the browser and logged into his email account. Meanwhile the undercover officer had typed in his emergency code alerting the police major incident room that their suspect was there. The police forensics IT technician had also noticed that Tristan had just logged into his email account, via the computer equipment that had been put in place previously. The SIO back at the police major incident room despatched two more undercover plain-clothes officers, so they could tail the suspect and go about their lifestyle assessment. Detective Maldini had insisted to his superior that he be one of them. He had changed from his usual expensive suit and Italian shoes, to an old pair of jeans, trainers, a T-shirt and a black leather bomber jacket. Maldini and the other undercover officer were a good fifteen minutes away, even with blues and twos at high speed with not much traffic on the roads.

The forensics IT technician had sent a message to the undercover officer at the internet café, informing him that reinforcements would be there in fifteen minutes and should the suspect leave before they arrived, that he was to tail him.

Tristan was only at the computer for ten minutes, and then got up to leave. The undercover officer noticed him leaving, so he quickly hit the send button on the keyboard to get a message back to the major incident room that he was on the move, and then he too got up and left, hot on the heels of Tristan.

As the officer left the premises, he was very careful to stay well back and out of sight. He watched the suspect walking around the corner at the end of the block. He pursued him, staying in contact with Detective Maldini via a tiny hidden microphone taped to his chest, and a wireless in-ear device. Maldini and the other undercover officer were still three minutes away, so the plain-clothed undercover officer was on his own until then. He followed the suspect around the corner and across the street. In the meantime, he continued to let Maldini know where he was, where the suspect was, which way he was heading, and relayed street names and other relevant information.

The undercover officer pursued the suspect into a multi-story car park, keeping a very good distance from him, continuing to relay information to Maldini, who in turn informed him that he was about thirty seconds away. Maldini had silenced the blues and twos of his unmarked police car, which only gave the car away when they were switched on as the blue flashing lights came out from behind the radiator grill. The undercover officer on foot had followed the suspect up onto the second floor and witnessed him getting into a black Audi RS 5 Coupe sports car. He informed Maldini of this, giving him the car's registration number.

Maldini and his colleague waited out of sight around the corner in their car and watched the car park exit and waited. As the black Audi came out, Maldini followed, keeping a reasonable distance between him and the Audi at all times. After about a mile, the Audi pulled over and stopped. Maldini quickly turned left into a side street and leapt out of his car. He carefully peeked around the corner and witnessed the suspect get out of the Audi and cross the street and into an alleyway between two buildings. Maldini instructed his colleague to stay and watch the Audi. Maldini then ran across the street in pursuit of the suspect.

When Maldini got to the alley, he saw the suspect disappear around the corner but he continued to follow him, keeping his distance. At the end of the alley, Maldini saw the suspect walk down into an underpass that led to three council estate tower blocks. When Maldini got to the underpass there was no sign of his suspect; he ran through to the other side, but when he came out, there was still no sign of his suspect. Detective Maldini spoke into his hidden microphone to his colleague who was watching the black Audi.

'I've lost him. Don't take your eyes off that Audi. I'm gonna take a look around here.'

Maldini headed across the communal concrete basketball court towards an underground car park beneath one of the tower blocks. He suspected this was one of the few places his suspect could have vanished to so fast. The underground car park was wide and vast with around thirty cars randomly parked. There were several very wide concrete support pillars, so wide that one of them virtually obscured an entire car. Maldini quietly walked around the car park, checking the various pillars and alcoves. He suddenly became aware of three young men in their mid-twenties who entered the car park from one of the lower-ground exit doors. He looked over at them as they purposely walked towards him.

One of them was white; the other two were black. Maldini recognised them from mug shots. They were known gang members. Just then he heard two more jump out from one of the large concrete pillars behind him. These two were less subtle, shouting and yelling, making chimpanzee-like noises. These two white dudes stopped about six feet from Maldini making intimidating sounds behind him.

'Well, looky what we got here, if it ain't the mother fuckin' Italian Stallion ... Detective Marion Maldini,' said one of the black dudes, cool as you like.

Maldini checked out the two white dudes behind him and recognised them as part of the same gang. It took Maldini a few moments to realise why they looked so familiar. The black dude doing all the talking had a younger brother, or at least he did until Maldini put him inside for a rather lengthy stretch.

'Kudos Touré, AKA The Saint,' said Maldini to the gang leader.

'I'm glad you remember me ... do you remember my brother too?'

'Look, I'm here on undercover police business, so fuck off and go and play somewhere else,' Maldini said sternly, in the hope that they would respect his police status.

Maldini was aware that his colleagues probably couldn't hear him, as his signal would be virtually non-existent in the underground car park. He also knew that trying to grovel and plead his way out of this situation wouldn't earn him any respect hence his use of the F word.

'I'll give you fuck off,' said Touré. 'My brother's doing a life term because of you, motherfucker!' he said curtly, while revealing his switchblade.

'Look, your brother stabbed and killed a man. I'm a police officer; I had to do what I had to do.'

'Yeah, well now I gotta do what I gotta do, bitch!'

Just then, one of the white dudes whacked Maldini in the lower back with a crowbar from behind, instantly dropping him to the floor in agonising pain. Touré stood there and watched as the other four proceeded to kick Maldini half to death. All Maldini could do was curl up into the smallest ball possible while four pairs of boots got to work on his body and head.

'Stop!' shouted Touré, taking control of the situation. 'Get him up.'

Two of them grabbed Maldini's arms and lifted him to his feet. Maldini stood hanging between the two white dudes with his legs dangling beneath him, barely able to stand. He was half-unconscious with cracked ribs, a broken arm and a busted up face with both eyes half-closed and swollen up. His blood was all over the concrete car park floor, so too was one of his teeth. He was a bloody battered mess.

Touré stepped up to him, grabbed his hair and lifted his head up so he could look into his eyes.

'Hey, wake up; I want you to see this, motherfucker … it's time to die,' he said, lifting his arm back high ready to come down in a stabbing motion with his switchblade in the direction of Maldini's chest.

Just as he launched his knife-wielding arm down towards Maldini, Tristan came out of nowhere and slammed into him at lightning speed, knocking him forty feet across the car park floor.

Chapter 16

Tristan had appeared out of nowhere, and had moved across the car park at what appeared to be bordering on the speed of light. The remaining gang members looked across to witness Touré being brutally attacked as Tristan sank his teeth into his neck, attacking his jugular artery. Touré screamed and thrashed about under him in agonising pain as the dark figure proceeded to tear his neck and throat to pieces.

'Kill that motherfucker!' shouted the other black dude to the remaining three gang members.

The two white dudes holding Maldini dropped him to the floor and sprinted across the car park to deal with Touré's attacker. Just as they approached, Tristan turned abruptly and looked up at them with blood dripping from his chin. His eyes lit up, bright white in the dingy car park; he looked eerie and ferocious like some sort of wild animal. The two dudes briefly looked at Touré on the ground, who now had blood jetting from his neck three feet across the car park floor and was spluttering and gagging for breath as blood pumped from his mouth, throat and jugular artery.

'Fuck this,' said one of them, and turned to run for his life.

Tristan sprang to his feet, grabbed the remaining dude's

head and swiftly spun it 180-degrees, breaking his neck and killing him instantly. Before he even hit the floor, Tristan got thirty feet across the car park to the other black gang member; it took less than a second. He grabbed his throat and lifted him two feet off the ground. As Tristan held him there struggling and thrashing in the air, like a fish out of water dangling from a line, the remaining two gang members ran like Olympic sprinters to get as far away from there as humanly possible, leaving their friend dangling and giving up any idea of actually rescuing him.

Tristan held the man in mid-air and squeezed his throat tighter until he eventually stopped thrashing about as his oxygen supply ran out. Tristan dropped him to the floor, and then turned his attentions to Maldini, who was writhing on the floor in agonising pain from the brutal beating he had just taken.

Tristan stooped down over him and looked him in his eyes. Maldini, half unconscious, looked back up at him.

'Why are you following me?' said Tristan, 'The man who I relieved of his head was a violent serial rapist. I did you a favour. You should be looking for the other vampire, Raven Xavier.'

'I know,' said Maldini, coughing up blood from his mouth, realising that the vampire had just saved his life. 'I need your help.'

'You want me to help you catch Raven Xavier?'

'Yes. He's running around the city killing innocent people and if he's what you say he is, and if you are what you say you are, then I'm going to need your help.'

Tristan looked at Maldini to analyse his wounds and the

severity of his beating.

'I can't feel my legs,' groaned Maldini, suddenly realising that the iron crowbar slamming into his lower back probably did serious damage to his spine. His head was spinning and he was feeling more and more dizzy by the second and his vision was starting to blur; things were not right for Maldini and he was in a critical condition after taking several severe hard kicks to his head.

'Do you believe in vampires?' said Tristan.

'I'm getting there,' spluttered Maldini. He coughed up more blood and could feel himself rapidly slipping away. Then it dawned on him that he was dying. On top of his broken arm, kicked out tooth and several cracked ribs, now he couldn't feel anything from the waist down and his brain was surely haemorrhaging. All he could do was lie there and die; hopefully it wouldn't take too long as the pain was agonising. His entire body felt like it was breaking down from the inside out.

Tristan put his left hand under Maldini's head, lifting it off the concrete floor. He then bit his right wrist and held his arm out over Maldini's mouth to allow his blood to flow down his throat. Maldini was in no state to resist; he coughed, choked, swallowed and spluttered as Tristan's blood ran down his throat. He couldn't understand why, but as Tristan's blood travelled past his pharynx and down into his oesophagus it felt incredible as a wonderful warm and energising feeling started to wash over his entire body. Tristan's blood seemed to race through his body at an incredible speed, like it was on a mission.

After thirty seconds of this treatment, Tristan gently lay

Maldini's head back down on the cold concrete car park floor.

'Pull your surveillance team and undercover officers off me and concentrate your full resources on Raven Xavier. You're going to need every man available to you,' said Tristan as he stood up and stepped back a few paces.

He turned his head away from Maldini as he prepared to vanish into the night. Then he slowly turned back and looked at Maldini on the ground.

'I'll help you catch him.'

Then like that, he was gone.

As Maldini lay there on the floor, he could feel the incredible healing powers of Tristan's blood taking fast effect. It was like some sort of super-human drug with immense healing powers. His coughing and spluttering slowed, his dizziness faded and his vision started to clear. He felt muscle, tissue and cartilage in his spine grind as it regenerated itself. The cracks in his ribs and the broken bone in his arm fused like new and healed. Feeling came back to his legs and he could wiggle his toes. The swelling, bruising and various gashes on his face diminished and returned back to normal. This entire body regeneration and repair process took less than four minutes to complete.

Maldini got up off the ground on to his feet. He felt great, he felt strong, like an athlete. He sprinted out of the underground car park so he could get a signal on his hidden radio transmitter and communicate with his other undercover officer who was still watching the Audi a block away.

'Mitch, I need backup at the Falcon Estate ASAP. I'm in the underground car park beneath the Kestrel House tower block with three dead gang members. Leave the Audi and get down here right away!' ordered Maldini.

'I'll be right there,' said Mitch.

Maldini headed back down into the car park and waited for backup to arrive.

Fifteen minutes later the place was crawling with police, a CSI team and a pathologist. The entire car park had been secured and cordoned off, including all exits. Maldini's superior, DCI Sean O'Connor had also arrived at the scene to get the full story directly from Maldini.

'So tell me again, why did you pull Mitch away from the Audi?' said O'Connor in disbelief, and angry as hell.

'I thought he'd be more use to me down here.'

'What, babysitting three corpses while our suspect jumped into his car and drove away … what the hell were you thinking?'

'Well, I guess after what just happened I wasn't really thinking straight.'

'You're damn right you weren't thinking straight. What the hell's going on here, Maldini? Is there something you're not telling me?'

'Look, it's two in the morning; I've just worked a straight sixteen hour shift and I'm exhausted. All I want to do is get home and get some rest.'

Maldini wasn't exhausted at all, in fact, quite the opposite after his boost of super-human vampire medicine in the form of Tristan's blood. But he really needed to get his head around this before going into any detail with his superiors.

'Yes, so do I, but before I do that I'd still like to know

why you created a gap, then let our prime suspect slip right through it?'

'Look, that's not what happened, it's not that simple.'

'Well make it simple,' he demanded.

'I can't do this right now okay!' Maldini said sternly as he walked away from O'Connor and grabbed the car keys for the unmarked police car off his colleague.

'Where the hell do you think you're going?' shouted O'Connor across the car park.

Maldini got into the police car without answering and drove out of there, leaving the crime scene with many of DCI O'Connor's questions left unanswered. He knew there would be hell to pay for that in the morning, but he just had to get out of there and go home. After all, it's not every day that you get beaten and kicked to within an inch of your life, only to be miraculously brought back to life from almost certain death by a vampire. He needed time to think, to reflect on everything that had just happened. O'Connor's reprimand was the least of his worries; it could wait until tomorrow.

After just four hours sleep, Maldini was up and out the door, heading straight to Tania de Pré's office. The funny thing was, he wasn't tired in the least. He felt as fresh as a daisy, like an eighteen-year-old athlete in his prime, and was super alert. As he pulled up at a set of traffic lights at a busy high street junction, he glanced over at a newspaper stand and noticed a man buying a copy of The Sentinel newspaper. Part five of Tania de Pré's vampire story had just been published in that very issue.

EMAIL FROM A VAMPIRE – Part 5
By Tania de Pré

Continued in the vampire's own words from yesterday.

As I moved out of the Middle Ages and through the centuries, many wars came and went and Europe became more divided. During this time I'd had a further five long-term wives and had been emotionally devastated with the passing of each of them. As the 18th Century progressed, I decided to leave Dijon in France, where I had been living for nearly 150 years, and travel to London, England.

It was 1774 when I began my journey with my faithful driver whom I had come to trust explicitly over the many years he had been in my employment. He knew about my vampire status and had done a great job of keeping my secret from the world, just like my faithful companions who had come and gone before him. It always took me many years to build up a good rapport with somebody to get to the point where I could trust them with my secret. My driver had already done this long journey in advance so he could recce the route and set up various inns beforehand. I had to be sure that the inns where we would be staying had rooms that were free from light during the day; however, we were packing lightproof material for emergency situations.

Transportation had come on in leaps and bounds since the Middle Ages. Old decrepit wagons had long given way to modern and much more comfortable horse-drawn stagecoaches with proper doors and windows and plush velvet interiors with comfortable padded built-in seats. Travelling during adverse weather conditions was much more civilised, at least for the passengers inside. However, travelling via stagecoach during the 18th century was not without its problems. It could be a very risky and dangerous prospect, especially for the wealthy. Most who travelled this way had to be very aware of highwaymen, and the rich would often employ an armed guard to make the journey with them, who would sit up top with the driver.

Everybody is familiar with the notorious Dick Turpin, probably the most famous highwayman of them all. But I can tell you that Dick Turpin's history does not bear looking into; the man was a sorry disappointment. He wasn't the great romantic that people mistakenly portray him to have been. He was nothing more than a failed butcher who turned horse thief and burglar. He occasionally robbed travellers in his spare time and when he did, he was usually quite brutal about it. From what I heard, back in his day before he was caught and executed in England in 1739, he was nothing but a low-life thief. Although Turpin would pose no problem for me, as he was long since dead and gone, Europe and England were riddled with hundreds of other highwaymen during the time I was travelling.

My 430-mile journey from Dijon to London via stagecoach took me forty days to complete – almost double what it typically took back then. This was because I could only travel after dusk when it was dark. Travelling during daylight hours was out of the question, as being a vampire the light from the sun's rays would have killed me. Even on cloudy, overcast, or rainy days when you can't actually see the sun, its harmful UV rays are still ever present. Any kind of daylight is produced by the sun, be it blindingly bright or totally overcast. Because of this I decided to start my long journey on December 10th, as the days are short during this time of year, giving me more travelling time during darkness. As a precaution, I had thick lightproof drapes installed inside my stagecoach just in case I ever was caught out and we found ourselves travelling during daylight due to some unforeseen delay.

Sometimes in bad weather, a stagecoach could get stuck in the mud for hours at a time. By now I had become a very wealthy man. I had been around for a total of 796 years, including my first 33 years as a human. During that amount of time you would be amazed at how one prevails in life and learns to capitalise on it.

I was travelling with a lot of gold, money, and valuables, so I still had to be aware of highwaymen, just like everybody else. Of course, being a vampire, I had some major advantages over mortal humans. I could not be killed with a bullet from a flintlock pistol, or by stabbing from a knife, and I had incredible strength and power, so highwaymen were nothing more than a minor inconvenience to me. I encountered six highwaymen in total on my journey across France to London, England. Three of them left me no choice but to kill them. These robbery attempts usually took place during the early part of the evening, just after dark.

I had to kill the first one when the stagecoach got stuck in a very boggy and uneven part of the road about thirty minutes before sunrise when we were only a mile from our next designated inn. My driver and I were stuck there for nearly two hours. With my help and strength we almost had the horses and stagecoach out of the mud, but then as the sun started to come up, I had to hide away in the coach with the blackout blinds closed and could no longer assist.

It was while my driver was gathering up more leaves and branches to put under the wheels that a highwayman attempted to rob the stagecoach. My driver had left his pistol in the compartment next to his seat and didn't see him coming. The highwayman hit the driver around the head with his pistol, knocking him to the floor. He then came around to the side of the stagecoach to open the door. I could not allow this to happen, as daylight would have got in, which could have potentially killed me. The stagecoach had been customised with little two-inch hinged sections of wood at various points around the inside of the coach. When I flipped one up, there was just enough room for me to poke the tip of my pistol through and shoot whoever was immediately outside.

With my acute hearing, I was able to pinpoint the highwayman's exact position to within a few inches. As he dismounted his horse and approached the side door of the coach, I slowly flipped back one of the tiny porthole covers and put the tip of my pistol barrel through it and fired. I heard the sound of the highwayman fall to the ground. I could hear him struggling to breathe while he lay there, then the breathing eventually stopped. My driver got up and pulled himself together after his minor head injury, and shouted into the coach to reassure me that the highwayman was dead. He managed to get us out of the mud and to the next inn safely.

Getting from the stagecoach to the inn during daylight was always going to be tricky. Of course, at night, I could just step out and walk right in just like everybody else. But during the day I didn't want to risk suicide-by-sunlight by doing such a thing. So my driver would go and assess the situation in advance and get the room ready, which sometimes meant hanging blackout material over the windows. He would also check just inside the main door to the inn and the walk from there to my room to check for light coming in through windows and such. Then when the coast was clear, I would make a quick dash from the stagecoach through the daylight wearing a large black lightproof cloak and hood that draped down over my face, so none of my skin was ever exposed to the daylight. Once inside, if there was no daylight spilling into the premises I would remove my cloak and hold it over one arm. If, on the other hand, there was daylight inside, I would remain cloaked until I got to the room that the driver had prepared for me in advance. In these instances, I always tried to do this while there was nobody else around to avoid arousing suspicion.

Some highwaymen were quite polite back in their day and even generous, leaving passengers the wherewithal to continue on their journey. Often, when caught, they would beg to be excused for being forced to rob. I could sense, using my mind-reading skills, that the three highwaymen I spared during my long journey were doing it out of bare necessity, to feed their families during the cold winter months when they had no crops.

However, two of them were vicious brutal thugs not doing it out of necessity, but for a living, being cruel and evil men. In one instance it was after dusk, so I could enforce my full vampire powers upon him. I also took the opportunity to feed from him. I would have spared the second man who tried to rob me but he left me no choice as it was during the early hours of the morning and the sun had already come up, so I had to shoot him from the confines of the stagecoach via one of the portholes.

When we got to Dover, England after the short channel crossing by ship, we had a different stagecoach and horses waiting for us that my driver had bought and paid for in advance during his previous recce. It was waiting about one hundred metres from where we docked, so I didn't have to go far wearing my big hooded lightproof cloak.

My driver had to guide me like a blind man as my face was totally covered. I boarded our new stagecoach while the driver loaded up the various chests and luggage. The new stagecoach had been customised just like the previous one. The final and shortest part of the journey from Dover to London proved fairly uneventful. It was raining quite heavily and it was a Sunday. Highwaymen didn't bother going out robbing on a Sunday. This was because stagecoach travel cost double on a Sunday, so people typically didn't travel much. Highwaymen chose instead to rest on a Sunday, like most other people. Fourteen hours later we eventually arrived safely at my new home in London.

Continued tomorrow.

***

When Maldini got out of the elevator on the fifth floor of The Sentinel newspaper offices, he found Tania busy at her desk writing up her column.

'Good morning,' said Maldini.

Tania spun around on her chair. 'Oh, good morning detective, I wasn't expecting to see you here this morning.'

'I need to talk to you. Is there somewhere private we can go?' he said, quietly.

Martin Lovejoy was standing nearby talking to a colleague and overheard.

'Hey, you can use my office if you like,' said Martin.

'Thanks Martin,' said Tania, as she got up. 'Okay, follow me.'

'Would you like a tea or coffee?' she asked, while they

crossed the office.

'No, thank you,' he said, wanting to get straight to the point.

Martin's office was pristine – immaculate, minimalistic and sleek. There was a large modern glass desk by the window with a tasteful leather swivel chair behind it. On the other side of the desk were a single chair and a smart two-seater sofa against the wall. Sleekly mounted along an elongated smoked glass wall shelf sat a modern Linn digital music streaming system with audio speakers sunk into the wall. Overall, it had a very plush and expensive feel to it. It was like sitting in a very large, expensive modern German car.

'Look, I'm going to be blunt and direct … I need you to be totally honest with me,' said Maldini.

'Okay,' she said, intrigued by his tone.

'Has the vampire been in touch with you?' he asked, looking purposefully into her eyes.

'Yes, you know he has. I've had emails from him.'

'No, I mean in person. Have you actually met him in person?' he said, more seriously now.

'No, no I haven't,' she said, putting her hand up to her face and gently stroking her right cheek and scar nervously; she never was very good at lying.

'Tania, I'm a detective. You're lying to me. I need to know when and where, and if you're going to meet him again.'

'You'll never catch him, detective. He's had a thousand years' experience of hiding from the world, and he's prevailed,' she said defensively.

'Look, we're on the same side,' he said in a softer tone. 'It's important that I find him again.'

'Again, what do you mean, again? You've met him?'

'Yes, last night ...' he paused, not quite knowing how to put it.

'Well, are you going to tell me?' she said, impatiently.

'We managed to track him down at an internet café in north London last night. I personally followed him, but I lost him on a council estate.'

'What was he doing on a council estate?'

'I think he knew I was tailing him, he was onto us. Anyway, something weird happened ... I was attacked by a gang.'

'A gang?'

'Yes, it was pure coincidence, five gang members just happened to be at the location at the same time as me and the vampire.'

'I don't understand why some gang members would attack a police officer. Did you identify yourself or show your police ID?'

'They already knew who I was, or at least the leader did ... I put his brother in jail for life last year.'

'What did he do?'

'He stabbed and killed somebody.'

'So that's why they attacked you.'

'Yeah, but that's just the beginning. They half killed me; my spine cracked when one of them hit me in the lower back with an iron bar. Then while I was on the floor, they kicked me all over until I was virtually unconscious. I took several serious blows to the head and body. I felt my ribs crack and I couldn't feel anything from the waist down. I felt dizzy and could feel myself dying.'

'I don't understand. You look fine from where I'm standing.'

'Yes I know, thanks to our mutual vampire friend.'

'I'm not with you, Detective?'

'Two of the gang members picked me up off the ground and held me upright. Just as their leader was about to stab me in the chest with a knife, the vampire appeared out of nowhere, killing three of them.'

'Oh, my god!'

'I remember exactly how I felt as I lay on the floor. If he hadn't done anything, I would have died within a few minutes. I was paralysed from the waist down with critical head injuries and was bleeding badly.'

'I'm still not clear. There's no physical sign that you were attacked, how did you survive? What happened?'

'My memories are a little hazy as I was on the verge of passing out and probably slipping into a coma and dying. My eyes were swollen and bruised and I could hardly see. But we spoke briefly and then I remember being aware of warm liquid running down my throat. Then he disappeared into the night, leaving me there on the car park floor. I felt my body heal right there and then. My cracked ribs, my spine, the feeling in my legs came back, the swelling went down. It was like I'd been fed some kind of miracle super fast healing potion. My body regenerated and today, well I feel like I have the body of 18-year-old.' The detective looked purposefully at Tania, awaiting her response.

'Wow, I don't know what to say.'

'It was his blood … he fed me his blood, and it brought me back from the brink of death. Now stop bullshitting me, and tell me what you really know,' he demanded.

'Why, what difference will it make?'

'It might mean the difference between life and death for someone. Raven Xavier's running around murdering innocent people. He's on a mad feeding frenzy and he doesn't care who he kills in the process. Your vampire can help me stop him, and last night he told me he would.'

'Look, I don't know how to get hold of him any more than you do. He emails me and phones me, and you know about that 'cos you're monitoring my calls and emails.'

'But you've met him … right?'

'Yes … yes I have, the other night he surprised me when I was walking home from my local off licence.'

'Do you believe he's a real vampire?'

'Yes,' she said, without hesitation.

'What makes you so sure?'

'He healed me … I dropped a bottle of wine on the pavement and cut my ankle on some of the broken glass. He cut his palm and applied some of his blood to my wound. It pretty much healed right in front of my eyes. Whatever it was he did, wasn't human, so yes, I'm pretty sure.'

'Okay, so we're both in the same ballpark playing the same sport. Fact is, I'm not sure how to handle this,' said Maldini.

'What do you mean?'

'Well, I can't just tell my colleagues and superiors that I was almost dead and a vampire saved my life can I? I've already missed this morning's briefing 'cos I know I'm in big trouble with my boss.'

'So what are you going to say?'

'I don't know. I'll figure it out eventually. But in the meantime, I suspect that you and I are the only two people who are convinced, as we've witnessed the vampire's power to heal. We need to work together to bring Raven Xavier down, you, me, and the vampire.'

'Just the three of us?'

'Yes, we're the only ones who know what we're dealing with. I can use the usual police tactics to try and track and trace him, but something tells me we'll need your vampire to finally bring him down. Only right now, I don't know where he is or how to find him.'

'Okay, you told me the vampire told you he'd help you last night, right?'

'Yeah.'

'Well then, I'm sure he'll find you, when he's ready.'

'I hope you're right, and I hope he does it before Raven kills any more innocent people.'

Chapter 17

Later that evening Tania was at home preparing some food in the kitchen. It was quite late as she'd been for a few drinks after work with Cora. As usual, she took her evening meal into the living room. Only this time, when she got there she noticed a necklace on the coffee table in the middle of her living room floor.

She put her meal down on the dining table, glanced around her living room, and then walked over to the necklace. She picked it up; it was quite heavy and very detailed and theatrical looking. It was totally festooned with what she assumed were fake diamonds. As she held it up, the light hit the stones and made them sparkle like nothing she'd ever seen; it was stunningly beautiful. Just as she was admiring it, her landline telephone rang. She walked over to answer it.

'Hello,' she said, in her usual polite evening tone.

'Pretty, isn't it?' said the deep eerie voice on the other end of the phone.

'Who is this?' she said.

'Oh come on, Ms de Pré, you know exactly who this is. The diamonds are real. I should know, I personally stole that necklace from Queen Marie Antoinette before she was beheaded. Tristan isn't the only vampire in town.'

'Raven Xavier?' she inadvertently said out loud.

'That's my girl' said Raven, toying with her.

'I'm not your girl, what the fuck do you want?' she said in a curt, but nervous tone.

'That's no way for a lady to talk, why don't you try it on for size?' he said.

'What are you talking about?'

'The necklace in your left hand,' he said, continuing to play with her.

Tania looked at the necklace in her left hand and took a sharp intake of breath. She frantically looked around and walked over to her living room window to look outside.

'Don't bother looking out the window for me Ms de Pré, I'm not there. I can hear the necklace jingling in your hand. I'm a vampire remember? I have pretty good ears, and as you're right handed, I'm assumed you picked the phone up with that hand.'

Tania wasn't totally convinced and still had a feeling of unease.

'So, try it on and take a look at yourself in that large mirror on your living room wall.'

'No!' she said, trying to take control of the situation.

'Don't argue with me, Ms de Pré, I think you already know what I'm capable of … just do it!' he demanded in a very loud angry voice that startled Tania.

She walked over to the mirror, put the phone on speaker, and placed it on the small shelf beneath the mirror. She put the necklace on, fixing the clasp around the back of her neck. Then, for a moment, she lost herself as she stood there admiring the necklace around her neck in the mirror.

'It belonged to Marie Antoinette.'

Tania was silent and became overwhelmed as she realised the necklace was probably the real deal.

'That's right, our mutual vampire friend isn't the only one who can prove he's been hopping around the planet for the last thousand years.'

'It's real?' she said softly, realising that it was a priceless piece of jewellery, one of a kind.

'Oh it's real, all right ... but don't worry, I wasn't responsible for Marie Antoinette's beheading ... but I will be for yours when I come to reclaim my necklace!'

Tania heard a static click, followed by a tone as Raven hung up. She frantically struggled to undo the clasp as fast as she could, then she threw the necklace across the floor as if it were cursed. She grabbed Maldini's card and phoned him.

'Maldini,' he answered.

'He's been here, he's been in my house today!' she said, all wound up and panicked.

'Who? The vampire?'

'No, the other one. Raven Xavier, he was in my house!'

'Whoa! Whoa! Whoa! Calm down. How do you know?'

'Because he just called me on the phone; he left me one of Marie Antoinette's fucking diamond necklaces on my coffee table!' she shouted, all hysterical and animated.

'Okay! Stay put and make sure all the doors and windows are locked. I'll be there in twenty minutes.' He hung up.

Tania paced up and down for a while before eventually sitting down on her leather sofa. She twiddled her thumbs and tapped her feet nervously while she waited for Detective Maldini to arrive.

Without warning her entire living room window came smashing in with an almighty crash. Glass, splinters of wood, net curtains, ornaments from the windowsill, everything came crashing into the middle of her living room floor with an almighty bang.

When the dust and wreckage cleared, Raven Xavier was standing there. He'd landed smack in the middle of her living room ten feet in from the window. He stood there perfectly motionless with his legs still half bent from his landing. One of his feet had gone through her glass coffee table. At no time did he take his eyes off Tania; every ounce of his attention was focused on her. It all happened so fast; one minute she was sitting on the sofa looking at the wall and mirror straight ahead, the very next instant, Raven came crashing through her window at lightning speed and now stood there in what looked like a very purposeful theatrical stance.

He gave her a look like that of a ferocious lion about to eat its prey. She remained frozen in her seated position on the sofa. Raven swiftly turned his head and glanced at the necklace on the floor.

'Hah, so you removed it; clever girl. And I was sooooo looking forward to having that pleasure all to myself,' he said in a deep evil mocking and sarcastic tone; the hint of Russian accent emphasising it.

'Get out of my house, you're not invited!' she said sternly, but nervously, in the desperate hope that the myth of vampires burning up and dying right in front of you if they entered your home uninvited was actually true.

'Ha! That old invitation bullshit doesn't work with me bitch; you've been watching way too many movies. Now I'm gonna make you famous … tomorrow, everyone can read about your imminent death in your very own paper,' he said, sniggering in his deep dark sinister tone.

In an instant, he leapt from his frozen stance and landed right in Tania's lap with his feet either side of her thighs, pinning her lower half to the sofa. He grabbed her hair violently with both his hands, causing her to let out a sharp yelp as he pinned her head back hard against the sofa. She put her hands up between his arms and scratched down either side of his cheeks really hard with her fingernails causing four elongated cuts to appear down either side.

'Oh baby, you know I like it rough,' he said, taunting and playing with her as he shook her head from side to side.

'Get the fuck off me!' she shouted, as she desperately fought and struggled under him, to no avail. Her attempts to get him off her were futile.

'Oh come on now, we're not done yet, there's still sooooo much fun to be had.'

She grabbed his hair with both hands and pulled as hard as she could.

'Get off me!' she protested, as she ripped some hair away from either side of his head.

'Get off me, get off me,' said Raven, in a high pitched mocking feminine voice.

Before she knew what had happened, he'd grabbed her arms and got both her wrists clamped in one of his large hands and had them pinned behind her head. He squeezed his thighs tight around her so she was locked and could not move.

Using the fingertips on his free right hand he stroked the scratches on his face and looked at his fingers to see blood on them. But then the scratches healed right in front of her, Raven laughed, and then turned serious.

'Bitch! … Please, allow me to return the favour. Let's see if we can mirror that pretty scar on your right cheek with an identical one on the other side, shall we?'

Raven swiftly reached across and grabbed a piece of glass from the broken coffee table that had conveniently landed on the sofa next to her. He dug it hard into her cheek and pulled it down slowly, but hard, ripping into her face. The excruciating pain as the jagged glass shard tore through her skin caused her to scream out loud; tears and blood ran down her face.

'Oh that's much better, now your pretty face has perfect symmetry,' he laughed.

She screamed as loud as she could. Raven darted his head forward mid-scream, faster than a viper striking an attack on its prey, and smacked his open mouth hard up against hers, instantly muting her screams. She struggled for breath as Raven thrust his tongue into her mouth and continued to play and toy with her. Her futile struggles were pointless, and she knew it. She bit down on his tongue as hard as she could, screaming at the same time. She could taste the blood from his tongue filling up in her mouth. Raven jerked his head back quickly, freeing his tongue from Tania's mouth.

'Fucking bitch!' he said, as he slapped her face really hard with his right hand.

'You're not invited!' shouted a male voice from across the room. Raven snapped his head around and looked back across the living room. Standing crouched on the windowsill was the very purposeful silhouetted figure of Tristan.

'Well, well, well, if it isn't the infamous Tristan Syhier Burnel. It's been a long time, Tristan. Won't you come in and join us?' he said, sarcastically.

'I said, you're not invited here,' repeated Tristan, in a more serious tone as he leapt off the windowsill and landed five feet from sofa.

'Yes, yes, yes, I know, we've been through all that already. Does it look like I'm on fire to you? Do you see me bleeding from my eye sockets?'

'You have to leave – now!' shouted Tristan.

'Is that so?' said Raven, leaping to his feet and squaring up to Tristan.

'You know, you and I are the same, we should team up and try to get along,' said Raven.

'I'll never be the same as you,' said Tristan, with utter contempt and disgust for his fellow vampire.

Raven stepped closer to Tristan and looked him square in the eyes. 'Oh yes you will, you just don't realise it yet. You've always been the same as me; you've just spent the last thousand years fighting it. Set yourself free, be part of my world.'

'Never, you can burn in hell.'

'Ha, that'll be the day.'

Raven appeared to vanish from right in front of Tristan and reappear eight feet across the room where the necklace was lying on the floor. He moved so fast, it even impressed Tristan. Raven picked up the necklace and turned to Tania.

'Well, it looks like your boyfriend turned up just in the

nick of time … that's right, your mind's like an open book to me, I know you have a little secret girlie crush on him.'

Tania realised that Raven had read her thoughts as she fleetingly daydreamed about Tristan even during their stand-off. Tristan was her brave knight in shining armour, with whom she would one day ride away into the sunset; at least that was her silly fantasy. Tristan was courteous enough to save Tania her blushes by not acknowledging the comment and keeping his eyes fixed firmly on Raven.

'Well, this has been an entertaining evening hasn't it?' said Raven mockingly, smiling a sinister smile. 'You can't stop me, Tristan. I'm stronger than you and you know it, you can sense it. I'm going to continue killing and feeding and there's nothing you can do about it. As for your pretty little girlfriend over there, I'm gonna have so much fun with her.'

Tristan flew across the room at Raven with lighting speed, but Raven was quicker. He leapt out of Tristan's way and landed on the windowsill, leaving Tristan to slam into the wall taking out a large section of the plaster in the process. Tristan got spun around, with white plaster dust dripping off him. He saw Raven perched on the windowsill looking at him.

'Until the next time, Tristan … this is going to be FUN!'

In an instant, Raven vanished into the night.

'Are you okay?' said Tristan, concerned for Tania and noticing the blood dripping from her face.

'Yes, I'm fine,' she said, standing up and composing herself, but finding that her whole body was trembling uncontrollably. 'Will he be back?'

'There's a good chance of that, yes … but not tonight.'

Tania felt reassured and safe with Tristan there. She looked in the large mirror on the wall and let out a shocked gasp for two reasons; one, she could not see Tristan's reflection in it, and two, she noticed the blood running down her face. She ran up to the mirror and examined the deep cut on her left cheek and put her hand up to her mouth and wept.

Tristan ran over to her, grabbed her shoulders and turned her face towards him.

'Let me see,' he said, 'keep still.'

He pricked the tip of his index finger on one of his still partly exposed fangs, causing it to bleed. He slowly ran the tip of his bleeding finger down the open wound on the left side of Tania's face, so his blood to run into it.

'So, your name's Tristan?'

'Yes, Tristan Syhier Burnel ... are you going to tell anyone?'

'No,' she said, in a reassuring voice.

'Good, let's keep it that way, for now.'

'Are you reading my mind right now?' she said, softly.

'No, I'm not, and I won't do that with you anymore.'

'How many times have you read my mind?'

'A few,' he said, not giving a figure away.

'But you're not going to do it anymore?'

'No, I'm not.'

'Why not, I mean, if you have the gift, why not use it?'

'Things have changed somewhat,' he said, continuing his skilled repair job on her face.

'Like what?'

'Well, I have to be quite physically close to you to read your mind. I didn't read your mind on the telephone, that's impossible for me, but I do have other vampire instincts that let me know what you are up to and what you were thinking while I was speaking to you on the phone. In the beginning, when I was doing my research on you, I got close to you a few times. Of course you had no idea that I was there. But when we met face to face for the first time down the street, I learned a considerable amount about you during our brief moment together. I can totally figure somebody out just by standing in front of them and looking into their eyes.'

'Like if they are a good or bad person?'

'Something like that, only in greater depth and with a lot more detail. I can absorb a person's entire character profile in just a few minutes – what kind of a person they are, what makes them tick, what they stand for, what morals they have, or don't have, their balance of love and hate, if there's an evil streak in them, if they're trying to be something they're not, what makes them happy, what makes them angry, what makes them cry – everything.'

'And you did all that with me the other night?'

'Yes, yes I did,' he said softly as he neared the end of fixing her wound, 'Tania, I'll never read your mind again … can you forgive me?'

'On one condition … you tell me what you found. What am I?'

'Don't do this,' he said, not wanting to reveal what he found out about her.

'No, that's not fair, you have to tell me. Sometimes I hardly know myself, and now, for the first time in my life there's a person standing right in front of me who knows who I am … tell me!' she demanded.

'There, you're done,' he said, removing his finger from her face.

Tania turned and looked in the mirror to witness the wound slowly healing up before her very eyes. Tristan paused for a moment, and then took a deep purposeful breath.

'Okay. The tough exterior that you portray isn't who you really are; locked inside is a very different person. Not only are you clever and sophisticated, but you also have so much love to give, and you're desperate to pour it into the right person. Being an only child and having a difficult upbringing meant that you had to be tough and even a little selfish as you fended for yourself during your childhood years.

'You have a zest for life and you're somehow able to approach each new day with a spirit of fresh inspiration while you block out the past. You only have a small handful of friends, but you would do anything for them and your loyalty doesn't waver. You find it hard making new friends because people don't really understand you, but deep down you don't mind because you know they probably never will.

'Even though on the outside you're the life of the party, you're on a different frequency from most people and you don't really fit into any specific social group and you never have. Deep down, you've always felt alone in this world and made your way through life suffering in silence.

'Your friends find you enigmatic, mysterious and sometimes even baffling, and they can't always work out where you're coming from. Your tastes and preferences are very eclectic in a way that most people would classify as just plain weird. However, you're consistent in your inconsistency and there's definitely method to your madness. Sometimes when you wake up in the morning you feel like you are one person, yet by the afternoon, you feel like you're somebody else entirely. You've never truly been in love before. You settled for your ex-husband the day that you married him, and you knew it, as did your father. Even though you're desperate to fall deeply in love now, you won't settle again. You'll wait your entire life for the right man if you have to, and deep down, you know it might never happen.'

Tania stood there looking at her reflection in the mirror with tears flooding down both cheeks. Although she could not see Tristan's reflection in the mirror, she could feel his hands on her shoulders as he stood behind her. By the time Tristan had finished talking, the wound on her face had vanished. She turned to Tristan; she desperately wanted him to embrace her in both arms. She was giving him a big bright green light; she opened up her innermost thoughts and feelings and was mentally begging him to read them, but he didn't.

As he stood there quite motionless looking at her, she could see pain in his eyes, pain that went back a long way in history. She tried to imagine how it must have felt for him to bury seven wives; the love, the pain, the on-going anguish. His eyes told a story, a story she could now see very clearly. The look he had in his eyes was like that of a man who had just come back from a war; several wars. He looked like an emotionally battered and beaten man. She couldn't even begin to imagine his pain and suffering, both past and present.

She was falling in love with him more and more, so quickly, and there was absolutely nothing she could do about it. And she didn't want to do anything about it either, her emotions were in overdrive and going full steam ahead, and she was personally greasing the rails to help them along. This man, this vampire, knew her so well and he even recognised himself in her, as she did him. Yes, he was a vampire, but she didn't care, because no human could ever compare to him. No mortal man had ever managed to bring her emotions to the surface and make her feel like this. She wanted him, and she could see that he wanted her too.

She stepped forward and gently cupped her hands on either side of his face. His skin felt incredibly soft and smooth, but quite cold too. She slowly and very carefully moved her face closer to his until she could feel his breath against her lips. He didn't move a muscle. He slowly inhaled through his nose to take in the scent of her skin and perfume as she moved in closer still. She tilted her head slightly to one side to gain easier access to his mouth. She closed her eyes, she could feel his energies, she could smell him, and she could feel his breath coming from his slightly parted lips. She moved a few millimetres closer and felt the skin of his surprisingly soft lips ever so lightly touch hers. She parted her lips slightly, but just when she was about to press her lips firmly against his, they heard a frantic banging at the front door.

'Tania, open the door, it's me, Detective Maldini!' Maldini continued banging and shouting.

'Oh no, I forgot,' she said, snapping back into reality. 'Can you wait ... will you ... I mean, you're not going to vanish while I answer the door are you?' she pleaded.

'Go and answer the door, Tania,' he said in a neutral nondescript tone, with an equally nondescript expression on his face.

Tania went off to answer the door, annoyed and frustrated at being interrupted at such a delicate moment. As she opened the door, Maldini barged past her with his gun in his hand and ran straight for the living room.

'Wait, what are you doing?' she shouted after him.

Maldini stormed into her living room, spun his upper body around and pointed his gun square into Tristan's chest.

'That won't do you any good, Detective' said Tristan, calmly.

Tania came running in after Maldini and jumped directly into his line of fire, acting as a human shield to protect Tristan.

'Detective, put the gun away!' she demanded.

Maldini assessed the situation and vaguely recognised Tristan from the underground car park and put his gun away.

'How are you feeling, Detective?' said Tristan, referring to the beating he had taken the night before.

'I feel great, thanks. What's going on? What happened to the front window?'

'Raven was just here,' said Tania, stepping back and standing by Tristan's side.

'You mean a second time, or was he here all along?'

'No, he must have put the necklace here earlier. He came crashing through the window after I spoke to you, while you were on your way over here. He left about five minutes ago.'

'Oh my god, I'm so sorry I didn't get here faster,' said Maldini, 'I'm confused.' He turned to Tristan.

'Tristan came along in the nick of time and saved my life. Raven was only here for a few minutes, but he didn't get chance to kill me because Tristan showed up. Lucky for me, Raven likes to play with his victims for a while before killing them. If he'd just got on with it, I'd be dead right now.'

'Shit, this is bad, this is really bad! … okay, you can't stay here, it's not safe,' said Maldini.

'She's coming home with me,' stated Tristan.

'I am? … I mean, yes, that's right, I'm going home with Tristan,' said Tania.

'I don't think that's a very good idea,' said Maldini, partly because he felt protective towards Tania and didn't like the idea of her being in a house alone with another man, especially a vampire.

'Detective, your police department and your gun can't protect Tania from Raven Xavier. I'm the only one who can do that.'

'How? And how are we going to catch him?' said Maldini.

'We're not going to catch him, Detective.'

'What?'

'We're going to kill him, or at least I am. It's something I should have done a long time ago.'

'Well, how are you going to do that?' asked Maldini.

'I'm working on it, Detective.'

'Well, can you work on it a little quicker, please,' said Maldini.

'Hey, give him a break; I don't see the police doing much. At least he was here to save my life!' said Tania, defending Tristan.

'That's not fair,' said Maldini.

'Well, you deserved it,' she said.

'Perhaps ... look, I never thanked you for last night,' he said, directing his conversation towards Tristan.

'No bother, Detective, you would have done the same for me.'

'Well, I'm not sure I would have done it in quite the same fashion that you did, but yes, I would have, it's my job.'

Maldini could see that Tania had taken to Tristan, and she was making it obvious. She appeared to be totally infatuated with him. He thought *Why? How could she have a proper life with him, how could she settle down and live with a vampire? Does he eat? Can he even have sex?*

'We should go,' said Tristan.

'Oh, okay, can I quickly gather a few things together. I mean, I'm assuming I'm going to be staying with you until Raven's caught.'

'Or killed,' said Maldini, in a serious tone.

'Sure, get whatever you need,' said Tristan.

Tania ran upstairs to load up a suitcase with clothes and feminine products.

Tristan turned to Maldini.

'Yes, I can have sex, Detective. But I think your imagination's running riot,' he said, smiling.

'You read my mind?' said Maldini, astonished.

'Yes, Detective.'

'How's that even possible?'

'Oh, I'm not really sure about the biological scientifics. It's just one of the perks that comes with being a vampire I guess.'

'Well, it's a pretty damn good perk if you ask me.'

'It has its advantages when it comes to trying to stay alive and knowing who you can and can't trust in the 21st century, Detective.'

'I can imagine it does.'

Detective Maldini wheeled Tania's suitcase out to Tristan's car, which was parked just around the corner. He wasn't happy about letting Tania go with Tristan to his house. But although Tristan was a vampire, Maldini knew that he wasn't in the business of killing and feeding off innocent people like Raven was. He also knew that he would not harm Tania, nor would he allow any harm to come to her, so he loaded the suitcase into the boot of Tristan's car and let them go.

Tristan did not give Maldini the address where they were going, and Maldini didn't ask as he figured that if Tristan wanted him to know where they were going, he would have volunteered that information. Besides, based on recent events, Tristan had a habit of showing up at just the right time. He did however insist that Tania kept her mobile phone with her so that he could keep in contact at all times.

As they drove away, Detective Maldini got one of his colleagues to arrange to get Tania's living room window patched up. He couldn't see the point in calling in a CSI team and creating yet another crime scene. Raven Xavier was running around the city creating enough of those already. In the grand scheme of things, Maldini was now past doing things by the book. He wanted Raven Xavier dead and he couldn't see the point in wasting time bringing in a forensics team just to look for DNA samples that they already had. No, Maldini was now going to introduce his own brand of justice – with the help of Tristan of course.

Tristan drove Tania through streets that were relatively free of traffic. There was a calm surreal feel about the drive. Tania liked it; they could have been a regular couple on their way home from the theatre or a restaurant. They didn't speak much while driving through London. Tania wasn't one for small talk; she was just enjoying watching Tristan drive. He kept his eyes straight ahead and didn't look at her much. She was thankful for this, as her scar was on the side of her face that he could see had he looked at her from his driving position. Tania always felt more comfortable driving, so her passenger got the view of her good side.

There's something very sensual about the way he drives his car, she thought. The way his hands and fingers caressed the steering wheel so delicately. The way he looked into the rear view mirror, the small movements of his head. Everything little thing he did was so incredibly magical and mysterious to watch; he was totally magnetic and addictive to her. She enjoyed the silence, it was so quiet in his super smooth Audi RS 5 Coupe, that she could have heard a pin drop as they drove through the dimly lit streets. The silence was so pure, so comfortable; she couldn't ever remember feeling so at ease and so relaxed with another person.

Sometimes he would rest his arm and hand on the centre console between the two seats. She desperately wanted to touch, or better still, hold his hand while he drove. His automatic car would have made this easily achievable. Tania rested her hand on the edge of her seat in close proximity to where Tristan's hand rested. Each time he lifted his hand to the steering wheel to turn a corner she would edge her hand a little closer to the centre console rest in the hope that when he returned his hand to its resting position he might accidently touch hers.

It was too much; she was going crazy inside, just to hold his hand for a few brief moments would have satisfied her at that moment. She was desperate to have physical contact with him, no matter how minuscule. She couldn't take it anymore, the temptation was just too great and she needed it so much. She waited until they were on a long straight stretch of road, then she slowly touched his fingernails with the pads of her fingertips. As she did so, she paused momentarily, just in case her action caused a negative reaction. It didn't, Tristan remained totally calm and relaxed, as if she had not even touched him.

She slowly drew her fingertips back across the tops of his fingers to the back of his hand; still no emotional response from Tristan, at least not outwardly. His right hand continued to softly caress the steering wheel as he drove around gentle bends. How she wished she were that steering wheel. She very slowly and gently slid her fingertips across the back of Tristan's hand, gliding over his incredibly soft skin, up to his wrist and back towards his fingertips again. Nothing, no reaction whatsoever. *Could he even feel my touch?* she thought.

She gently manoeuvred her fingers between his and slowly drew them together until the pads on the tips of her fingers touched the top part of the palm of his hand. Then it happened, his fingers suddenly sprang closed around hers like a Venus flytrap clamping around an insect. His grip on her fingers was firm, his skin was as smooth as silk and his touch totally electrified her. She looked at him; he closed his eyes while squeezing her hand. *What is he feeling; what is he thinking?* she thought.

He continued to drive with his eyes closed, she didn't think to look at the road, she had no fear, and she somehow knew they were not going to crash. Even though his eyes were closed, she suspected that he had some kind of vampire sense that was guiding him through the streets. A few turnings later, he opened his eyes and slowly turned his head and looked deep into her eyes. If she could have frozen that moment in time and made it last forever she would have done so.

Tania thought about the brief conversation that she overheard between Tristan and Detective Maldini while she was packing her case back at the house. When she heard Tristan tell Maldini that he could have sex, she almost jumped for joy and had to put her hand up to her mouth to prevent an excited scream from coming out. To say she was thrilled about this would be the understatement of the year. It was something that she wanted to know, and now she didn't have to worry about how she would put the question to him. She couldn't control her emotions or the feelings that she was fast developing for Tristan. They were coming on thick and fast and she couldn't slow them down even if she wanted to.

They drove through the large iron electronic gate at the entrance of Tristan's estate and up the winding driveway between the woodland areas. Tania admired the trees and flowers on this tranquil night. Even though they were on the outskirts of London, Tania felt like she was in the middle of some surreal and secluded fairy-tale land.

When they got to the house, Tristan got out of the car and opened the door for Tania. He then got her case from the boot and carried it into the house for her.

'Let me show you to your room, so you can get comfortable,' he said, leading the way across the marble hallway and up the winding stairs. As they entered the main master bedroom, Tania was totally overwhelmed by the beauty and taste of the décor.

'Is this your bedroom?' she asked.

'I'd like it to be, but no, unfortunately not. I rest in a secure lightproof room in the basement during the hours of daylight.'

'Oh,' she said, surprised as he had obviously gone to great lengths to make this room beautiful and perfect.

'Although the drapes in here are lightproof, I simply could not risk using this room as my place of rest during daylight hours. If anything was to accidently happen, and light got in … well, you know.'

'Yes, I understand.'

'I've never slept in here, but, I will spend one night in here … soon,' he said, cryptically.

'Make yourself comfortable, I'll be downstairs in the living room.'

He left Tania to unpack her things. When Tania had unpacked her suitcase, she made her way downstairs and found Tristan standing by the window in the living room. She walked over and stood next to him.

'The sky is so clear, I can't believe how bright the stars look,' she said as they both admired the night sky.

'Follow me,' said Tristan.

He led Tania upstairs, then through a door that led to some more stairs. When they got to the top of the second set of stairs there was a secure door that led out onto the roof. It was a large flat concrete roof with a low castle-style wall around the edges. He led her across the roof to the edge so she could get a better view of the grounds.

She rested her hands on the wall and leaned forward slightly to look down. Although they were only two floors up, it felt a lot higher. She was in awe of the beauty of the grounds and how beautiful everything looked. Even though there was only a crescent moon, it was surprisingly bright. She had a clear panoramic view of the entire estate.

'It's so beautiful!' she whispered.

Tristan could see that she was feeling the night-time air on her bare arms as she was only wearing a thin blouse. He removed his coat, and from behind he gently placed it around her shoulders as she admired the view. He put his arms around her waist and delicately wrapped his jacket around her and embraced her from behind.

Tania melted like butter in Tristan's arms as his body pressed into hers and his arms held her in a firm embrace. She could no longer see the crescent moon or the stars; her eyes had closed as she sank deeper and deeper into Tristan's dreamlike embrace. She let go emotionally and any defences she might have kept up in the past, had been let down entirely. She could feel the presence of his head just inches behind hers. His chin was almost touching her shoulder and she could feel his breath on the side of her neck. She tilted her head back and to the side slightly, inviting him to kiss her neck; but the kiss never came. She could feel that he wanted to and was fighting the temptation, *but why,* she thought, *why?*

Tristan slowly turned Tania around so she was facing him.

'We should go inside, it's late and I have some things I need to take care of,' he said, as he led her back across the roof and downstairs into the house.

He showed Tania where the kitchen was and made sure she had everything she needed.

'Get some rest; I'll be back before dawn. Oh, don't open any of the drapes, not if you want to see me in one piece during daylight hours that is,' he joked.

'But where are you going, what do you have to do?'

'There are certain things I need to do, some of which are similar things to what you would do during the course of the day. The first thing I have to do is eat, I'm famished,' he said smiling, as he walked to the door.

What does that mean? she thought. *Was he going to visit one of his hospital nurse friends to illegally buy some blood from their reserves, or was he going to visit some sleazy willing female donor?* She didn't want to go there. Thoughts of Tristan feeding off a glamorous young female while she lay naked on a bed getting off on it was something Tania didn't want going through her head while she lay in bed trying to get to sleep. Jealousy was not an emotion she wanted to feel right now. So she let him go without asking any more questions.

Chapter 18

The next morning Tania woke up feeling totally energised, like she'd had the best night's sleep ever. This surprised her, as she usually didn't sleep well in strange environments. She always dreaded having to stay in hotel rooms if her work demanded it, as she would usually have a terrible night with just a few hours broken sleep. But here, in Tristan's house, she felt completely comfortable and relaxed.

She got up and went to take a shower in the en-suite. While showering, she wondered if Tristan was in the house. *Is he in his secure resting place in one of those basement rooms, or perhaps he's in the living room or study behind the safety of his lightproof drapes sitting in artificial incandescent lighting?* she thought.

After her shower, she got dressed and went downstairs. She looked in the living room and study, but there was no sign of Tristan. She went into the kitchen and made a cup of tea, then returned the living room with her laptop and mobile so she could phone Jack at the office to explain that she was going to be working from home for a few days. As she sat down on one of the long black leather sofas, she noticed a copy of The Sentinel newspaper right there on the coffee table. Tristan must have returned before dawn, as the newspaper couldn't have got there by itself, and his car was parked right outside. Perhaps he was in his resting place downstairs. She looked at the cover of the paper, but didn't bother to pick it up and read it. After all, she already knew what the column said, as she was the one who wrote it.

EMAIL FROM A VAMPIRE – Part 6
By Tania de Pré

Continued from yesterday in the vampire's own words.

Settling in London and building a new life came easily for me. Learning the English language didn't pose any problems. After becoming a vampire, my brain seemed to learn a lot quicker, and absorb and retain information like never before. It was almost like every single brain cell had been unlocked and I now had a brain capacity that was a thousand times what it was before. I leaned to speak English very fast. After just four weeks I was speaking and sounding like a native.

I spent the first five years establishing myself and building a few trustworthy contacts. I had a large house with a secret secure basement room where I would often sleep or rest during the daylight hours. During these early years I kept a relatively low profile, but I did go out and socialise some evenings. In 1779 I met Hannah, who later became my seventh wife. Being a vampire, I have to be quick in evaluating potential long-term partners or wives. After all, it didn't take women too long to realise that I only met them during the hours of darkness, which was why I rarely met potential new female partners during the summer months.

It is very difficult trying to build a relationship with a woman when you cannot spend any daylight hours with her, at least not outside. Because of this, it takes a special and certain type of woman to go the distance with me. All my previous wives were unique and special women and I had very deep meaningful and long-term relationships with all of them.

Hannah, who I met in London in 1779, was one such lady. I revealed my secret to her after ten months. Being able to read people's minds is a big advantage, especially in this situation. I trusted her explicitly, and she did me. I knew my secret was safe with her and would be for life. We married three years later in 1782 and spent the next 64 years together until she died in 1846 aged 90. As with my previous wives over the centuries, I was devastated, heartbroken and totally inconsolable for three years after her death and during this time I kept to myself, rarely even leaving the house.

I spent the next one hundred years alone, and then in 1946 I met Elizabeth. We never married, but we had a very strong and loving relationship and she was comfortable with what I was. She moved in with me at my house and eventually we set up an antique business in Chelsea, London, which she ran with two employees. Of course my involvement in this business was minimalist due to my allergy to daylight.

I had already acquired a very large collection of relics, artefacts and other valuable items over the centuries while living in Europe, and these later become incredibly valuable antiques. Since my arrival in England in 1774, I had continued to build on this collection, adding to it over the years.

I would rarely show up at the business premises, and whenever I did, it was typically late in the afternoon during the winter months after twilight. This had become a primary source of income, not that we needed it financially speaking, but it made Elizabeth happy. Of course, I'd had a major head start and had many advantages that other antique businesses did not have. As the years went by, we made a fortune. We loved each other intimately and trusted each other implicitly, and everything was perfect. I always knew that Elizabeth's death would one day come, but it came a lot sooner than I expected. In January 1972 she was killed in a car accident when she was 52 years old. Elizabeth was the passenger in a friend's car. They were hit by another car; the other driver had lost control of his car on an icy road, and swerved over onto the wrong side, hitting Elizabeth's car head on. I'd already taken a vow to myself never to marry again as it was just too painful when my wives died. But just because Elizabeth and I were not married, did not mean the pain was any less. I suffered, just like I'd always suffered. I struggled through the next few years, feeling very lost and very alone; again!

One of the staff members at our antique business took over as manager and ran things. He also took on another member of staff to help out with the workload. In 1974 I could no longer stand living in the house where I had spent 26 amazing years full of joy and love with my beautiful Elizabeth. The surroundings, the memories, were all too clear and all too painful; so I decided to move. I bought a large house on the outskirts of London, which is where I live today. It has several acres of land, and is totally enclosed. I spent a considerable amount of money getting the conditions of the house perfect for my vampire requirements, as well as making provisions for the storage of valuables and antiques. By now I probably owned the single largest and most valuable collection of antiques in Europe, most of which had to be securely locked away. I contracted builders to build three secret underground rooms, which were accessible via short corridors from two of the basements that were already there. The builders were led to believe that they were going to be wine cellars. I later contracted different people to convert two of them into walk-in vaults with nine-inch thick steel doors, which are alarmed and are only accessible via an eight-digit security code. The remaining one is equally secure, but this one is used for my secure place of rest or sleep during the hours of daylight.

The house and grounds are also secure with high walls and fencing securing the perimeter of the estate and a large electronic gate at the only entrance with an intercom system communicating with the main house. All the windows of the house are fitted with black lightproof drapes. The drapes are drawn in reverse to that of mortal humans i.e. I will have them closed during the hours of daylight, allowing me to move freely around the house safe from rays of light. Then at night I open them to reveal the view of the stars and moon in the night sky.

The years quickly went by and in the summer of 1978 on 20th June I celebrated my birthday, my human birthday that is. I had been on this planet for exactly 1000 years, 967 of those as a vampire. I spent that evening alone, reflecting on my life through the centuries; my wives, the people I'd known, the places I'd been, and the things I'd seen and experienced. It conjured up very deep emotions for me as I remembered all of my wives so very clearly; it was as if their deaths were only yesterday.

Since the late 1970s getting my dietary needs met, i.e. blood requirements, was much easier and more straightforward and a lot less complicated. Unlike the Middle Ages, these days I had several different sources of blood to meet my requirements. I no longer had to go out hunting to kill animals; instead, I sourced pig's blood from a contact at an abattoir and stocked it in my fridge at home. The abattoir was great, as that particular source never ran dry. Pig's blood was my preferred animal blood as it contained all the right types of nutrients that I needed. I still occasionally went out and hunted animals at night, I imagine it was the wolf instinct in me that sometimes needed to be satisfied.

For human blood I had a janitor friend who worked at a hospital, who I paid to supply me with the discarded blood that had been suctioned from patients during major operations. However, this was a little risky as blood diseases were rife during the late 1970s and although AIDS infected blood would not kill me, I could be laid up for a couple of weeks while my body fought the disease off.

Because the discarded blood method had its risks, I later befriended a hospital nurse and got to know her very well. I would pay her to relieve the hospital blood banks of some of their stock once in a while, which she was happy to do, as her salary at the time was not great and she appreciated the extra cash.

But every now and then, I just couldn't resist the taste and sensation of lovely, fresh, warm human blood straight from the artery. But I never killed anybody for their blood. Believe it or not, I actually had four young ladies dotted around London who were more than happy to let me feed off them. I would typically drink between a quarter and half a pint from two tiny puncture holes in the wrist, which I would make with my razor-sharp fangs. This usually took place on a bed in the privacy of either their bedroom or a hotel room. I later found out from my willing donors that the very act of me feeding off them was incredibly erotic and gave them amazing sensations. The ecstatic sexual feelings that these women experienced were probably down to a combination of my mild unintentional hypnosis and tiny amounts of venom escaping involuntarily from my fangs and finding its way into their bloodstream. I've since learned that very tiny amounts of my venom can get a human slightly high and trigger incredible sexual feelings. I have also been told that the sensation coming from the light touch of my lips and hands on the flesh on their arms feels incredible while I'm feeding; like some kind of sexual electricity.

One young woman told me that while I was feeding, she could feel strong static-like charges coming out of my fingertips and lips, and any other part of my skin that was in contact with hers. She said it fired off electricity inside her, giving her multiple sexual thrills. One young girl in her early twenties asked me if she could taste a few drops of my blood once, and afterwards told me about the incredible "high" she got from it, making her feel strong, energetic and sexy.

It wasn't uncommon for a woman to reach orgasm while I was feeding from her. Other women would sometimes bring themselves to orgasm with a little encouragement. Either way, my willing donors were happy for me to feed from them on a regular basis in exchange for a few drops of my blood coupled with the amazing sexual experience that it gave them. Just as their warm blood was almost like a drug to me, the feelings I gave them were equally addictive, so everybody was happy.

Continued tomorrow.

Later that evening, Tania caught up with Tristan in the living room. She didn't ask where he had been all night, knowing that it was not her place to enquire. She assumed that he had been locked away in his secret basement room during the hours of daylight.

She could sense that Tristan was a little on edge and very alert. As twilight passed and it became dark outside, Tristan opened the lightproof drapes and stood by the window, scanning the grounds.

'What is it,' she said softly, 'you've been on edge for the last thirty minutes.'

'Something's wrong,' he said.

'What do you mean?'

'Raven's close, I can sense it.'

'What!' she gasped, 'how do you know?'

'Vampires can sense each other when another is in the immediate neighbourhood. It's like a mix of our sixth sense and mind reading capabilities.'

'Well how close is he, I mean, how accurate is your vampire detecting radar?' Immediately after she said that, she realised how stupid it must have sounded.

'It's hard to tell with any degree of accuracy. Raven's a lot stronger than me and he's learned how to mask his presence quite effectively. He's masking it right now, but I'd say he's definitely within half a mile.'

'On your estate?' she said, sounding worried.

'Possibly, he's using his blocking defences to mystify his exact location,' said Tristan, with his eyes closed in total concentration. 'His physical presence is rapidly shifting all over the place. I can't pinpoint him.'

Tania could see that he was frustrated, so she got up off the sofa and walked over to the window to be near him, to try and comfort him. As she stood there with her hand on his shoulder, he suddenly sensed that something else was wrong. He sniffed the air and his wolf-like sense of smell picked something up.

'Something's on fire,' he said, continuing to sniff the air.

'I can't smell anything,' said Tania, also sniffing the air.

Tristan ran out of the living room, across the hallway and right up to the patio window in the study with his face virtually pressed up against the glass. He looked out across the grounds of his estate and over to the far right corner through the trees. He saw flames and smoke coming from what could only be the cottage where Will and his mother Angela lived.

Tania caught up and entered the study just in time to watch Tristan smash through the glass patio doors. He wasn't going to waste valuable time fiddling with a key, unlocking the doors and sliding one of them open. He vanished with incredible speed off the patio, across the open expanse of grounds and into the wooded area, leaving Tania standing there with her jaw on the floor after witnessing his incredible speed. It reminded her of one of those cartoon scenes where a character instantly vanishes out of a shot, leaving behind an airborne dust ball right where they were just standing. She raced back to the hall, rang the fire brigade, and then ran outside in the same direction as Tristan, towards the fire.

Tristan arrived at the blazing cottage seconds later. Thick, black clouds of smoke billowed into the air. Angela and Will were upstairs at Will's open bedroom window screaming for help. It was too high for them to jump, and the ground floor of the cottage was now a mass of flames, which were fast taking over the first floor as well. Tristan sprang from his standing position and landed in a crouched position with his feet on Will's bedroom window ledge. With his free hand he ripped both the wooden windows off their hinges and tossed them to the floor, creating a larger opening so he could enter. Inside, the flames were moving into Will's bedroom and advancing towards them fast. The room was starting to fill with smoke, causing Angela and Will to cough and choke.

Tristan picked Will up and leapt out of the window to the ground, bending his knees and cushioning the landing for Will. He put Will down then leapt back up into the window. He picked Angela up in his arms and leapt down, landing with her safely on the ground. They retreated away from the burning cottage and watched as pieces of timber started to collapse. Flames and smoke lifted high into the night sky. Angela and Will stood, holding on to each other, and watched their home and all their earthly possessions go up in flames; they could do nothing to save any of their belongings.

The fire brigade arrived swiftly to deal with the blazing cottage. Later, when they'd all accepted that there was nothing they could do, Tristan took Will, Angela and Tania back up to his house. They all stood in the large marble hallway while Tristan explained his plan.

'Angela, you already know about the two secure rooms under the house,' said Tristan.

Will looked at his mother questioningly.

'What secure rooms?' said Will.

Tristan turned to Will.

'Will, when I bought this house, I contracted various builders to add some secret rooms that are only accessible from the basement. I then had a security specialist firm turn two of them into vaults, or in this case, panic-rooms. These two rooms are incredibly secure. I used to store antiques in them, but these days they're simply extra rooms. Inside, there's furniture, a TV, fridge-freezer; all the regular things you would find in a normal house. The doors are opened via electronic combination codes, from both inside and out.'

'And we're going to stay in them,' said Will, sounding a little down.

'Yes, you can both stay here, and don't worry about the cottage or your things. I'll help you out with that. I want you and your mother to stay in one of these secure rooms until I figure out what happened. I want to be sure that you're not in any danger from Raven. Will, I promise you, everything's going to be okay,' said Tristan.

'Oh, how very touching,' said Raven, appearing at Tristan's living room door where he had been sitting waiting for them to return from the fire. Raven slowly and arrogantly walked across the marble floor towards Will and Angela, while looking at Tristan.

'My, my, you really are Mr Compassion aren't you? Why do you care so much for these pathetic mortals?' he said, in a scathing tone. 'That was a very heroic rescue, and after all the trouble I went through to watch them burn; you disappoint me.' Raven gave Tristan an evil smile.

Without hesitation, Tristan flew twenty feet across the hallway at lightning speed, his feet barely touching the ground. This time, he was fast, faster than he had ever been, fuelled by anger greater than he had ever felt before. He slammed hard into Raven, knocking him a further ten feet back. The pair of them hit the marble stairs so hard that part of the staircase exploded under the impact, sending small fragments off in all directions.

Raven laughed hysterically as Tristan pinned him to the stairs underneath him.

'You think you're stronger than me, you think you can defeat me?' said Raven. At that moment, he flew forward with such velocity it carried the two of them to the other side of the hallway sending Tristan's back slamming into the wall, causing several cracks to appear under their impact. They both fell to the floor; Raven had Tristan pinned down beneath him in a stranglehold.

Tania, Angela and Will retreated into the corner out of harm's way, and could do nothing but stand by and watch.

'You don't have my strength, you're weak, you can't defeat me; you have nothing to fight for,' said Raven, angrily.

Tristan reached up and grabbed Raven's throat with both hands.

'I do have something to fight for,' said Tristan.

Tristan squeezed Raven's neck hard enough to almost make his head explode, and then forced his head backwards. Raven looked momentarily shocked at this surprising bout of strength from Tristan. Suddenly, Tristan pulled Raven's head towards his own and brought his left knee up hard into Raven's groin in one lightning quick movement, knocking him clean over his head and sending him skidding twenty feet across the marble hall, crashing into the far wall.

Raven jumped to his feet, angered that Tristan had temporarily overpowered him. He stood there looking like an agitated and angered bull about to charge a red rag. But instead, he turned and got to Angela in a fraction of a second and grabbed her by the hair with one hand, and neck with the other.

Tristan looked at Raven gripping Angela around the throat, and tried to figure out the best line of attack.

'Don't even think about it. I'll snap her neck like a twig before you get half way across the floor!' Raven was raging furious.

'Now, here's how it's going to be. You're taking up too much space in this city and there isn't enough room for us both anymore, so one of us has to go. And guess what, it's not going to be me; you're the one blabbing our secret all over the media. You just lost all your UK privileges, so now you've got two choices; get the fuck off this island and go back to Europe,' Raven demanded as Angela choked and struggled for breath under his tight grip.

'You said there were two choices,' said Tristan.

'You know the second choice … Aniguias reverso morvphius,' said Raven slowly, with a cold stern evil look on his face.

There was silence between them as Tristan contemplated what he had just heard. Tania was perplexed by what Raven's Latin phrase meant, while Angela was trying to fight for breath under the vice-like grip Raven had on her neck. Will was panicking as he watched his mother struggle, but there was nothing he could do.

After a brief pause, Tristan answered. 'I'm not going anywhere,' he replied adamantly.

'I was hoping you'd say that. Monday at midnight … you know where, history man,' said Raven, whilst Angela's face turned a shade of purple.

Raven released his grip on Angela's neck and pushed her across the hallway causing her to fall to the floor at Tania and Will's feet. She coughed and spluttered while trying to take in some large gulps of air. Will knelt down to help his mother, while Tania waited anxiously for the confrontation to come to an end.

Tristan calmly walked over to the door and opened it wide, as a gesture for Raven to leave. Raven sped twenty feet across the hallway to the door in less than a second, leaving a blurred trail as he did so; he stopped at the door and turned to Tristan, who was standing a few feet away.

'Until Monday night,' said Raven in his usual deep evil tone.

He vanished in a flash out of the door and across the grounds of Tristan's estate. Tristan calmly closed the door behind him and turned to look at the others.

'What the hell does *Aniguias reverso morvphius* mean?' said Tania.

'It's a sort of ritual for when two vampires can't agree on something.'

'What does it involve?' asked Will.

'It basically involves Raven and me meeting up at a secret historical location.'

'Where?' said Tania.

'I can't say. I don't want you to get involved with this.

In fact I want you to be as far away from it all as possible.'

'Today's Friday, why does Raven want to wait until Monday?' said Tania.

'There's always a three day grace period after the proposition ... three's the magic number right?' joked Tristan.

'Are you serious?' said Tania.

'It's just the way it's always been, it dates back a very long time.'

'What if he comes back over the weekend?' said Angela.

'He won't,' said Tristan, adamant.

'How do you know for sure,' asked Tania.

'There isn't much that Raven respects, but he does respect this particular law as it's one of the fundamentals of vampirism. Trust me; he won't do anything until Monday night. Between now and then he'll be too busy planning how he's going to kill me.'

'Well, that's not very reassuring?' said Tania, sounding panicked and upset.

'What are you going to do?' said Angela.

'Right now, I'm not entirely sure.'

'Do you have to go?' said Will.

'Yes, otherwise I'll have to go back to Europe and never return to England again.'

'Well what happens at this ritual?' asked Angela.

'The two of us will go in, and only one will come out ... that's about the crux of it.'

'You mean you'll fight to the death?' said Will.

'Something like that.'

'But one of you will die!!' said Tania.

'Yes.'

Everyone stood silently, reflecting on the gravity of the situation. Tania was not happy about it at all. Just as she was falling in love, the object of her affections might be taken away from her.

Chapter 19

Knowing that Raven wasn't going to return to the house that weekend, Tristan decided that the security of the panic rooms was not needed, so he allocated some of the spare bedrooms upstairs to Angela and Will. While his new guests familiarised themselves with their temporary living quarters, Tristan went downstairs to the living room where they shortly joined him. It was 1:30am, but Tania, Angela and Will were far from sleepy considering the evening's events. They were deeply concerned and there were too many questions that needed answering and a plan of action needed to be worked out – and fast.

'Is Raven really stronger than you … could you beat him? How do you know he's stronger than you?' said Will.

'We can just sense it. We don't fear anything, but we have a survival instinct that tells us when another vampire is stronger. I've looked into Raven's history; I know he was born in Russia in the late sixteenth century, and became a vampire when he was thirty-eight. Soon after that, he moved around Western Europe for quite a while. He only came to live in England in 1930.

'When he was turned into a vampire back in Russia, it

was via a vampire who came from a pure line background. Although Raven's only been a vampire for a short time, compared with me, he's a lot stronger for several reasons. First, when I was transformed, I already had wolf DNA in my blood from when they attacked me. Because of this, I'm not a pure vampire; I still have a tiny amount of both human and wolf DNA. Although I consider my remaining human and wolf DNA an advantage, they are a weakness against pure vampires. Raven is one hundred per cent vampire, a pure bred.'

'How did you find all this out?' said Tania.

'I called in a favour.'

'From who?' said Tania.

'Another vampire.'

'How many vampires are there?' said Will.

'In Great Britain? Fifteen to twenty that I'm aware of, but nobody really knows for sure.'

'Who is this other vampire you called in the favour from?' said Tania.

'Someone just like me, living a relatively solitary life and keeping a low profile.'

'Have you met this vampire before?' said Tania.

'No. When I had to go out and leave you the other night, that was the first time we'd met.'

'How did you manage to track another vampire down?'

'We're quite resourceful; a vampire can't find another vampire that easily. However, a vampire can be found by another vampire if they actually want to be.'

'I don't understand. How does that work?'

'Okay, imagine if London had a fifty foot high wall all

around it and there was no way in or out, and you and twenty other people lived there, but you all lived alone and none of you had any idea where the others lived. How would you attract attention and get one of them to come and seek you out?'

'I don't know, I'd probably find the tallest building I could and set fire to it, then wait for someone to show up.'

'Exactly, well, a vampire would start a telepathic fire, send out the signal, and then wait for another vampire to show up. It's like a telepathic beacon that we all have.'

'And that works?' said Tania.

'Yes.'

'How long did you have to wait, after sending out this signal?' said Will.

'Not long; about forty minutes, this particular vampire was local, she lives in London.

'She!' said Tania, sounding like a jealous girlfriend.

'Yes, not all vampires are male.'

'Of course, I knew that,' said Tania matter-of-factly, 'so how did this female vampire know so much about Raven?'

'When she first arrived in London, she sent out a signal for other vampires and he showed up. She was with him for a few years after that.'

'What, like dating?' said Tania.

'Yes, I guess so.'

'Okay, can we get back to subject of dealing with Raven now?' said Tania, not wanting to hear any more about Tristan's late night encounter with a female vampire.

'It's late; you should all get some rest. I have some things I need to do,' Tristan said, tired of the questions.

He got up from the sofa and headed for the door. Tania hated not knowing where he was going, but didn't feel that she could really ask. Although Tristan's duel with Raven was only a few short days away, she didn't want to come across like a sad controlling girlfriend. After all, she had no right as they were not in a relationship and they hadn't even kissed. Tristan paused at the living room door and turned to them.

'Good night,' he said, in a neutral nondescript tone.

Nobody really knew what to say and there was an uncomfortable silence mixed with a feeling of anxiety in the room.

The next morning was even worse as Tristan had returned in the early hours and had locked himself away out of sight and away from light in his secure basement room. Tania, Angela and Will spent Saturday morning discussing the imminent ritual between Tristan and Raven, but they were clearly out of their depth when trying to find a solution for Tristan. They were all incredibly frustrated, this was no ordinary problem. It definitely wasn't one of those *helping a friend move a sofa* sort of problems. How were three mere mortals supposed to figure out how to get rid of one unwanted vampire to save another?

The entire nightmare revolved around Raven. All they had to do to end the nightmare, was eliminate the problem – Raven Xavier, and this would almost certainly mean killing him – but in practice, the task was going to be near impossible.

The hours were ticking away at a frustratingly fast pace and they still didn't have a plan of action. The rest of

Saturday flew by, and night-time had arrived before Tania barely had time to think.

Tristan appeared from the basement, but not long enough for Tania, Angela or Will to see him; he simply came up from his safe room, disappeared out the door and drove off. All Tania heard was his car screeching off the gravel drive outside. She didn't know what she hated more, him just leaving like that at the speed of light without even saying good evening or goodbye, or wondering if he was off out to put out another vampire beacon signal, or worse still, go to feed off one of his sexy willing female harem.

She had to check herself. Tristan wasn't her boyfriend and this was no ordinary situation. She had fantasised about life with Tristan, getting married etc. But she knew that even if she did end up with him, and she desperately wanted to, it would be no ordinary relationship. He could hardly make romantic gestures like bringing her breakfast in bed with a rose, drawing the curtains and saying, *"Honey, it's a beautiful day outside, we should go for a walk in the park."* No, that would never happen. The only time they would be able to go shopping together would be in the wintertime when it got dark at three in the afternoon. The list was endless, but in truth, she didn't care. She had fallen in love with this mysterious man in a way she never knew was possible and if it came down to it, she would change her body clock and work at night and sleep during the day so she could be with him.

Tania left her bedroom door open and hardly slept a wink that night as she listened out for Tristan's return. She didn't hear him come back, perhaps because she fell asleep at about 3am. The next morning she wondered if he was resting in his panic room. It was totally frustrating, waiting again, waiting until nightfall for Tristan to re-appear.

Later that evening, Tania, Angela and Will were in the living room when they heard the front door open. A strange man entered the living room, which immediately put Tania on edge.

'Good evening Angela ... Will,' said the stranger, in a very familiar and polite voice.

He was tall and slender and wore a midnight blue suit with a black shirt with the top two buttons undone. He had light mousy brown hair and an impeccably shaped pencil moustache. Although he was 72, he didn't look a day over 55 years old, and was fit as a fiddle.

'You must be Tania. Please, don't be alarmed. I'm a good friend of Tristan,' he said. Just then, Tristan walked in.

'Ah, Michael, I sensed you were back ... how was Russia?' said Tristan, looking at the wooden case that Michael was holding.

'Successful ... mission accomplished.'

'Good,' said Tristan, sounding very satisfied, 'Tania, let me introduce you to my very good friend, Michael. Michael knows all about you and I brought him up to speed on the phone this morning regarding Raven's recent activities.'

'You must be the Michael I've read about in Tristan's story?' said Tania.

'The very same,' said Michael.

'I've known Michael for over forty years now and he's the closest thing to family I have,' said Tristan. 'He lives here in the house and takes care of things for me.'

Tania stood up and went over to shake Michael's hand.

'It's a privilege to meet you. I feel like I already know you,' said Tania. She then stepped back and stood next to Tristan, making herself comfortable with her shoulder touching his. This caused Michael to give Tristan a questioning and concerned look.

'May I,' said Tristan, gesturing for Michael to hand over the wooden case he was holding.

'Of course,' said Michael, lifting the case to chest height with both arms, inviting Tristan to open it.

Tristan stepped forward and flicked the two catches open and slowly lifted the lid to reveal four rather old looking wooden crossbow bolts with metal pointed arrowheads on them. Angela and Will remained seated and were polite enough not to jump up to try and catch a glimpse of what was inside the case.

'Excellent!' said Tristan, gently closing the case.

'What are they for?' said Tania.

'I'm going to use one of them to kill Raven,' said Tristan. 'Well, Michael is actually.'

'You're going to kill him with a crossbow? ... Why a crossbow, surely there's an easier way?'

'Cool,' said Will from the couch.

Angela gave Will a firm parental slap on the knee, suggesting this was no time for witty remarks.

'Well, how would you suggest we kill him? He's a lot stronger than me and there aren't many things that can actually kill him.'

'And an arrow shot from a crossbow will?' said Tania.

'Yeah, it's like a wooden stake through the heart,' said

Will, excitedly, which warranted another *look* from his mother.

'Well the old *stake through the heart* routine doesn't really work, at least not with Raven, but I'm hoping this one will.'

'But how can it, you just said a stake through the heart won't work with Raven,' said Tania.

'That's right, but there's an exception to this rule, an exception I'm rather hoping Raven either doesn't know about, has overlooked, or has long since forgotten about.'

'Do you want to share this information with us?' said Tania.

'Okay. Like me, he can't be killed with silver bullets, a stake, or any of that other mythological stuff. Daylight will kill him, but as this is taking place at midnight, that's not going to help us much, besides, the daylight would kill me too. Also, holy water and crucifixes have no effect on him. In fact, he can bath in holy water and use garlic cloves for bath salts and nothing would happen to him. Now, although a regular wooden stake through the heart won't kill him, an older stake or pointed wooden object that was made *before* he became a vampire will. But, it must have been made in the same region that he was born as a human, by a craftsman in that region and before he became a vampire ... does that make sense?' said Tristan.

'Erm ... I think so,' said Tania, thinking through what she had just heard.

'The crossbow bolts that Michael kindly brought back from Russia today were made by an Artillator in Moscow in the fifteenth century, before Raven was born.'

'What's an Artillator?' asked Will.

'An Artillator is a person who makes bows, arrows and

other archery devices,' said Michael, sounding like a school lecturer.

'Raven was born in Moscow?' said Will.

'That's correct,' said Tristan.

'And how did you come by these bolts?' asked Tania.

'They were stolen from a historical museum in Moscow,' said Michael.

'You stole them!' said Tania, sounding shocked and surprised.

'Oh heavens, no!' said Michael. 'I'm too old for running around playing cat burglars. I paid a professional over there to break into the museum and steal them for me. I simply went over to Russia to collect them and pay the man for his skills.'

'And one of these antique arrows can kill Raven?' said Tania.

'I'm hoping so, yes,' said Tristan, 'but it has to be fired straight through his heart, and that's going to be tricky.'

'Okay, now I'm more confused than ever,' said Tania. 'You're just going to show up tomorrow night at this secret location and shoot Raven through the heart using a crossbow?'

'Not exactly, I can't do that. It's against the rules.'

'What, you mean these things have rules and are actually governed?'

'It's like a vampire code of practice, and it's a code that all vampires respect.'

Tania gave Tristan a perplexed look.

'All vampires except Raven, right?' said Tania.

'Raven respects the code of practice; most of it anyway.

But he's always been rebellious and reckless throughout his entire life. I can assure you that Raven isn't going to turn up tomorrow night to play fair. It won't be a level playing field and he's going to bring every dirty trick to the party that he can think of.'

'I don't get it. You're not allowed to shoot him with the crossbow?' said Tania.

'That's correct. No weapons can be used by either of us. But if a vampire breaks the code, he can be killed using any means necessary, weapons included. But I won't be able to just turn up holding a crossbow, as that would show my intention to break the code from the word go. And Raven knows this, so he won't be showing up with anything either, at least nothing that I'll be able to see.'

'So how are you going to play it?' said Tania.

'I'm going to be there,' said Michael.

Tania turned to him, surprised that Michael would be capable of using such a weapon, let alone killing a man, well, a vampire.

'Don't look so surprised, my dear. I practiced archery with a local club right up until last year. A few of the other archers at the club had crossbows. I was fascinated, so I decided to get one. I got pretty good at it too.'

'You can use a crossbow?' said Tania, surprised.

'Yes, and it's even easier to use and aim than my old longbow, especially at my age,' said Michael.

'Do you still have this crossbow?' said Tania.

'No, but I will have. After doing a little research and getting some advice from a nice gentleman at a dealer in Yorkshire, I ordered a new one online from my laptop while

I was waiting in the airport lounge for my flight out to Russia. It's a rather splendid model too, with a lightweight composite plastic body and fibreglass bow, complete with an optimiser speed dial and scope – and all for under £600. Mind you, I had to spend an extra £1,400 on a full night vision aiming scope, but it'll be well worth it,' said Michael, proudly.

'You're cutting it a little fine aren't you … I mean, all this is taking place tomorrow night,' said Tania, sounding quite anxious.

'Oh don't worry. I'll have the whole day to practise and get back up to standard. It's just like riding a bike, once you learn, you never forget.'

'This is crazy,' said Tania, looking at Tristan concerned.

'Well, we don't have that many options open to us,' said Tristan.

Michael turned to Tristan and looked at him seriously.

'I'm going to make a much deserved cup of tea … Tristan, I need to speak with you privately for a moment … please excuse us,' said Michael, leading the way to the kitchen.

'She likes you, Tristan,' said Michael.

'Yes, I'm aware of that,' said Tristan.

'Come on, Tristan. I've known you a long time. You know what I mean … it's clear that the girl has feelings for you,' said Michael as he filled the kettle with water.

'I'm aware of that too.'

Michael gave Tristan a questioning look while raising his eyebrows.

'Don't give me that look; nothing's happened,' said Tristan.

'I'm just trying to protect you, Tristan. You know what

will happen, the same as what always happens.'

'I know,' said Tristan, deep in thought.

There was a momentary silence as Michael poured his cup of tea. He turned to see Tristan staring down at his hands, deep in thought.

'Oh, no! You like her, don't you?' said Michael.

Tristan looked up sheepishly at Michael and said nothing.

'I hope you know what you're doing, Tristan, I don't want you to get hurt again,' said Michael, sounding apprehensive.

'Let's just stay focused on tomorrow night and Raven, shall we?' said Tristan.

'You're right, that's a much more pressing matter. Well, I'm going to take my cup of tea upstairs and get my beauty sleep. I'm going to need all the strength I can get for tomorrow.'

'Goodnight, Michael ... and thank you,' said Tristan, sincerely.

Chapter 20

The next morning Tania woke up and looked at the clock, which read 9:40am.

'Oh god, how did that happen?' she groaned, still half asleep.

She was surprised to wake up so late, but she hadn't slept much the previous night so her body had some catching up to do. She dragged herself out of bed, put her robe on, went over to the window and parted the drapes slightly. As she looked through the chink, she saw Michael outside in the grounds away in the distance, shooting at what looked like a life-size mannequin with his new crossbow. He was lying flat on the grass like a combat soldier. Will was standing behind him, watching. The mannequin was clothed in black trousers and a black overcoat. It was just as well that this was private land that could not be seen from the main road otherwise it would have looked pretty damn spooky to passers-by.

Tania was surprised at how far Michael was from the target. It looked like he was a good seventy metres away. She was even more surprised at his shooting skills and accuracy, going by the two bolts already stuck in the mannequin's chest. She stood there and watched Michael shoot another bolt, hitting the tall, black plastic figure straight in the chest again just inches from the first two. He re-cocked the crossbow and loaded another bolt, took aim and fired; another direct hit straight into the mannequin's chest.

'Wow, you're pretty good!' she whispered to herself, as she watched him get up and walk over to the mannequin to retrieve his wooden bolts.

Tania took a shower, got dressed and went downstairs to make herself a *wake up* coffee. Angela was in the kitchen when she got there. She was sitting at the kitchen table in a daze, with her head in her hands, staring at the cup of coffee in front of her.

'Good morning,' said Tania in a soft tone desperately trying not to jolt Angela out of the place she was in.

She slowly looked up at Tania. Her eyes were red, she had obviously been crying.

'Oh, sorry, I didn't notice you come in,' said Angela.

Tania went over and put her arm around her shoulder in an attempt to comfort her. As she did so, Angela hugged her tight and sobbed into her blouse. Tania stroked her hair and held her for a minute. Angela slowly pulled back and wiped her watery red eyes.

'It's going to be okay,' said Tania in a reassuring tone.

Angela turned and reached for her coffee.

'There's a fresh pot on the side if you want a cup,' said Angela.

She made no attempt to sound cheerful. Tania gave Angela's shoulder a gentle squeeze before getting herself a coffee.

'Are you alone this morning?' she said, hoping Angela

might have seen or heard from Tristan during the early hours.

'Yes. Michael's outside on the grounds practicing with his crossbow, and Will's out there with him.'

'Yes, I noticed them out of the bedroom window.'

Tania pulled up a chair at the kitchen table and sat with Angela. She noticed a copy of The Sentinel newspaper open on her column page. Angela had obviously been reading it.

'I read your column this morning. It's quite interesting seeing Tristan's entire life story condensed down into such a short abridged format,' said Angela.

'Have you read the complete unabridged version?' asked Tania.

'No, I'm assuming you have, being the journalist he chose to contact?'

'Kind of, he sent me the entire thing, only I felt the final section left some unanswered questions.'

'How do you mean?' asked Angela.

'I'm not sure, but I think there's something he's not mentioning, not yet anyway. I don't know. I can't quite put my finger on it; just a feeling I have.'

'Well, I wouldn't worry too much. I'm sure if there is anything else to his story, it will all come out in good time.'

'I guess so,' said Tania, pondering.

'It's an incredible story, but the column couldn't possibly accommodate all 81,000 words of it, so I had to cherry pick the most relevant parts and seriously edit them down, which was a really hard thing to do. The readers are only really getting a very small snippet of his story.'

'Oh, I know that. I still think it's a real shame. Perhaps one day the entire thing could be published as a book, an autobiography maybe?' said Angela.

'Perhaps. I'm just going outside to speak with Michael for a minute, will you be okay?'

'Sure. Would you be kind enough to ask Will to come inside now? I don't want him getting in Michael's way.'

'Of course, and look, if there's anything I can do to help, I'm here,' said Tania sincerely.

'Thanks, I appreciate that.'

Tania grabbed her coffee and went outside.

EMAIL FROM A VAMPIRE – Part 7
By Tania de Pré

Continued from Friday, in the vampire's own words.

The early 1980s arrived and the world had gone technology mad. VCRs, CD players, computers, games consoles and all kinds of other weird and wonderful electronic gadgets were springing up all over the place. Everything appeared to be great and very exciting in the so-called western civilised world. Like everybody else, I embraced our new technological world and tried to keep up with the times, something I'd had a lot of practice at.

All this new technology was working in my favour and it certainly made my life a whole lot easier as a vampire. Over the centuries, I'd had many faithful and trusted friends whom I could rely on to keep my secret from the world and now was no different.

My loyal friend, Michael, is a huge fan of technology and pretty streetwise too. Michael was 30 years old when we became friends in 1970. I met him through my last partner, Elizabeth. She had known him for six years and trusted him enough to introduce him to me and let him in on our secret. After Elizabeth died, Michael was amazing; he stepped in and helped me, as he knew I needed a "day friend" to make my life easier. He dealt with certain day-to-day things such as modernising the security at my house and dealing with certain officials as more and more red tape was introduced into the system of the modern world.

If emergencies came up, I could even get around during daylight hours if needed. I'd bought a couple of cars; one of which was an Audi S8. Michael arranged to have the rear windows blacked out with a special one-way lightproof film that protected me from the daylight. He'd also had a black screen fitted between the front and rear cabin inside the car, like those found in limousines. It was great as I could see through the windows during the day, even though the lightproof film made the view a little dark. However, it was rare that I went out in the car with Michael during the day, it was strictly for emergencies. Although I was protected from the light, and the central locking system gave me some security and prevented people from opening the doors from the outside, I always feared being involved in a traffic accident, or being stopped routinely by the police. But, for emergencies, I at least had the choice. After dark I would drive myself around in my own car, an Audi RS 5 Coupe.

Then the millennium arrived. It was the year 2000 and I found myself in the 21st century, and when that happened, I had an icy cold realisation that sent a shiver down my spine. It was like somebody had walked over my grave. I realised that in just eleven years' time it would be my 1000th anniversary as a vampire. Come 2011, I would have been around for a total of 1033 years and would have been a vampire for 1000 of those.

It was a very scary thought, a thought that filled me with horror.

However, the internet had arrived and home computers were becoming more and more advanced by the month. The internet helped me enormously. I could order certain products online and carry out other duties without ever having to leave the house. It had so many great advantages and it was a total lifesaver for me.

Michael was still my faithful companion and although he was now 60 years old, he was as fit as a fiddle, though on a few occasions I did have to give him some of my blood as a health booster to regenerate and eliminate a few ailments that came up from time to time. When a human drinks my blood, it acts like a kind of super-steroid, only without the side effects, and it's more permanent. My blood has massive healing properties for humans and it also makes them immune to diseases and everyday coughs and colds. It's like a super-human intravenous immunoglobulin, but one that lasts a lifetime and never wears off.

Over the years I've saved many people's lives this way. I was able to save people who were dying from a terminal disease, or who had been in a major accident leaving them in a critical condition in hospital. Once I even brought a woman out of a coma. In most cases, these people had no idea that I had saved their lives. Often doctors were totally perplexed as to how their patients suddenly made a miraculous recovery. A few of these patients' stories were published in national newspapers with the word "Miracle" in the headline.

I started doing this on a small scale to relieve the boredom of my life some nights. Sometimes it was easy, and sometimes it was a bit more challenging. My coma patient for example was easy, as she had no idea that I was there or what happened. I simply went into the hospital at 3am undetected and using a portable intravenous kit, I administered 50 millilitres of my blood directly into her vein. It didn't take much of my blood to complete the regeneration process of her entire body, covering every single cell. Sometimes, depending on the severity of the disease, or accident, just a few teaspoons full of my blood taken orally would suffice.

On other occasions where the patient was awake, I would hypnotise them first, so they were still capable of swallowing a small amount of my blood, but without really knowing what was going on. Of course, I could only do these duties after twilight when it was dark.

I'd acquired a doctor's coat from one of my nurse friends and Michael had a fake hospital ID made for me via one of his contacts. The fake ID was a bit tricky, but if you have the money, you can buy pretty much anything. I didn't feel bad about having to go down this illegal route as I was doing it for a good reason, to save people's lives. I could hardly walk into a hospital and offer my services in an honest way through the proper channels.

Of course these days hospital security is a lot tighter, so saving people's lives is not without its problems. I don't believe in playing god on a mass scale, so I don't spend my entire life running around hospitals trying to speed-save as many people as possible. I simply reserve my healing powers for people I know and their immediate family and friends; that's just the way it had to be.

I don't know a lot of people and I only have a few very close friends. Over the centuries I have had to keep it that way. But once, back in the 19th century, I slipped up. I wanted to test the water, so I rented a small house temporarily in London's Whitechapel area, which was a good twenty miles from where my main house was on the north-west outskirts of London. Back then, that was a good enough distance away, so if my plan did not work I could return home and never be seen again.

It was a very big mistake, and one that I would never make again. It was the year 1888 in the East End of London. Capital cities have always had an exciting nightlife, and back then was no different. Over a very short period of time I built up a lot of friends in London's East End and even got to know a lot of their families; only in the evening, of course. Then, late one evening, on August 14th 1888, the younger sister of one of my new friends was stabbed in a vicious attack in London's Whitechapel area.

The attack took place just two streets from where she lived. She was stabbed nineteen times in her abdomen. We heard some commotion outside and people running down the street shouting. My friend and I went outside and headed around the corner to where it was all going on. When we got there, she was almost dead. Due to the multiple stab wounds her intestines, liver and stomach were all severely damaged and she had lost a lot of blood. Everyone thought it was another attack by Jack the Ripper, as only a week earlier in the same district another woman was stabbed 39 times.

My friend was inconsolable as he and a small crowd stood there watching her die. I had a serious dilemma. I knew I could save her life, but by doing so, several onlookers would witness the event. But I had no choice; I could not let my friend's younger sister die right there on the pavement in front of his very eyes in a pool of her own blood.

Her breathing was slowing and she was going into shock. I could see that she had just minutes left to live, if that. I needed to get my blood into her system while she still had a pulse strong enough to carry it around her body. I pushed my way through the onlookers and told them that I was a doctor. I bit my wrist, severing a main artery. I then lifted her head off the cobbled pavement, put my wrist against her mouth, and told her to drink. I told her that if she drank she would live. She struggled to drink, coughing and choking as my blood gushed from my wrist down her throat.

Back then, things were a little more primitive than they are today, and the common folk that had gathered around had no reason to question my technique for trying to save her life. After all, bloodletting continued to be in practice right up until the early 1900s, so I suppose some of these simple folk might have considered this some sort of reverse version of the bloodletting technique. Besides, nobody else had anything better to offer, and so they let me go about my task, making her drink the blood from my wrist.

After a few minutes, she stopped drinking; her brother put his coat on the ground and I gently laid her head back down onto it. Within a few minutes her breathing returned to normal and she appeared to be much more comfortable. Colour started to come back to her cheeks right in front of our eyes. The bleeding from her abdomen stopped and the multiple stab wounds closed up and healed. All this happened in less than four minutes, witnessed by several onlookers. She got to her feet as if the attack had never taken place with no physical signs that she had been stabbed.

Of course, after this the word got around that I could perform miracles. The locals had mixed feelings about me. Some thought I was some kind of saint who could heal the sick, while others thought I was the devil straight from hell. Sick and injured people were constantly trying to seek me out to ask me to heal them, while others put together a lynch mob and went on a witch-hunt for me. Either way, I could not stay and I did not return to the Whitechapel district of London for many years. After that, I vowed I would never publicly help anyone again, or let my powers be known.

Continued tomorrow.

***

Tania couldn't just sit back and do nothing, so she got on the phone to DI Maldini and brought him up to speed with the latest developments. She gave him every piece of information she had in the hope that there might be something he could do. Then she sat back and waited.

The rest of the day seemed to go by in a flash. Whenever Tania looked at her watch, it was as if the hour hand was being sucked towards the twelve position via some unknown force. She was on edge and incredibly anxious. The sun had gone down and it was now twilight. Tania just wanted Tristan to emerge from his resting place in the basement.

She opened the drapes in the living room and paced up and down looking out of the window at the darkening sky. She kept looking at her watch and glancing towards the doors that lead to the basement for any sign of Tristan. She was frantic with nervous energy in abundance, and the fact that it was Monday 18th June with the first day of summer only a few days away meant that twilight didn't kick in until just after half past nine. She realised that it must be an incredibly horrible and frustrating time of year for Tristan, with the very long days.

As she turned, deep in thought, to pace back across the living room floor from the window she jumped with shock. She had not noticed Will enter the living room.

'Will, you startled me,' she said, holding her chest and catching her breath.

'I'm sorry. I'm not your typical noisy teenager, I tend to creep around,' he said, apologetically.

'Well, can you try and creep around a little louder, please,' she joked. 'Have you seen Tristan this evening?'

'No, but I imagine he'll make his presence known soon enough, it's dark outside now,' he said, looking towards the window.

'Where's your mother.'

'She's been out most of the afternoon, sorting stuff out to do with the house, or rather lack of house ... there's not much left of it.'

'I'm sorry,' said Tania.

She felt pretty stupid saying that. Somehow, sorry, just didn't seem to do it. What are you supposed to say to console somebody whose house and belongings had just burned to the ground?

'Thanks ... I'm sure we'll be okay,' said Will, putting on a brave face.

'You're going to be just fine young William,' said Tristan, who suddenly appeared at the doorway to the living room as if by magic. Relief washed over Tania in an awesome way.

'Oh,' said Will, turning around, 'good evening, Mr Burnel.'

'Good evening, Will. I'd like to speak with you, if you

have a moment,' said Tristan.

'Er, yes, sure,' he said, surprised that Mr Burnel would want to speak to him.

'Tania, would you mind leaving Will and me alone for a moment?'

'Oh, certainly, I'll go and make myself a drink in the kitchen,' she said, feeling a little thrown out.

'Thank you, I'll come and find you in a few minutes.'

Tristan closed the living room door behind Tania.

'Will, sit down and make yourself comfortable; there's something I need to tell you.'

'Okay,' said Will, sitting down on one of the sofas. Tristan sat on the other sofa facing him.

'It's about your father.'

'My father?' said Will, surprised.

'Yes … you're aware that he died when you were just two years old.'

'Yes, my mum told me the whole story. You saved my life. You prevented me from being dropped over the balcony.'

'That's right, Will. But there's a little bit more to that story that you don't know about. Did your mother ever tell you how your father actually died?'

'Well, no, not really, based on what she did tell me, I figured he fell over the balcony when he was drunk.'

'Well, that's the part of the story that isn't strictly accurate. Of course, he was drunk and he did fall over the balcony and he did land on the concrete four floors below … but with a little help from me.'

'I don't understand,' said Will, confused.

'I threw him over the balcony, Will. Do you understand

what I'm telling you? It wasn't an accident … I killed your father.'

'What!!' said Will, shocked and trying to come to terms with the idea. 'No … it can't be … you … you murdered …' he got up and made hastily for the living room door.

Tristan stood up. 'Will, wait!'

'Stay away from me!' shouted Will, as he ran across the hallway towards the front door.

Before he got to it, the door opened and his mother walked in. Will ran straight past her and out into the night.

'Will,' she shouted after him.

Angela turned to Tristan, who stood by the living room door, silent.

'What happened?' she asked.

'I told him … I had to tell him the truth.'

'The truth about what?' Then it dawned on her that he must have told Will about how his father really died.

'Oh my god,' she breathed, putting her hand to her mouth.

'Shall I go after him?' said Tristan.

Angela just shook her head no, while pondering for a few seconds.

'I'm assuming by his speedy exit, that it didn't go down too well?' she said.

'No, I'm afraid not.'

'I'll go and find him.'

'Do you need my help?'

'No, I know where he'll be.'

'You do?'

'Yes, whenever he's had trouble at school or is unhappy about something he goes and sits at the base of a tree in the bluebells just off the driveway. It relaxes him and gives him a chance to be with his thoughts.'

'I see.'

'He'll be okay, Tristan. He always has a knee jerk reaction to bad news. He'll come around, I promise,' she said, trying to reassure Tristan; she could see that he was upset.

'I hope so,' Tristan said, in a soft sincere tone, now wondering if telling Will was the right thing to do.

But he felt that he had to clear his conscience in case he died at Raven's hands. Tristan closed the front door behind Angela and went to the kitchen to see Tania.

'Sorry for keeping you waiting. How are you feeling?'

'I'm freaking out, that's how I'm feeling. It'll be midnight in just over two hours and I have absolutely no idea what's going on. I don't know where you're going or if you'll even be coming back at all! What if you die, what if I never see you again!' she said, frantically.

Tristan walked over to Tania and cradled her face in his hands and looked purposefully into her eyes.

'Tania, I need you to trust me. I have to do this,' he said, softly.

'But I need to ...'

Tristan cut her sentence short by planting a very firm kiss on her lips. He held this position with his lips pressed closed and hard against hers for about ten seconds, and then very slowly he released the pressure to the point that their lips were just faintly touching.

For a minute, Tania totally lost herself and parted her lips slightly then started to caress the crease between his lips with her tongue while trying to encourage a small opening between them. Tristan parted his lips slightly to allow her to gently venture into his mouth with the tip of her tongue. He reciprocated and their tongues proceeded to do a slow sensual intimate dance. Tania felt her muscles clench in the most delicious way deep down below. She ran her fingers through his hair on the back of his head, while involuntarily lifting her right foot slightly off the floor behind her. She was somewhere else; she had left this planet and was now floating on some heavenly cloud somewhere.

But then she was brought crashing back down to earth with a jolt. She couldn't feel Tristan anymore; no tongue, no hair, no body – in an instant it had all gone as Tristan had stopped kissing her. She opened her eyes. Tristan was standing there looking deep into her eyes; she looked back into his and started to feel herself instantly slip into a deep dreamy state.

Her eyes slowly closed and she felt her legs buckle beneath her. As she collapsed, Tristan caught her before she hit the floor and gently laid her down.

'I'm sorry I have to do this to you … forgive me,' he whispered in her ear.

He vanished at lightning speed. Before one second had passed, he was out of the front door. He started up his car and screeched down the drive. He was gone.

***

'Tania, wake up, wake up!' said a faint distant voice, 'wake up, Tania, wake up!' The voice got louder. 'Tania, wake up!' much louder now.

Then the sound and pain from the slap on her face brought her round. Her eyes opened and she saw Detective Maldini and Angela looking down at her. She sat bolt upright on the kitchen floor and noticed Tristan was not there.

'Tristan!!!' she screamed.

Chapter 21

Tania jumped to her feet in a state of anxiety and panic.

'Tania, he's not here, but I think I know where he's heading, but we've got to go right now!' said Maldini.

'Wait, how did you find me, how did you get in?' said Tania, still in a half-hypnotised state.

'I tracked your mobile phone position when you called me earlier. Now come on, we've got to go right now.'

'Of course you did. Do you know where Tristan is?' said Tania.

'I think so, yes, but we must go, now!' he commanded.

He looked at his watch, grabbed her arm and proceeded to drag her out of the house with Angela in hot pursuit right behind them.

'Wait, how did you get through the main gate and into the house?'

'I'm a police detective, getting into places that are designed to keep people out is part of my job. The electronic gate didn't pose much of a problem for me. Now get in!' he said, opening the car door.

'But how did you get in the house and into the kitchen?'

'I let him in,' said Angela, 'Will and I were just about to

let ourselves back into the house when the detective pulled up in his car.'

'Where's Will now?' said Tania.

'Tania, we've got to go!' said Maldini, looking at his watch and getting more anxious.

'Go! I'll stay here and look for Will,' said Angela.

Tania got into Detective Maldini's police car, a Volvo V70 estate, complete with police Battenberg pattern down the sides and blue and white lights on the roof.

'Belt up,' he said, as he started the engine and wheel-spun off the gravel to speed down the winding driveway to the main gate.

'Well, this is hardly subtle,' said Tania, commenting on the brightly coloured police car.

'Trust me, we're going to need this,' he said, as he hit the blues-and-twos switch on the dashboard.

Suddenly Tania's head was forced back into the headrest as Maldini floored it and accelerated like a Saturn rocket. The sirens wailed and the blue lights flashed. Within minutes they were on the M1 motorway heading north at well over a hundred miles per hour.

'Sorry about the speed, but we need to move fast, it's gone 10pm and we have to cover 120 miles to get there before midnight, and we still need time to find the exact spot when we arrive!'

'Arrive where? Where are we going?' said Tania.

'Nottinghamshire … Sherwood Forest to be exact.'

'What! As in Robin Hood, Sherwood Forest?'

'That's the one.'

'Tristan and Raven are meeting at Sherwood Forest? I

don't understand, it doesn't sound very symbolic,' she said, bewildered at the strange choice of location for a ritual showdown.

'Well, it might just be a little more symbolic than you think.'

'How's that?' she asked.

'There's a place in the middle of the forest called Thynghowe. It sits amidst the old oaks of an area known as the Birklands. Historically, this area in the forest functioned as a place where people came to resolve disputes and to settle issues.'

'How do you know all this?'

'I'm a police detective, remember? Oh, and Google helped me a little,' he joked.

Tania was in no mood for jokes, and she let it be known via the stony expression on her face.

'But how do you know for sure that's where Tristan and Raven are going to be?'

'I've spent the whole day on this, I made a lot of phone calls, spoke to a lot of people and I dug deep, very deep ... remember the After Dark club?'

'Yes, of course, the place where Raven killed those people.'

'Well, one of the human vampire members was convinced that a real vampire showed up there a few years ago. She said she sat and talked to him for the best part of the evening.'

'And she told you all this Sherwood Forest stuff?' she said, in disbelief.

'Yes, she told me that this vampire had told her about a place where real vampires meet to fight to the death if they can't agree on something or have a disagreement.'

'And you believed her?'

'Look, she told me some things that rang true. Tristan saved my life by giving me his blood and I'll never forget the feeling it gave me for as long as I live. This woman told me that she begged the vampire to allow her to drink a little of his blood, out of curiosity. He made a tiny nick in the tip of his finger. She explained the feeling it gave her ... the feelings were exactly the same as the ones I felt when I drank Tristan's blood. There's no way on earth she would have been able to describe how that felt it if it wasn't true.'

'Did she tell you anything else?'

'Yes. She thinks there're about twenty real vampires in England, and according to the vampire she spoke with that evening, only once before have two vampires met at this location to resolve their differences.'

'When, and what was it about.'

'It was in the sixties, two female vampires fighting for the sole right to a male vampire.'

Tania slid into a short girly daydream fantasy about Tristan fighting Raven over the right to be with her.

'Look, I don't know what to expect when we get there, or how this is going to pan out. It's 120 miles away and, even at this speed, we'll only just get there for midnight. According to Megan...' Tania interrupted him.

'Wait, Megan?'

'The girl from the After Dark club,' said Maldini.

'Okay, continue,' she said, shaking her head.

'According to Megan, the two vampires involved in the dispute can't use any weapons to kill each other, just their hands and other physical and mental psychic powers. They can enter the location from anywhere, north, south, east, or west, then set about tracking the other down ... kind of a hunt to the death, like in the movie *The Hunger Games* ... but ...'

'But what?'

'Megan told me that the vampire mentioned Raven in passing. She said she could never forget a name like Raven Xavier.'

'What did she say about him?'

'That he was evil and the one thing we could be certain of is that he would play dirty.'

'Oh great!' she sighed. 'So, what are we going to do?'

'I'm not sure. I got a rifle and two handguns from the police armoury, for what good they'll do. They're on the back seat in that long holdall.'

Tania looked over her shoulder.

'What are those strange binocular looking things?'

'Night vision glasses. Tonight's a new moon, meaning there isn't one, it's going to be virtually pitch black in the forest.'

'Do you have some for me?'

'Yes, there are two pairs on the back seat, as well as a spare pair in the boot.'

'Shouldn't we have more police backup?' she said.

'We should, but we don't. I wasn't about to go to the superintendent and ask for a back up team for a showdown between two vampires in Sherwood Forest was I? ... no, we're on our own.'

'You know, the guns won't kill Raven. There's only a few ways that he can be killed,' said Tania.

'I kinda figured that, so what are these other ways?' said Maldini.

'Well, I'm assuming that he can be killed by another vampire, and of course, sunlight. But for a human to kill him, you have to use a wooden stake through his heart. But there's a caveat.'

'And what's that?'

'The stake must have been manufactured before the vampire, well, became a vampire. And it must have been made in the same region that the vampire comes from, and to make things worse, it must have been made by a craftsman from that same region.'

'Well, I guess I'm shit out of luck then,' said Maldini.

'Well, maybe not.'

'What do you mean?'

'Tristan has a good friend called Michael, who's going to be helping him, kind of as a back up in case Raven decides to play dirty.'

'I'm listening,' said Maldini, waiting for more information.

'He's got some crossbow bolts that were made by an Artillator in Moscow during the fifteenth century, before Raven became a vampire. These bolts are capable of killing him.'

Maldini shook his head in disbelief.

'Crossbow bolts ... I don't even want to know how he got hold of those,' he said.

'No, it's probably better you don't,' she said.

'So let me get this right. This Michael's going to be at the location, hiding away somewhere secretly watching Tristan's back?'

'That's about the thrust of it, yeah.'

'This just keeps getting better and better ... I'll be glad

when this night's over,' sighed Maldini.

They arrived at the perimeter of the forest close to the Birklands area with about fifteen minutes to spare. There was no moon and it was incredibly dark. They got out of the car and Maldini grabbed the holdall, night vision goggles and a map from the back seat and placed them on the bonnet. He removed a rifle and two handguns from the holdall.

'Okay, we know these won't kill Raven, so the name of the game is to add extra back up for Michael, as he's the one with the only weapon that can kill him.'

'But how are we going to find him?' asked Tania.

'I don't know. I'm making this up as I go along,' Maldini said, spreading the map across the bonnet of the car. 'We're here, and we need to get to this point here,' he said, pointing. 'It should only take about ten minutes on foot.'

'Take this,' he said, handing Tania a small, but rather heavy handgun, 'just slide this safety leaver to the OFF position, then point and squeeze.'

'Look, I don't know if I'm comfortable with this,' she said, holding the gun awkwardly.

'We're just going to go in there and try and find this location. You probably won't need it, but it's there if you do. Let me put these on you,' he said, fitting some night vision goggles over her head and securing the Velcro straps before flicking a switch on the side.

'Oh my God, these are amazing! I can see everything!' said Tania, totally blown away at the clarity of her night vision.

'£3,000 state-of-the-art police issue; you should be able to,' he said, fixing up the straps on his own night vision glasses.

'Okay, this way,' Maldini said, leading the way to a rather high fence.

'Wait, how are we going to get in?'

'We're going to climb over,' he said.

'I can't climb over that! It's got to be ten feet tall.'

'Yes you can, just grab hold like this, and put your toes in the gaps, and climb,' he said, leading by example.

'Fuck it,' she said, stuffing her gun into the waistband of her jeans.

Thinking of Tristan on the other side needing all the help he could get, she climbed over the fence and dropped to the forest floor on the other side rather clumsily. Maldini looked at her and half smiled as she dusted herself down and pulled a leaf out of her hair.

'Don't say a damn word. I can see your facial expression perfectly clearly through these you know.'

'Hey, I didn't say anything. Okay, keep quiet, don't step on any twigs or make any sounds. Stay close and keep your eyes peeled in every direction at all times,' he ordered.

He paced rapidly through the forest, seemingly knowing which way to go.

'Okay, according to the map, the exact spot should be about a hundred metres ahead, so keep dead quiet,' whispered Maldini creeping forward as quietly as he could.

He looked at his watch, which read 11:53pm. There were just seven minutes to go before whatever was going to happen was due to start.

They arrived at an opening in the middle of the forest. It was a small expanse of open land about half the size of a football pitch. In the middle, about twenty metres away, was an oak tree stump about one metre wide and one metre high. It looked like it could be used as a picnic table. Maldini and Tania remained under cover of the trees at the edge of the opening.

Tania was anxious and shaking like a leaf, but she just kept thinking of Tristan; she didn't want anything to happen to him. She didn't know why, but she was willing to risk her life for him.

Although Maldini had experienced this kind of situation, this one was somewhat different as there were a couple of vampires involved; hardly a routine police bust scenario.

Tania was freaking out inside, she could hardly bear it. The waiting, the not knowing what was going to happen, it was horrible. She just wanted whatever it was that was going to happen, to hurry up and happen. To make things worse, she kept hearing things rustling in the forest behind her, but every time she turned and looked, there was nothing there. Maybe it was just the wind rustling through the trees, or perhaps a badger or fox, she thought as she tried to reassure herself.

Maldini tapped Tania on the shoulder and pointed towards the old oak stump in the center of the opening. Tania gasped as she noticed Tristan standing on it and facing to the left. *Where the hell did he come from and how did he just appear there like that,* she thought. It was as if by magic, one minute there was no sign of anybody, the next minute, Tristan was standing there on the tree stump, totally motionless; just like a statue.

'What's he doing?' she whispered quietly in Maldini's ear.

'Keep quiet and don't move a muscle,' he whispered back

as he scanned the area.

Maldini spotted something over to the left, just at the edge of the forest, camouflaged in the undergrowth. There was a slight movement, and then he realised what it was. He could see the front end of a crossbow very low to the forest floor. Somebody was lying on the ground holding it, but they had done a good job of covering themselves up with branches and leaves and they were wearing a camouflaged cap and had their eye up to the telescopic sights of the crossbow.

'I can see Michael,' whispered Maldini.

'Where?' whispered Tania.

'Tristan's looking in his direction. He's lying on the ground at the foot of the trees over to the left.'

'Where, I can't see anything?' she whispered, as she tried her hardest to spot him in the undergrowth.

'Trust me, he's there, he's covered in branches and wearing camo clothing.'

Tania looked back across to Tristan, who remained motionless on the oak stump, but not for long. At that precise moment, Tania and Maldini witnessed Raven slam into the back of Tristan with unbelievable speed and force, knocking him a good thirty feet off the oak stump.

'Shit!' whispered Tania, 'we need to help him.'

'Wait, our bullets won't do anything, remember. Let's just see what Michael does with that crossbow.'

'You're making this too easy for me, Tristan,' said Raven as Tristan got to his feet.

'I wouldn't say that,' said Tristan, stepping to the side slightly, as he realised that he was blocking Michael's line of fire. 'You know it's funny, I was convinced that you'd play dirty.'

'Oh don't worry, the night's young,' said Raven, with an evil glint in his eye.

'Shoot, Michael, what are you waiting for!!' whispered Tania.

'He only has one chance so he has to pick the right moment. If he misses his heart, he won't have time to load up another bolt before Raven spots him. Besides, Raven isn't showing any signs of playing dirty, so it might not work.'

Just then, two more people appeared from out of nowhere at un-human speed and slowly circled Tristan.

'What the hell's gong on!!' said Tania.

'Oh shit!' said Maldini.

'What?' said Tania.

'He's brought help; two more vampires.'

'Well, where the hell did he find them?'

'I don't know, but it doesn't look good.'

'I thought I'd bring along a couple of little helpers for entertainment value. Not that I can't take you on my own, of course,' said Raven, grinning to himself.

The two little helpers were young, aged about fifteen. What used to be two innocent teenage boys, were now evil sinister vampires with a taste for blood. They continued circling Tristan, looking menacing and intimidating. They hissed and growled at Tristan. It was obvious that they wanted to attack, but they had to wait for the word from their creator, Raven.

'You immortalised two innocent kids ... you're a monster!' said Tristan.

'Yeah, ain't it cool,' said Raven, laughing and smirking.

But at that instant the smirk was removed from Raven's

face as a crossbow bolt struck him in the base of his neck, causing him to splutter and cough. The two teenage vampires hissed and started going frantic while scanning the area. Raven let out a loud roar; he was angered beyond belief. He grabbed the bolt and pulled it out of the base of his throat in one swift movement. The two young vampires hissed and sneered in the direction from where the bolt had been fired, focusing their attention on the small area where Michael was hidden in the undergrowth.

'Shit! He missed,' said Maldini, as he scanned right to left to see if Michael could re-load undetected and get another shot off.

But it was too late, Raven had spotted him.

'Kill!' shouted Raven, giving the order for his two vampire helpers to attack, as he pointed towards Michael, who was struggling to re-load his crossbow.

The two teenage vampires got across the 30 metres open expanse of land to Michael in less than three seconds. While Tristan was distracted by this and looking in Michael's direction, Raven took advantage of the moment. He grabbed Tristan by the throat and sank his fangs deep into his neck, paralysing him almost instantly with his venom.

The two young vampires snatched Michael from the undergrowth and hauled him to his feet just as he managed to load the crossbow. But he had no time to aim and fire as Raven's two minions simultaneously sunk their fangs into his neck, one on either side. The crossbow dropped to the ground as the vampires tore into Michael's flesh, horrifically ripping his neck and throat to pieces and feeding from him while he was still alive and screaming. It was their first kill. There was no subtlety or skill; they were ravenous and cannibalistic. Just days earlier they had been two innocent teenage brothers, but now they had become two evil cold-blooded killers who needed to feed.

Tania could not stand by and watch the same thing happen to Tristan. She jumped to her feet and ran across the open land towards Tristan.

'Wait!' shouted Maldini, getting up and running after her. 'Shit!'

'Let him go!' shouted Tania, running towards them with her handgun.

Raven lifted his head up from Tristan's neck and looked in her direction.

'Oh, how romantic, the lovely Tania de Pré comes to save her boyfriend; how very sweet of you,' said Raven, sarcastically.

'Let him go, Raven!' she said, 'you've had your fun, now leave him alone.'

'Or what, you'll shoot me with your little gun?' he sneered.

Tristan was well and truly paralysed from the neck down due to the copious amounts of venom that Raven had pumped into him via his fangs. Tania pointed her gun straight into Raven's face. Raven then played with Tania by moving Tristan left to right, placing his head into Tania's line of fire.

'Be careful with that, you wouldn't want to shoot the wrong vampire in the face now,' said Raven, continuing to laugh and joke and make a mockery of the situation.

Maldini stopped ten feet short of Tania and Raven and turned to the left and aimed his gun at the two young minion vampires, who were still feeding off Michael. He fired off two shots into the chest of the one to his left, then aimed and fired off three shots into the chest of the other one. They both simultaneously dropped Michael to the floor, leaving him to die, blood still pumping from the many wounds on either side of his neck. They ran at breakneck speed and got to Maldini in just a few short seconds. One of them grabbed Maldini's handgun before Maldini knew what had happened. Maldini took his rifle off his shoulder, but before he could raise it to fire a shot, the young vampire shot Maldini in the shoulder with his own handgun, dropping him to the floor in agonising pain.

Raven was still having fun and games with Tania and Tristan; to Raven, the whole situation had now become a very funny and entertaining situation.

'You know, all this excitement has made me a little ... peckish,' said Raven.

In an instant, he sank his fangs deep into the side of Tristan's neck from behind. Tristan let out a scream as Raven fed off him – savagely, in an attempt to weaken him further and eventually kill him. Tristan's blood jetted all over Raven's chest as he fed. Tania stepped forward and pressed her gun up against Raven's head while he continued to feed off Tristan and pulled the trigger. The recoil from the powerful handgun sent Tania's arms up in the air and her body backwards, causing her to trip over and land on her backside.

The bullet went straight through the side of Raven's head and out the back; the force caused his head to jolt back. He looked down at Tania, very angry; but then he started to laugh loudly as the bullet hole in the top of his head stopped bleeding and instantly healed. The other young vampire saw this and flew at Tania, knocking the gun out of her hand. One of them grabbed Tania tight and held her in a bear hug grip from behind while the other grabbed her by the hair, pushed her head backwards and grabbed her throat. He was just about to rip into her neck with his fangs when Raven shouted at him.

'No!! ... She's mine!' shouted Raven.

The young vampire looked long and hard at Raven and knew that he must resist the temptation, or his creator would surely kill him right there on the spot. Raven held onto the paralysed and bleeding Tristan and gave his young apprentice a stern look to make sure he was going to obey; he did. But he still held her hair tightly and continued to squeeze her throat.

'Let him go,' said a young male voice, as a slim figure appeared out of the dark woods holding what looked like Michael's loaded crossbow.

'Will, what the hell are you doing here?' screamed Tania, under the tight grip of the young vampire.

'I don't have time to go into it right now,' said Will, not taking his eyes off Raven.

'Oh, how very fetching, first the lovely Tania, now a pretty blonde teenage boy ... how would you like to join me and my two companions, I'll make you immortal?' said Raven, smiling a sinister smile.

'Put Tristan down and prepare to go straight to hell,' said Will, very seriously while aiming the crossbow squarely at Raven's chest.

'Oh this is going to be fun, first Ms de Pré with the little bullet trick, and now you with a fucking crossbow. Do you even know how to aim and shoot that thing, boy! Well here, let me make it a little easier for you.'

Raven threw Tristan to the ground like a rag doll, pulled open his jacket and ripped his shirt open, revealing his chest.

'Here,' Raven pointed to the exact spot on his chest where his heart was. 'Be sure to enjoy the moment, because after I've allowed you this little pleasure, I'm going to pull that bolt out of my chest, remove those night goggles off your face and gouge out both your pretty eyes with it … didn't anyone tell you that wooden stakes through the heart don't work with me, boy! You've been watching too many vampire movies.'

Raven fumed, hardly able to constrain himself from launching forward and ripping the boy's head off right there.

'They do if they were made six hundred years ago by a Russian Artillator!' said Will, calmly.

Raven looked closely at the suspiciously old looking wooden bolt loaded up on the crossbow. The realisation washed over Raven quicker and colder than an arctic blizzard. Every muscle in Raven's face dropped and quickly turned into a look of fear.

'That's right, bloodsucker,' said Will.

Raven growled and lunged forward to attack Will, but it was too late. Will released the trigger sending the antique Russian-made bolt straight into Raven's chest and through his heart, knocking him backwards, counteracting his lunge attack attempt in the process.

Raven looked down at the bolt jutting out from his

chest and clamped his fist around it. But his strength had been sapped; he couldn't remove the bolt. Something was happening to him. His two young apprentice vampires started to scream, freak out and panic. Something was happening to them too. Raven started to cough and gasp for breath; blood began to run from his mouth and down his chin. Tears of blood ran down his face. Blood streamed out of his nostrils, then his ears. He dropped to his knees, with blood flowing freely from all his orifices.

The two young vampires started to lose their strength. Their grip on Tania weakened as they both thudded to the floor either side of her, landing on their backs, both doing the dying-fly dance in fast motion as they continued to writhe, fit and spasm right there on the ground. Their creator was dying, which meant they were dying too. Tania, now free from the choking grip, stepped back and watched.

Will stepped up close to Raven, who looked up at him with one hand clutching his chest and the other outstretched towards Will, as if gesturing for his help and compassion.

'This is for burning down our house!!' said Will, as he kicked Raven hard in the bridge of his nose, with the heel of his boot, sending him flying backwards flat onto his back.

With their creator's imminent death, the two young vampires imploded in perfect sync, into an ever-decreasing ball of blood, flames, bone and ash, most of which, after a few short seconds, vaporised into the night sky, leaving two smouldering areas on the ground where their bodies used to be.

Raven wasn't making such a fuss; instead, he was somewhat more dignified, lying flat on his back almost motionless except for the odd twitch from his arms and legs, with more and more blood streaming out of every orifice in his body. Will and Tania looked down at him, while Maldini looked across the ground from his lying position where he slowly squirmed and clutched the bullet wound in his shoulder.

Raven started to tremble and shake violently in a large pool of his own blood that was slowly soaking into the ground beneath him. He coughed and spluttered and made strange muted screeching sounds. *Is this what the death rattle of a vampire sounds like?* thought Tania, as she stood there watching. Then the shaking stopped, fading to a few faint twitches in his hands. Finally, there were a few final faint metallic screeching sounds from the back of his throat, and then a momentary pause before his body burst into flames that emerged from his head, and then swept spectacularly down his torso to his feet. In an instant, there was nothing but a flat layer of bloody jet-black ashes in the shape of what used to be his body.

Tristan let out a faint whimpering noise, which got Tania's attention. She ran to him and cupped her hand under his head, raising it off the ground.

'Oh my god, what can I do?' she cried.

'I can't move. I have too much of Raven's venom in my system,' he struggled even to talk.

'There must be something I can do?' she said, with tears in her eyes.

'No, there's nothing you can do, but don't worry; I'll be okay in about eight hours when his venom wears off. Don't forget, a vampire can completely regenerate.'

'Thank god!!' she said, overjoyed that Raven was dead,

but most importantly, that her beloved Tristan was still alive.

Tania drove Tristan's Audi, with Tristan lying across the back seat, while Will, with his limited driving experience, drove Maldini's Police car. Maldini lay across the back seat with his shoulder in agonising pain from his bullet wound. They made the short journey to the nearest hospital Accident and Emergency Department in Nottingham first, to drop Maldini off so he could get treatment. Will then got into Tristan's Audi, with Tania driving, to head home, leaving the police Volvo in the hospital car park for Maldini. By the time they arrived back at Tristan's estate on the outskirts of north London it was nearly 4am.

Chapter 22

It was 11am at the Burnel estate, and all was quiet. Tania had just stirred and had thrown her robe on and made her way down to the kitchen to make some coffee and reflect on the previous night. Although it was all very brutal, and it wasn't every day that one woke up from witnessing vampires bleeding to death and bursting into flames, she felt surprisingly calm.

Knowing that Tristan was resting and recovering in the basement from the paralysing effects of Raven's venom and that he was going to be okay was a huge relief. What was an even bigger relief was the knowledge that Raven was gone – forever. Tania smiled to herself and was overwhelmed with a wonderful warm fuzzy feeling deep down inside as she fantasised about how she and Tristan could now finally move forward.

After Tania made herself a coffee, she called Maldini on his mobile to find out how he was.

'Maldini,' he answered in a somewhat subdued tone.

'Hey, how are we feeling today?' said Tania, in a friendly voice.

'Hey you! I'm fine thanks, how are you?'

'I'm good. How's that shoulder?'

'Shoulder's good, I'm gonna be fine. They removed the bullet and patched me up. It was a glorified flesh wound really. The Doctor told me to rest up and wear a sling for two weeks, and then I'll be as good as new.'

'That's good news, I'm really pleased. Look, did I thank you for last night?' she said.

'No, I don't think you did.'

'I will,' she laughed. 'So, when are they letting you out?'

'This afternoon.'

'Wow, so soon?'

'Yeah, well it wasn't that serious an injury. They've given me some pain killers, I'll be fine.'

'Do you need me to come and collect you?'

'No, you don't have to worry about that, I'm fixed.'

'Okay, I'll catch up with you real soon.'

Just as Tania hung up the phone, Will walked in.

'Hey,' he said, making his presence known.

Tania turned around and saw Will standing there, wearing black jogging bottoms and a Jack White T-shirt and one seriously messed up hair do. She walked over to him.

'Good morning,' she said, kissing his cheek. 'So – how's the hero this morning?'

'Okay, I guess,' he said, in a sleepy voice.

'Just okay? Well, you should be more than just okay after what you did last night!'

'Well … Mum's still kind of upset with me for pulling that stunt and disappearing last night. She was worried sick, but I think deep down she's happy I saved Tristan's life.'

'Saved all our lives! You saved us all, Will,' she said, with both her hands pressed firmly on his cheeks. 'So, how exactly did you get there, and how did you know where we were?'

'It was no big deal really. Last night, Mum and I were just coming back to the house when I saw the detective banging on the front door trying to get in. Mum let him in with her key. When we found you on the kitchen floor he tried to wake you up, then as you started to come around he said he knew where Tristan was and that he was in a hurry for you both to get to him. That's when I ran outside and hid in the back of his police car.'

'But I didn't see you when we got in?'

'I know. I was in the estate section at the very back, hidden under the cover.'

'And you spent the entire journey hidden there?'

'Yeah,' he smiled, all proud of himself.

'So what did you do when we got there?'

'Well, I waited until you and the detective got out. I could hear you talking near the front of the car, then as soon as I heard you walk away, I slid the back shelf cover open and looked out the window … I saw you fall off the fence,' he smiled.

'Yeah, not one of my finest moments,' she smiled back.

'Anyway, once I saw you go into the forest, I got out of the car and brought the spare pair of night vision goggles that were in the back and followed you.'

'So you saw everything?'

'Yeah, I went around to the left from you and was hiding about twenty metres away from where Michael was standing. I saw the two vampires kill him,' he said, in a more melancholy tone.

'I'm so sorry you had to see that,' said Tania, putting her hands on his shoulders, 'but, if it wasn't for you, they would have killed all of us.'

'I usually hate confrontation, but when I saw them kill Michael like that, my adrenaline kicked in and I found an inner strength I never knew I had. That's when I picked up his crossbow.'

'Well, I'm glad you did.'

Chapter 23

'Good morning, Detective,' said a young black female nurse, 'how are you feeling today?'

'My shoulder's got a constant dull ache, but I guess that's to be expected after having a bullet pulled out of it,' he joked.

'Don't worry. It'll subside in a few days. The doctor's going to come and see you soon, and then you should be able to go. Is somebody coming to pick you up?'

'Yes.'

'Good, would you like a copy of today's paper to read until the doctor comes?'

'That would be great, thanks.'

The nurse returned a minute later with a copy of The Sentinel newspaper. Knowing that this was the paper Tania wrote for, he thumbed through the pages to seek out her column.

EMAIL FROM A VAMPIRE – Part 8
By Tania de Pré

Continued from yesterday, in the vampire's own words.

Over the centuries I have had my fair share of tough times and incredibly difficult moments, mentally, physically and emotionally. But, the past ten years have proved to be the toughest, by a long way.

Life has become more challenging than ever before, and trying to keep up with everyday life with my vampire status has become difficult and tiresome, especially from an emotional standpoint – seven wives and seven major heartaches would be enough to emotionally destroy anyone.

As a mortal human, I always used to think that time was absolutely priceless, the most precious gift in the world. I would treasure each moment, as if it were the last. But my lifetime's tune changed drastically when I became a vampire. You would be amazed at how your attitude changes when you become immortal and you realise that you are going to live forever, into infinity, and that you will never get old and you will never die. Time is no longer precious, in fact it becomes quite the opposite; time becomes a very heavy burden that you have to carry on your shoulders for the rest of time.

Just stop and ask yourself, what would you do, and how would you spend the rest of your life, if you found out tomorrow that it was never going to come to an end? Imagine for a minute that you don't have to plan your retirement or worry about seeing all those places in the world that you have always wanted to visit before you die. You no longer have to worry about writing up a bucket list of all those great things you have always wanted to do, as there is no longer any great urgency. You don't have to worry about your health anymore; having a heart attack would never happen to you. What would you do, how would you live?

Well, let me answer that for you. The cold fact is you wouldn't do anything. You would actually "stop" living. Why? Because with your new immortal status comes an all-new mind-set. Because you know that you don't have to worry about the inconsequential things in life anymore and there is no rush for you to make any decisions about things, you simply don't bother. The next thing you know, a hundred years have gone by and you haven't done anything with that time, then another hundred go by, and so on and so forth. Until one day, you realise that you are sick of living, or at least existing as the undead.

When you are a mortal human, you live your life; the emphasis here is on the word "live". But once you have an eternity to live it, you stop living it; instead, you merely exist and get through it the best you can. Life is no longer precious or valuable and you no longer treasure the moment.

The fact is I stopped living the day I became a vampire back in the year 1011. I can tell you wholeheartedly that a mortal human lifetime is more than long enough, if you live it right.

Over the centuries I've seen many wars come and go, some small, some great. I've seen many devastating disasters happen, some taking thousands of lives, some taking hundreds.

I've noticed one common denominator in every one of these instances. Be it a tsunami, a hurricane, a terrorist attack, a collapsed coalmine, a sunken ship, starving and poverty-stricken children, a crashed passenger airliner, a motorway pile-up or a missing child, whenever disasters strike, people come together; there's love, warmth, compassion, civility, humanity, generosity and help in abundance.

Humans are at their best, when things are worst.

The question is: why do we have to wait for death before our decency and loving nature comes into play. Why can't people just be like this all the time?

My parting advice to you is this – LIVE & LOVE!!!

This has been the last column in my own hand. Ms de Pré will sum up when she writes her concluding part to my story in due course.

Goodbye,

Tristan Syhier Burnel – The Vampire.

Why would he say that? Why would he publicly reveal his real name? thought Detective Maldini as he placed the newspaper on the table next to his hospital bed. *Is he going somewhere? What's he up to? Does Tania know something that I don't?* He sat there on the bed and mused over it.

Chapter 24

As the late evening twilight approached, Tania found herself, yet again, frantically pacing up and down in the living room, waiting for Tristan to emerge from the basement. She was going crazy and was desperate to know that he was okay, that Raven's paralysing venom effects had worn off completely, and his neck wound had healed up.

It got to 10pm and it was well and truly dark. *Where is he?* Tania thought. 10:30pm arrived and there was still no sign of Tristan. She knew that he hadn't gone out without her noticing as she could see the hallway and front door from the living room. 10:45pm and still nothing, no sign of him. Tania was going crazy, internally at least. *Where is he? Why hasn't he emerged from his basement? Is he okay? Is he alive?* She walked over to the drapes and, just as she opened them to look outside, she heard his voice from behind her.

'Come to bed!'

Tania spun around on her heels and saw Tristan standing in the open living room doorway. She ran over to him and threw her arms around him, squeezing him as tight as she could.

'Thank god, thank god you're okay,' she said, stepping back and looking him up and down and checking his neck.

'You're okay, aren't you?' she said, anxiously.

'Yes, never better,' he smiled.

'The venom effects have gone?'

'Yes, and as you can see, the wound on my neck has also gone.'

'So … there's no more Raven and you're okay?'

'That's right,' he smiled again.

Tania let out a huge sigh of relief and embraced Tristan in her arms with her head neatly nestled against his collarbone.

'Wait a minute. You said, "Come to bed!" not "Go to bed!" didn't you?' she said, loosening her embrace and looking up at him.

Tristan stepped backwards away from Tania.

'That's right.' He held out his hand as a gesture for her to go with him.

She felt like her whole life had been leading up to this very moment, and now it was here, she didn't quite know what to do, or how to handle it. She slowly stepped forward and gently took his hand. He led her across the marble hallway to the stairs.

'Wait, don't we have to go downstairs to your basement room?'

'Not tonight. I've never spent a single night in my main bedroom, the proper bedroom. Tonight I want to fall asleep when it's dark, and in the arms of a beautiful woman. Tonight is different … it's special,' he said, looking meaningfully into her eyes.

Oh my god, she thought. *This is it; I'm going to sleep*

with the devastatingly handsome Tristan Syhier Burnel; and he wants to sleep with me.

'But what about in the morning, when the day breaks? I know there are light proof drapes in the bedroom, but what if something happens and light gets through?'

'Don't worry about the morning. Let's enjoy tonight,' he said, mesmerising her with his soft tones and incredibly attractive eyes. To her, his eyes were not fierce; they were expressive and full of emotion, and tonight, there was a longing in them. For the first time, she could clearly see that he needed her. *But why now, why tonight?* she thought. It didn't matter; she was here for him, not just tonight, but forever.

As he led her up the stairs and into the main bedroom, she had a sudden attack of butterflies in her stomach, but very pleasant ones. Her knees turned to jelly when he led her over to the large four-poster king size bed, the very same bed where she had slept alone since arriving at Tristan's house. She had not noticed him come out of his basement room, but he must have been up a short while as there were two red candles burning either side of the bed.

Tristan stopped a few feet from the bed and turned to face Tania. He manoeuvred her so that the bed was immediately behind her. He stood close to her, looking deep into her eyes. *Oh my god*, she thought, *this is it, he wants me … he actually wants me.*

He gently placed the palms of his hands on either side of her face and purposely leaned forward to kiss her, brushing her slightly parted lips ever so gently with his own. The light and delicate contact sent sparks of electricity through her entire body. She unhurriedly moved her hands up from the small of his back, to his shoulders, and then gently ran her fingers through the hair on the back of his head. She had wanted to do this for ages, and it felt every bit as good as she had imagined.

She parted her lips wider and ran her tongue along his bottom lip. He masterfully, but gently, tilted her head to one side slightly and started to explore inside her mouth with his tongue. Tania felt things stirring deep inside, her muscles clenched with excitement and anticipation, down *there*.

He pulled his head away and allowed his fingers to gently move down the sides of her face, lightly brushing over her scar. It was funny, but she no longer felt self-conscious of it, not anymore. He unhurriedly undid the buttons of her blouse revealing her cleavage and midriff. He brought his hands back up to her neck, and his slender fingers delicately traced a line across her collarbones to her shoulders, making only the faintest contact with her skin as he did so, but enough to send delicious spasms through Tania's upper body. He hooked both index fingers under the shoulders of her blouse and leisurely slid it across until it fell off her shoulders and dropped to her wrists. She went to remove the trapped garment from her wrists, but he grabbed her arms.

'Don't!' he demanded, making it very clear that he didn't want her to remove anything.

'Let me enjoy this moment, let me enjoy you,' he whispered sensually.

She stood perfectly still, looking into his mesmerising eyes. He reached down and slowly undid the cuff buttons allowing her blouse to move over her wrists and hands freely, dropping to the floor. He quickly yanked her close to him in a masterful way using his hand in the small of her back with the other gripping the hair on the back of her head. She let out a pleasurable and excited gasp as he did so. He kissed her, hard and passionately, with purpose. Their tongues danced and entwined as he gripped her hair tighter and moved his hand languidly up her naked back, eventually finding the horizontal bra strap between her shoulder blades. He skilfully and swiftly undid the fastening using just one hand. *Wow! How the hell did he manage that?*

He stepped back and gently slid her bra straps off her shoulders, allowing her bra to drop to the floor by her feet. Inch by inch, he ran his fingers across her shoulders before tracing lines across her collarbones to the centre of her chest ... then down and outward over her breasts, pausing momentarily with the tips of his fingers resting sensually on her nipples. Her entire body twitched with excitement as his touch triggered every nerve ending in her upper body to react. She felt her nipples harden up almost instantly under the sensual touch of his long slender fingers; their eye contact never broke, not even for a moment.

Tristan delicately moved his hands down Tania's body with the tips of his fingers making only the faintest contact with her skin. He drew them south to her stomach, over her pubic bone and down the front of her thighs, before finally breaking off to allow his arms to come to rest by his side.

He stepped back and looked at Tania, inviting her to remove his shirt. She obliged by decisively undoing the buttons on his expensive immaculately pressed white shirt, starting at the top then slowly moving down, revealing his slender, but incredibly well toned body. She gently placed the palms of her hands on his stomach and little by little, she sensually moved them up his body over his chest to his shoulders, then slid his shirt off and down over his arms. *Wow, what an amazing body. So firm, yet so soft and smooth to touch.*

She pulled him in close to her so she could feel his bare skin pressed up against hers. Her nipples pressed hard into his chest; it felt incredible. She placed delicate kisses on his cheeks, chin and neck while pulling him hard up against her using her hand in the small of his back. As she did so, she felt his erection pressed up hard against her stomach. This was agony, she wanted him more than anything else in the world, and she wanted him now!!!

She continued to tentatively kiss his neck, working her way down to his chest. *Wow*, she thought, *what a gorgeous chest*. It had only the faintest, hardly noticeable, short downy hairs congregated in a tiny pool right in the centre. She planted soft sensual kisses all over it, caressing his nipples, in turn, delicately between her teeth while flicking her tongue over them. He let out a light groan and arched his back while the muscles in his chest tightened in response to Tania's skilful tongue and mouth work.

She pulled her face away from Tristan's chest and stepped backwards until her calf muscles came into contact with the bed; looking intently into his eyes as she did so. Tristan stepped forward and gently placed the palm of his left hand in the middle of her chest, and then, without warning, he pushed her hard, causing her to land on her back on the firm mattress. He then broke eye contact as he stood there and watched her chest heave up and down under her deep breathing as her excitement heightened.

Tristan knelt down and took Tania's right foot in his hands and slowly removed her shoe. Supporting her lower leg by her calf muscle with his left hand, while gently holding her foot up with his right, he delicately drew his tongue up the instep of her foot, eventually reaching her toes, where he continued to push his tongue between them, one at a time until all five of her toes had been expertly explored. Finally he took her big toe in his mouth and firmly sucked on it, while drawing circles around it with his tongue. Tania was going crazy as her upper body writhed and swivelled from the waist up. She grabbed her own breasts and squeezed them hard while biting her lower lip. *How is it possible that this kind of foot treatment can have such an incredibly erotic effect on me?*

Tristan gently placed her foot on the floor and repeated the entire process with her left one. Then, he purposefully moved up onto the bed with his extended arms walking up either side of her legs. He reminded her of a tiger slowly stalking forward, his shoulder blades prominent as he moved seductively and gracefully up to her navel, staring deep into her eyes as he moved. He undid the button at her navel and deliberately unzipped her trousers, pulling them open at the top to reveal her skimpy black lacy knickers. He leaned forward and drew some small circles around her belly button with his tongue then continued down over her stomach before finally pushing his tongue under the thin waistband of her knickers. He licked side-to-side over her neatly groomed pubic landing strip, sending Tania climbing the walls with manic anticipation and excitement.

He continuously moved both his hands outwards across her waistline and hooked his index fingers under her knickers either side of her hips. She gently lifted her behind a few inches off the bed inviting him to slide them down, which he did, very slowly. Everything he did, every movement he made was like witnessing a graceful art form, accentuated even more in the dim flickering candlelight. As he delicately pulled her knickers over her thighs he enjoyed the view of her impeccably trimmed pubic area and the way the slight bulge of her pubic bone looked with her thighs pressed so tightly together. Tania could clearly see that the sight of her naked body excited him greatly. His eyes were feasting on her body, absorbing and taking in every inch of her flesh while letting out a slow pleasurable gasp between his slightly parted lips.

He then stood up at the foot of the bed and elegantly kicked off his shoes. Then, using those long slender fingers, he undid the button of his black neatly pressed trousers and unzipped them allowing them to fall from those incredible hips to the floor. Even the way he gracefully stepped out of them was nothing less than poetry in motion. She propped herself up on her elbows to view him and was amazed to see that he wasn't wearing any socks. *Wow, what beautiful feet*, she thought. Feet aren't usually the most attractive part of a man's body, but these were something else. They looked incredibly smooth, with immaculately defined toes and a slightly feminine instep. In fact, if they were two sizes smaller, they could almost belong to a female ballet dancer.

They looked like they had recently had a pedicure; sheer perfection.

He teased his tight-fitting trunks down and over his nifty snake hips to reveal his ... W*ow! Oh my god*, she mentally gasped. *Tristan Syhier Burnel is standing totally naked at the foot of the bed, looking at me and feasting his eyes all over my body. He is so handsome, so beautiful, so slender, yet so masculine all at the same time.* His bone structure was just incredible, like a male supermodel; a thing of sublime male beauty. His waistline was astonishingly attractive, almost womanlike. *Oh my god, take me now!!!* her body screamed for him as she lay there trying to hide her involuntary writhing movements as she felt herself getting very hot and moist down *there* in anticipation of what was going to happen next.

Tristan slowly moved up onto the bed, looking so seductive, stopping at her knees. He leaned forward and delicately stroked her pubic landing strip with his nose, gently sweeping it up and down over the narrow strip of short soft hair. He could smell her sex and feel the heat emitting from between her thighs.

'Have you any idea how intoxicating you smell, Tania?' he whispered excitedly, as he drew his tongue down her pubic bone towards her clitoris.

Tania was about ready to explode and could hardly contain herself any longer as she outwardly gasped and moaned. He delicately drew his tongue in long strokes up and down her vagina lips, sometimes pushing it between them. All this skilful tongue treatment sent Tania into spasmodic turmoil. Her body writhed and her hips moved up and down as she ground harder into his face and mouth. By now, Tania was quite literally dripping, *there*. She could hardly contain herself any longer as Tristan started to draw intricate circles around her clitoris with the tip of his tongue.

'Oh fuck, that's so good!!' she gasped.

He increased the speed and pressure of his tongue, pausing every now and then to press the tip of it hard into her clitoris. Tania gasped and let out moans of excitement as Tristan continued to pleasure her in the most skilful way she had ever experienced. Her body convulsed and continued to spasm violently. She lifted her behind off the bed slightly and pushed herself harder into his face, grinding up and down.

'Don't stop, oh please don't stop!!!' she begged, as her body continued to coil up tighter and tighter like a spring as the intense sexual feelings heightened beyond belief getting stronger and stronger.

'Oh my god ... don't stop ... oh please ... aarrrrrhhhhhh!!!' she screamed, as an incredibly strong orgasm exploded both inside and out at the same time.

'Oh my god!!!' she gasped, panting, moaning out loud, as her exquisitely deep strong orgasm continued. Her body was no longer her own, it was possessed by an incredible force. Her body spasmed, twitched, writhed and convulsed as her orgasm started to gradually wind down; Tristan's tongue still lightly pressed up against her genitalia. The aftermath left her wanting him more than ever.

'Now, I want you now!' she demanded as she grabbed the hair on his head and tried to pull him up towards her.

Tristan slowly started to move up her body with his tongue pausing at her navel before continuing his journey north. He planted lots of soft delicate kisses all over her chest and breasts. She could feel his solid erection hovering over her pubic area and pressing gently into her navel. She couldn't stand it anymore; the anticipation was driving her nuts. She reached down between their bodies and took hold of his penis in her hand and gave it a gentle squeeze. *Wow, oh my god … I so want that inside me.* It was absolutely rock solid, but reassuringly smooth and soft to the touch. She squeezed him again, harder this time, and moved her hand slowly up and down its length, to his delight. He let out some soft pleasurable moans as he kissed and licked his way up her neck to her left ear.

Tania's pleasurable panting turned into full on hyperventilation. She couldn't stand it any longer, she felt like she was about to explode; the anticipation was having an overwhelming effect on her entire body. She just wanted him, and she wanted him inside her right now! She squeezed him hard while grabbing a handful of hair on the back of his head.

Tristan's excitement grew; he grabbed the hair on the back of Tania's head and yanked it back hard, forcing her head backwards and her neck to thrust out forward. His head snapped forward like a viper striking its prey as he bit her on the side of her neck. She yelped and gasped with the mix of pain and pleasure as his fully exposed fangs penetrated the surface of the skin on the side of her neck. He gently toyed with her, refusing to enter her just yet, instead drinking a few drops of her blood.

She jerked under him, moving her hand up and down his length harder and faster, desperately trying to encourage him to penetrate her. He continued to lick the small traces of blood from her neck that had trickled from the two tiny surface puncture wounds, which excited him greatly. He brought his thumb up to his mouth and punctured the tip of it on one of his fangs, causing a small drip to appear on the end. He pressed it hard up against the two tiny wounds on her neck and held it there for a few seconds until the holes closed and healed, moving himself excitedly back and forth in her hand as he did so.

Tania was now out of control. She grabbed his hair and pulled his face close to hers, thrusting her tongue deep into his mouth, tasting her own blood in the process. She released the grip she had on his penis and wrapped her legs around his back and squeezed him hard with her thighs. She felt Tristan's powerful erection pressed hard against her pubic bone; she manoeuvred her behind up the bed until...

'Oh my god!' she moaned, with ecstatic pleasure as Tristan entered her and they became one.

How on earth can lovemaking feel this incredible? she thought, as he slowly and sensually moved in and out of her. It had been quite a while for Tania, but she had never experienced anything even remotely close to this, she was in total ecstasy. He had only been inside her for a few moments, but it was too much, she couldn't control it, there was no way that she could hold back. She felt her lower muscles tense up and her body writhed all over again as she felt another orgasm building up. She dug her fingernails hard into Tristan's back and as she climaxed, she ripped her fingernails down his back, the pain causing Tristan to arch his back and thrust into her one final time; hard.

'Aaaahhhhh ... OH MY GOD!!!' she cried out loud.

She was in ecstasy. This was something else, totally out of this world. She had never experienced anything like this in her life.

Tania screamed and moaned as Tristan continued to move slowly inside her; her breathing became manically sporadic as her entire body jerked up and down violently underneath him. She resembled a woman who was having electrical cardiac defibrillation treatment. She continued to scream out one very long continuous note as her orgasm lasted an absolute age; *holy fuck, is this ever going to end!* She was going to have to breathe in at some point, but she was unable to draw breath as her sexual pleasure sustained.

Tania eventually came back down to earth. Her erratic breathing steadied as she slowly regained some kind of control over her body and senses. Tristan withdrew from inside her and lay next to her, stroking her body as she lay in a state of total blissed-out afterglow. Her chest heaved up and down; she breathed deeply, taking in much needed oxygen. Her body tingled all over, her skin baked in sweat; *what on earth just happened*? She lay there feeling the most intense pleasure imaginable.

Tristan was generous enough to allow her a few minutes to enjoy the moment and come back down from her orgasms and regain her senses. Then he gently manoeuvred her onto her side so she was facing away from him. He then proceeded to enter her from behind, only this time, making love to her faster and harder. She felt every inch of him from this angle, and loved every second.

'Oh my ... god ... oh please ... yes, Yes, YES!!!' she

moaned, as he thrust himself into her, faster, deeper, harder!

If she thought the first two orgasms were out of this world, this was something else entirely. Her senses were now heightened after two spectacular orgasms and every second was incredible, she was in sexual utopia. She felt herself building up to third orgasm as he continued to thrust harder and faster. *How can this be?*

Never in her life had she experienced such out of this world lovemaking before.

She continued to move in perfect rhythm with him, getting higher and higher as her body started to wind up tighter than a drum. She was on the edge, she moaned, louder and louder as Tristan moved in and out of her creating feelings and sensations that she never thought were possible. Every muscle from her waist down was clenching and tightening up. Every single nerve ending *there* was firing off rapid static charges that spread through her entire lower body. Tristan thrust himself hard and fast, deep into her, while squeezing her right breast and delicately pinching her nipple with his free hand.

'OH MY GOD!!!' she moaned, 'don't stop, faster, oh please, please, I'm coming!!

Then it happened, spectacularly.

Tristan slowed slightly, and then thrust himself hard and deep into Tania one final time as he exploded inside her, letting out a loud groan of satisfaction. At that moment, Tania let out an almighty scream as she had the most breath-taking orgasm ever, over and over again. Multiple orgasm after multiple orgasm; they just kept on coming. *Where the fuck did all these come from?*

'Oooooohh ... Aaaahhhhhh ... oh my god ... I love you!!!' she screamed.

It was like a year's supply of orgasms all coming out at once. It couldn't get any better; *it doesn't get any better,* she thought, as they enjoyed synchronised orgasms. Her body writhed as Tristan continued to hold himself still, but firmly inside her; deep inside her.

Tania was absolutely shattered, in the best possible way. She reached behind her and grabbed Tristan's head, heat radiating off her body. She turned her head and pulled his face into hers, kissing him hard and passionately as her body continued to twitch and squirm involuntarily. Gradually, her body transitioned into a state of relaxation as she lay there reeling from the most extraordinary physical reaction she had ever experienced. Tristan delicately pulled out of her, allowing her to gently fall backwards onto her back. She laid her head on the pillow, closed her eyes and tried to regain her senses.

The total wonder that he had introduced her to was beyond anything she could have ever imagined. He had taken her to places she didn't know existed. As she lay there in a tranquil state of pure ecstasy and afterglow, Tristan gently stroked her hair, forehead, eyebrows and cheeks, slowly and repeatedly, until she drifted off to sleep.

Chapter 25

Tania stirred, turned over and reached her arm across to hold Tristan. Her arm landed in an empty section of bed with her hand on an empty pillow. She opened her eyes and realised that Tristan was not in bed with her. She turned and looked at the clock on the bedside table, which read 4:15am. She propped herself up on her elbows and looked around the room. The candles had been blown out and it was quite dark, except for a single light coming from the en-suite.

'Tristan,' she called.

There was no answer.

Then she noticed a piece of paper on his pillow, she picked it up and unfolded it. There was writing on it, but it was too dark to read. In her tired state she got out of bed and ambled naked, with her eyes still half-closed, to the en-suite. Although the mirror light was switched on, there was no sign of Tristan. She looked at the note; it was hand written with a fountain pen, on expensive embossed paper with a watermark.

Dearest Tania,

Words are so pitifully inadequate, and can hardly begin to convey the true depth of my feelings for you. Last night was indescribably wonderful; my feelings of love and passion reached new heights and depths. Our ecstatic lovemaking was like a furnace, fuelled by passion, desire and mutual joy, melting our two hearts together forever into one. Your total acceptance of me for who I am is a rare and precious gift, and one that I did not expect to receive. I am humbled, exalted and soothed.

Tania, I have loved several women in my very long life. You know this. Each has been precious, each has been entirely different. You are my last and final love, and I love you from the bottom of my heart. Your very openness and depths have enabled you to reach out to me, to embrace and love me in an entirely new way, which has renewed my love. During the past few weeks you have made me feel human again for the first time in many years. But the fact is, I am not human, and I can never return to my former human status.

But I am tired, Tania. Living in this way

over the centuries has finally taken its toll on me. I have lived and loved for years beyond human comprehension. My physical body is unchanged, perpetual and strong. However, my spirit and my emotional being are shredded, stretched beyond endurance, patched several times over for my darling wives. I cannot continue to grieve over my past lost loves, or for my past faithful and devoted friends, such as Michael, who have eased my life over the centuries

I cannot continue; this is my time, this is where it has to end for me.

Forgive me, my love. I know you will remember me always. I will take your love with me; your heart I will carry in my being as I greet the sunrise for the first time in a millennium on this, my final day.

Farewell, my beautiful beloved. Live as if this too is your last day, and love always, for I truly believe that our spirits will one day be united, and come to rest together in eternity.

I love you,

Tristan

'Tristan!!!' Tania shouted.

She ran out of the bedroom and into the corridor; 'Tristan, where are you?' she shouted again, now wide-awake.

While standing there looking along the corridor, she became aware of a light breeze against her naked body. She ran along the corridor; the door to the roof was slightly ajar.

'Tristan!' she shouted, as she opened the door and ran up the stairs.

At the top, the exit door that led out onto the flat roof was also slightly ajar. She pushed it open, and then she saw him. He stood over on the other side, totally naked, near the low wall at the edge of the roof with his arms resting by his sides. He was facing east, looking directly towards where the sun would be rising in about ten minutes' time.

'Oh my god!' she whispered.

'Tristan, what are you doing out here!' she shouted, running across the rooftop towards him.

He didn't turn to look at her; instead, he kept his head and eyes facing straight forward, looking directly at the horizon beyond the trees on his estate.

'Tristan, please, come back inside, the sun will be coming up soon, please!' she pleaded.

Again, he retained his stance and kept his eyes focused on that spot on the horizon, right where the sun would soon be appearing.

'Tristan, I beg you, please come inside, we'll talk about this!' she said, more anxiously.

'Tania, my darling, I need you to understand that this is my time, I have to go,' he said, softly, but with purpose.

'But why? Why do you have to go?' A single tear escaped

from her left eye.

'Life has become tiresome and meaningless, there's nothing left for me now.'

'That's not true, there's a lot to live for.'

'Try saying that after a 1033 years, when you've been dead for 1000 of those.'

Tania pushed herself directly in front of him so he had no choice but to look into her eyes.

'What about me, what about us?' she said, as a few more tears ran down her face from her right eye.

'Tania, I have to leave, it's time for me to depart this earth so that my soul can finally come to rest.'

'Tristan, please, I don't want you to go, you'll get hurt by the sun's rays!' she begged and pleaded as she tugged at his arms.

'Tania, I haven't seen a sunrise for nearly a thousand years.'

'Tristan, you can't watch the sunrise, it will kill you'

'Tania, I've been a vampire for quite a long time now, don't you think I'm aware of that fact? I want to see it, and I want to feel the sun's warmth on my skin.'

'But it's early in the morning; the sun won't be that warm.'

'Tania, I'm a vampire, trust me, I'll feel the warm rays on my skin.'

'But it will kill you!'

'Yes it will, but not straight away. I'll have a few brief moments to see the sun rise and to enjoy the warm sensation on my skin.'

'Tristan, you're really scaring me,' she said hysterically. Tears now streamed down her face as she sobbed uncontrollably.

'We can make a life together, I'll work at night and sleep with you during the day, please!' she pleaded. 'I love you, I love you so much!'

'Tania, it's not possible. Yes, you would spend your entire life with me. I, on the other hand, would only spend a short chapter of mine with you, a chapter that would end in misery as you grow old and eventually die, leaving me alone, mourning your death with a broken heart; yet again. I've had seven wives and been left a heart-broken widower seven times. I can't do it again, Tania. I've had a thousand years of misery and I don't want a thousand more; please don't ask me to go through it again,' he said softly, almost in a whisper, as he looked into her eyes.

'My darling, I love you, I will always love you!' she said, as she looked into his eyes through her tears, beginning to realise that he was not going to move on this.

'I never thought I would love anyone again, Tania, especially after such a short time. I love you too, my darling, and I'm so grateful for what you've given me.'

She hugged him and squeezed as tight as she could, crying tears into his naked chest. He held her, delicately, while stroking her hair.

'My darling, today is the first day of summer. To most people this is a good thing, long hot summer days. But for me, the days are incredibly short. I'm about to enter the worst time of year. This is my millennium; it's my 1000th year as a vampire.'

'I don't want you to go,' Tania cried as she continued to squeeze him really tightly.

'My darling, do you know what my name means? It was

influenced by the French term *triste*, which means, *sad*. My name reflects my mood over the centuries.'

'I'm so sorry … I love you so much!' she said, trying desperately to slow her tears.

'Tania, I've been a vampire for a thousand years and I don't want a thousand more. If you truly love me, you'll understand and you'll let me go,' he whispered into her ear, as he continued to stroke her hair.

Tania pondered for a moment, then suddenly pulled back from him, turned and looked towards the horizon. The sun would be appearing any minute now.

'I want you to bite me on the wrist and drink some of my blood,' she said, urgently.

'What are you talking about, why?' he said, turning to face her.

'Please, just do it. I want some of my blood to be inside you, running through your veins.'

'I don't understand, when the sun comes up in a minute, I'll cease to exist.'

'Yes I know, and when you die, I want a part of me to be inside you. I want a part of me to die with you, Tristan. So a small part of me can go with you and be with you.

Tristan looked deep into Tania's eyes; he could see that she was deadly serious. He glanced at the horizon, then took her right hand in his, turned it wrist-side up and lifted it up to his mouth. Without breaking eye contact, he sank his fangs deep into her wrist, causing her to wince for an instant. He gently drank, while looking into her eyes.

As Tania looked back, deep into his eyes, she noticed a change. As her blood ran down his throat, his eyes slowly began to change. Their wolf-like appearance started to subdue as they transitioned into more human looking eyes. They slowly became a beautiful warm hazelnut colour; they were Tristan's birth eyes.

'Oh my god,' she whispered, tears running down her face, 'so that's what you look like.'

Tristan slowly removed her wrist from his mouth and went to prick his thumb on one of his extended fangs to he could heal the two puncture wounds.

'No!' she said, and grabbed his hand to pull it away from his mouth.

'Tania, I need to heal the two wounds on your wrist.'

'I don't want you to. I want to keep them … forever.'

Tristan leaned forward and kissed her gently on the forehead, then pulled her into him and squeezed her tight, looking at the horizon over her shoulder, the sun only seconds away from appearing.

'It's time,' he whispered, slowly.

Tania gently released her tight embrace on him and turned to look over her shoulder, just in time to see a sliver of sunlight appear over the horizon. She moved from in front of him and stood by his side and held his hand.

'Tania, I only have a vague idea of what to expect. Holding my hand might not be a good idea.'

'It's a perfect idea … I want to be with you, touching you … right to the end.'

Tristan turned to watch the sunrise, while Tania watched his face intently. He looked so innocent, with his beautiful hazelnut eyes, like a child witnessing something incredible for the very first time.

As the sun came up further, they both saw its light travelling fast across the earth's atmosphere from the horizon towards them. Closer and closer it came, until its light hit the outer perimeter of Tristan's estate. Tania squeezed his hand tighter. Then the sunlight hit the base of the house and crept up the outside wall. She squeezed his hand even tighter as her body tensed up.

'It's okay, my darling,' he whispered.

The sunlight struck his bare feet and slowly travelled up his body and onto his neck and face.

'Oooohhhhhh,' he quietly groaned in pure pleasure from feeling the intense heat on his body and face; he enjoyed the view of the sun, then closed his eyes and savoured the moment.

'This feels incredible,' he gasped.

Tania watched the look of immense pleasure on his face. She smiled, tears gently running down her face. Then he turned to face her and slowly opened his eyes.

'Goodbye, my darling,' he delicately whispered, and looked purposefully into her eyes; he looked so calm, so at peace with himself.

Tania felt his hand starting to get incredibly hot, but she was determined to hold on tight. She looked deep into his eyes as more and more of his human side started to appear, cutting through the vampire that he had been for the past 1000 years. His pale white complexion slowly diminished as colour started to appear in his face. His hand got hotter and hotter as the skin on his face and body slowly started to smoulder, and light grey and white smoke started to rise into the air off his body.

'Don't forget me,' he smiled.

'I'll never forget you … I love you … I will always love you, my darling.'

At that moment, it happened. In an instant, in a fraction of a second, Tristan burst into a cloud of grey and white ashes. Tania's hand closed on itself as Tristan's hand turned to ashes.

There was no fire, there were no flames. Tristan died incredibly delicately, quietly and gracefully. As his ashes lifted gently into the air, Tania looked down at her closed fist and opened it. His remaining ashes lifted from the palm of her hand and were carried high into the air by the gentle early morning breeze. She looked up at the ashes as they were carried higher and higher into the summer sky. They sparkled and glittered in varying shades of silver and gold. Tristan Syhier Burnel was at peace; finally.

Tania looked down at her wrists, at the two small puncture wounds made from Tristan's fangs. A few tiny droplets of blood still lingered from each one. The holes would eventually leave two perfectly formed little round scars exactly 36mm apart; scars that she could look at whenever she wanted, scars that would act as a reminder of her brief time with him, for the rest of her life. Scars that she would be happy to bear for her dear, darling Tristan – forever!

For more information about the author visit
www.nigelcooperauthor.com

Follow Nigel Cooper on Twitter
@nigelcooperuk

EMAIL FROM A VAMPIRE

GENERIC POOL PUBLISHING

ISBN 978-0-9573307-0-2